THE FAMILY STONE

Also by Michael R. Lane

THE FAMILY STONE

Michael R. Lane

BARE BONES PRESS
P.O. Box 9653, Seattle, WA 98109

Published by Bare Bones Press, Seattle, Washington.

The characters and events in this book are fictitious. Any similarity to real persons, living or dead, is coincidental and not intended by the author.

Design: Bare Bones Press
Production: Bare Bones Press
Cover Art: Monika Younger

Bare Bones Press
P.O. Box 9653
Seattle, WA 98109

www.michaelrlane.net
www.michaelrlane.com

Second Edition: September 2023

Dedication

To Civil Rights, long may you reign.

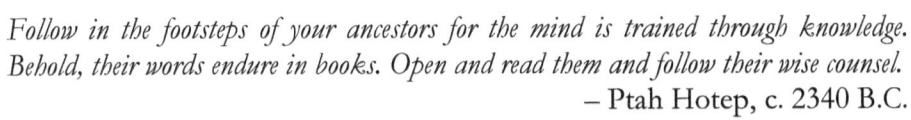

Follow in the footsteps of your ancestors for the mind is trained through knowledge. Behold, their words endure in books. Open and read them and follow their wise counsel.
                                                        – Ptah Hotep, c. 2340 B.C.

CHAPTER ONE

Winona Sissieretta Stone stared into the blackness of early morning, her back pressed hard into the firm mattress. Bright red numbers projected on her brown cheek from the electric alarm clock on her nightstand. She turned her head to see the clock. *Time to wake up Dwight*, she thought.

Her body felt leaden. Her movements showed it. Winona slipped her feet into the corduroy slippers on the floor. When she stood, her flannel nightgown tickled her ankles. It was the winter of 1965. The house was warm. Outside, it was cold and snow-laden. She plucked her cotton bathrobe from the chair near her side of the bed. One arm worked its way through, then the other, with no thought of movement: reflex brought about by hundreds of pre-dawn repetitions. From these things she garnered security, but little solace.

Down the hall, then to her right, she walked, with slow, compulsory movements. Before her stretched a dazzling runner that protected the hardwood floors. Under an ivory ceiling hung flowered wallpaper that halted above dark oak baseboards. On a dainty end table, near the head of the stairs, a small crystal lamp softly lit her way.

Knocking with her knuckles against the thick wood door, Winona yelled, "Dwight! Time to get up!" Dwight rolled over, suspended between sleep and wake, time and timelessness; not knowing which world was his.

"Dwight, are you up? It's time for school!"

Dwight did not move. He tried to fight through the fog of sleep that threatened to reclaim him. His eyes half-opened, then closed, then half-opened again. He was losing the battle. Sleep would have had its way had it not been for Winona, who now rapped on his bedroom door with the heel of her fist. It startled Dwight enough to thrust him through the fog into a room dim with pallid morning light.

"Dwight, are you up?"

"Yes, ma'am!"

"I don't hear you moving!"

"Huh?"

"Don't have me come in there!"

"I'm up! I'm up!" Dwight said; the first time to convince his mother and the second to convince himself.

Dwight bent forward and shoved the top sheet and blanket away before he fell back onto the bed. His head struck the pillows with a muffled thump. His mouth was dry. He rubbed his face with his hand. His eyes remained shut.

"Aw man, better get up," he mumbled. He slid his feet from the bed until gravity pulled them down to the carpeted floor.

"Man-o-man-o-man, I'll be glad when school's over so I can get some sleep."

"Dwight!" Winona yelled, louder than before, hammering the door again with the heel of her fist. "Are you up?"

"Yes!"

"Pardon?"

"Yes, ma'am!"

"I still don't hear you moving!"

"Ain't school canceled?"

"First I've heard of it." There was a moment of silence.

"Dwight?" No response. "Don't make me come in there!"

"I'm up."

"What?"

"I'm up!"

"All right then, let's get a move on it!"

Dwight put on the blue flannel robe draped over the footboard. He liked its soft weight and delicate warmth. It was an extension of his comfortable bed. He took a few steps toward his door before he realized he had forgotten his slippers; an oversight that would release a tirade from his mother, if she saw it. The pale yellow light from a full moon spotlighted his drawn winter drapes. It did not help Dwight see any better as he walked back to the bed to search for his slippers.

He felt around on the floor for the slippers but could not find them. Then he remembered he had accidentally kicked them under the bed after his third trip to the bathroom. Too sleepy to go rooting around in the dark, he'd decided to get them in the morning. He reached under the bed as far as he could. The carpet tickled his cheek. He closed his eyes and smelled a hint of baking soda.

Pleasant memories of that odor lingered in his subconscious. It made him smile for a moment. His hand found a baseball card, two marbles, a tennis shoe, and what felt like crumpled candy wrappers before finally locating one slipper. In pulling it out, it bumped against the other, which he also retrieved.

He sat back on the bed to put his slippers on. Soon he found himself, eyes half-closed, drifting back to sleep. He gently shook himself awake and stood up. In a motion that resembled languid ice-skating rather than walking, he made his way out of his room, down the hall, and into the bathroom.

Winona was making breakfast downstairs when she heard the familiar sound of water spilling into the upstairs basin. Dwight's mother was a stern woman with handsome features—her hands' long, elegant fingers would make any pianist proud. When Winona smiled, another world entered her eyes. As defiant and threatening as she could appear, she could become equally tender and open. Mr. Stone brought this quality out the most, in her, followed closely by Dwight. Once exasperated, as she was now, Winona was inconsolable; as Dwight would soon discover.

Despite her verbal prodding, it took Dwight thirty minutes longer than Winona expected to ready himself for school. When he appeared, books in hand, groomed, dressed, and in front of the table, she stood there and glared at him.

Winona had awoken that morning with a troublesome headache, having not slept well the past few days. Christmas and New Year were over. Each had gone well, in her household. They had been much-needed distractions, keeping her away from the recent past.

Watts had rioted, that summer. This followed the '64 summer of race riots that flamed in Rochester, New York, Philadelphia, Jersey City, Patterson, Elizabeth, and Chicago. Winona had watched the Watts rebellion unfold on television. Oppressed frustrations from chronic, systematic abuse erupted within the California district's ghetto communities, not much different from her own. Armed National

3

Guardsmen supported police in riot gear who made certain of no breach in containment. There was burning, looting, and rants of revolution: one that would not be televised. Martial law was enacted. Lives were lost.

When the spent masses of humanity exhausted themselves, all that remained were incinerated shadows of neighborhoods. Charred, gutted businesses became monuments of a brief revolt. Wisdom did not emerge from the ashes of carnage; nor did harmony and acceptance. People who had desperately hoped for understanding discovered that deaf ears belonged to those of resolved ignorance, victims of their own demise.

Winona had felt a strong connection to the rioters on the evening news; people whose actions she intimately understood. Their faces were contorted with rage. Cursing, name-calling, and violence burst through their hoary dams of civilized behavior. It frightened her, as it did many. Heated rhetoric pointed at an inevitable race war, armed militias combating on all fronts. In that caldron of fury and fear, vengeance and justice, there were no peaceful havens or room for compromises; only a world of corpses afloat in blood. She imagined it as Armageddon in her own backyard. That's when the migraines started.

"Where's Dad?" Dwight asked, eyeing the bacon and eggs on the serving plate.

"Where is he every day at this time?" Winona snapped.

"At the store," Dwight said, looking as though he were puzzling why he'd asked such a ridiculous question.

"You better give me my breakfast and put a lid on that lip, woman." Dwight grinned, hoping for the same response from his mother. Winona Stone put a hand on her hip and cocked her head to one side. Even in an unflattering robe, no makeup, her comfortable, oversized slippers, and a white cooking apron spotted with renegade spatters of bacon grease, she looked regal.

"Who do you think you're talking to?"

Dwight sat at the kitchen table where a plate, paper napkin, glass of orange juice, and silverware were neatly arranged on a cloth placemat.

"I'm talking to you, Dwight."

"Ma'am?"

"What's your answer?"

"Don't have any." Dwight was confused. He did not realize he was late, since he had not yet looked at a clock that morning. He assumed his mother was having a bad day. The only way he knew how to remedy her bad mood was to either give her a gift or joke her out of it.

"You getting smart?"

"I'm intelligent. Kids are smart."

"I see." Winona Stone strode over to him and pinched his nose between her forefinger and thumb.

"Okay-okay-okay!" Under this pressure, she stood him up and led him into the kitchen before she let him go with a sharp jerk of her wrist.

"Mom, that hurt!" Dwight rubbed his nose, checking it for blood.

"You think you got a maid around here?"

"I was kidding."

"I'm not. You're ten years old. Past time you learned how to cook, and we're going to start right now."

"Why I got to start now?" Dwight pointed in the direction of the food. "There's bacon and eggs and toast right there. Why can't we eat those?"

"You took so long getting ready, they're cold. We want a hot breakfast to get us going in the morning." Dwight looked resistant. Smells of fried bacon and eggs hovered in the air. Winona made her fingers into a crab-like pincher and reached for his nose. Dwight jumped backwards.

Dwight wiggled his nose and rubbed it again, not satisfied the painful throb resonating from it wasn't a sign that something was wrong.

"I think you broke it."

"Boy, shut up about that nose or next time I'll snatch it right off your face."

In frank disbelief, Dwight stared at his mother. *What is wrong with her this morning?* he thought, keeping his hand over his nose to prevent her from having a clear opportunity.

"I asked you a question."

"What?"

"What do you want for breakfast?"

"Cereal." Without realizing it, Dwight edged away from his mother.

"Get back over here." Dwight walked over to his mother, protecting his nose with his right hand.

"I think you broke it," he repeated.

"I'm going to break your behind if you don't stop all that whining. Take your hand away from your face." Dwight did as his mother commanded. "Now, what do you want for breakfast?"

"Cereal."

"You don't want scrambled eggs, bacon and toast?"

"No, ma'am. Cereal'll be fine. I ain't that hungry."

"You'd better get that hungry, because this morning you're going to have bacon and eggs and toast made by your own hands."

Winona snatched away his hand, which had crept back in place over his nose. Dwight flinched. They looked at each other. Her stare defied him to put it back. She folded her arms across her chest and waited.

"What's the holdup?" she asked.

"I don't know what to do."

Her hands placed on his shoulders, she squared up with him as two boxers about to do combat in a ring. "First you need something to cook them in, right?"

"Un-huh."

"And what do you see your mommy cooking bacon and eggs in?"

"A frying pan."

"Very good; now get one." Dwight looked around the kitchen as if he were lost.

"Where they at?"

Winona twisted her lips to one side. Her head throbbed, not from the acute ache she'd experienced before, but from miniature cluster bombs of pain. She kept reminding herself, *Dwight is not the cause of this. Don't take it out on him.*

"The question is," she said aloud, "where are they? Where do you put them on the few occasions you wash dishes?"

"In the drawer under the stove."

"Then that's where you'll find one, sweetheart."

They stared at each other. Winona then leaned into Dwight until their noses touched. Dwight got the message, and with a nervous grin he retrieved a frying pan from the drawer.

"That one's a little small. Try again." The next one he held up was a cast iron ten-and-one-half inch.

"Now we're making progress. What's next?"

"Mom, I'm going to be late for school."

"So what! What's next?"

Dwight looked around the kitchen. Clean, neat, organized. To him, it might as well have been a question on World History. He could not begin to think of what to do. He had watched his mother cook bacon and eggs for years, yet he had no inkling how to prepare them himself.

Winona thought a clue might help.

"What do you usually do with a frying pan?"

"Fry?"

"Right; so put the frying pan on one of the burners and get something to fry."

"Like what?"

Winona shook her head. "Like bacon and like eggs, son." Her voice had the tone of a hissing teakettle.

"Where are they?" The tone of her voice told Dwight he had asked another dumb question. He elected to figure it out for himself. No sooner did he detach himself from his mother's heated stare then he realized that everything he would need was in the refrigerator. Six eggs (he was really hungry), bacon wrapped in white butcher's paper (cut fresh by his father last evening), and one stick of butter. Winona watched. Both fists had found their way to her waist. Her lips had relaxed but her brow had furrowed and her eyes burned from the inside. *God give me the strength not to kill this child*, she thought.

"Come on, Dwight, you don't have all morning. And you're still going to school."

Dwight set the items on the sink near the stove. He looked at them, then at his mother. Then back at them.

"Okay." She said the word as if to release pressure that would otherwise make her explode. Had it been a stranger, a cousin, a friend, or someone she loved less than this child, she may not have held back. Even with Dwight having what she would describe as that stupid look on his face, she found restraint. God had once again answered her prayer.

"Now unwrap the bacon, honey." Winona forced a smile. They both knew it. Just as her voice had a false sweetness when she said, "honey," coming from a place outside of her heart. Dwight did as he was told. Bacon unwrapped, he stood back and waited for further instructions.

"How many pieces of bacon do you want?"

"Six." Dwight waited. Winona reached over and placed an arm around him as his father would do. "Peel off six strips of bacon and lay them inside the frying pan."

He did as instructed.

"Turn on the burner. Not so high. You want the bacon to cook thoroughly. That means you need to keep the flame low."

"Don't you want any?"

"No thanks, I've lost my appetite. While the bacon is cooking..." Winona guided Dwight by the shoulders to the left cabinet above the sink where she instructed him to select a small mixing bowl. On their way back to the stove, she obtained a wire whip from a utensil jar and handed it to him.

The remainder of the lesson went that way. Winona Stone told her son precisely what to do and how and when to do it. He carried out her instructions explicitly.

With scrambled eggs, bacon, and buttered toast still steaming, Dwight filled his plate and asked his mother to join him. Winona declined, but agreed to sit with him. Dwight ate as if he had not eaten in days. Winona would casually snare an occasional nibble of bacon or toast or eggs. Her headache was subsiding.

"Can I cook again tomorrow?" Dwight asked with his mouth filled with half-eaten eggs.

"I'll think about it."

"I want to make waffles next time."

If he were sincere about learning how to cook, she would teach him on the weekends. There was too tight a schedule to maintain during the week. Winona had to admit that his bacon and eggs weren't bad; though they were not as good as his father's.

CHAPTER TWO

"Have you made up your mind, Kirby?"

"No, sir."

"What about you, Clyde?"

"Gimme two jawbreakers...one fireball...two sourballs and—"

"Cousin Abe, how much for a banana Popsicle?" Marvin Bankhead's face was moist from freezer mist. His caramel skin shined. Abe did not mind Marvin making their family ties public as long as he did not attempt to use their familial relationship to gain favor when it came to store dealings. Family was treated like every customer at Willie's Market: with respect and dignity, but no special allowances—a fact that Marvin's mother had yet to accept.

"Same price as the cherry one you asked me about a minute ago, Marvin: five cents." Marvin got up on his tiptoes and stuck his head so far into the freezer, his face was out of view.

The cowbells over the front door clanged. Theresa Peoples walked in wearing a peach housecoat, white granny boots, and a pink montage of sponge hair curlers tucked beneath a tightly-wrapped red scarf. She was a tall woman who worried too much and thought too little. At least, that was the consensus of the liberal-minded barbershop Abe Stone attended. Theresa was a hair stylist during the week; nude dancer on weekends.

Every man in East Liberty had seen her limber body prowl the stage of the Carlisle Club. Most she knew by first name. This was, in part, why many women in East Liberty despised her, blacklisted her from involvement in community and church projects, rolled their eyes when she said hello or attempted small talk, and referred to her as a whore, trollop, and husband-stealing wench.

They had heard stories regarding her private life: everything from orgies to lesbianism to sadomasochism to husbands who bragged to other husbands that they'd had sex with her. None of which was true. While she preferred the company of men, she had allowed only one lover into her life since the birth of her son fourteen years ago. There had been no room for any other male. Only recently had she yearned for more.

"Have you seen Anthony, Abe?"

"Saw him earlier this morning."

"Was he with Perry and Dog?"

"Don't you think you should've put some clothes on before you came out in this weather, Theresa?"

"I don't have time for that. Was he with Perry and Dog?"

"Yes."

"Damn that boy! I told him to stay clear of those fools." She opened the door and placed one foot out before she remembered something. Cold air raced inside. "If you see Anthony, will you tell him I'm looking for him?"

"Sure thing."

Theresa looked at the boys as if seeing them for the first time. She smiled. They smiled back. She left, leaving warmth to reclaim its dominion.

"Mr. Stone." Clyde had gotten impatient.

"Sorry about the interruption. What else did you want?" Abe had the opened penny candy bag planted in his right palm. Clyde had ordered thirty-four cents worth of candy and had sixteen cents to go.

"Three root beer barrels…some peppermints—not that many, two; five nut bars—make that seven. I like nut bars."

"Cousin Abe?" Abe held up his hand. Marvin waited with another Popsicle held as high as he could reach. Clyde and Kirby peered through the glass case, their faces inches away from its side.

"And—and—three butterscotch. And—two licorice twists."

"That'll be fifty cents."

Clyde gleefully pushed forward a collection of dimes, nickels and pennies that added up to fifty cents. Abe handed him the bag of candy. Clyde politely accepted it.

"Cousin Abe."

Abe again raised his hand toward Marvin. "You decided on anything, Kirby?"

"Give me a Grape Stix and an Apple Stix."

Kirby never purchased anything until Clyde bought what he wanted. It was tradition. Abe suspected they shared candy and did not want to duplicate tastes.

"Ten cents, please." Kirby placed a dime in Abe's waiting palm. Abe handed him his candy. Kirby carefully guided the candy into his coat pocket, still wearing his winter gloves.

"Cousin Abe, how much for the blue Popsicle?"

"Five cents, Marvin. On a cold day like this, why do you want a Popsicle?"

"I like Popsicles."

"If you don't have a nickel then you can't have one."

"I don't have a nickel. All I got is a quarter."

"Then what's the problem?"

"I'm doing what my dad says he does when he goes shopping."

Abe waited for Marvin to finish. When he didn't, Abe asked, "And that is?"

"My dad says no one should buy the first thing you run across. Chances are good you'll find a cheaper one right in the same store if you look hard enough."

"Popsicles are a nickel no matter where you go, Marvin."

"Oh!" Marvin appeared stunned by the news. He stood on his toes again and emerged with a banana Popsicle. Kirby and Clyde waited for him by the front door.

"Five cents." Abe gave Marvin two dimes for change. Marvin put them in his pocket, holding his savory treat aloft, to be paid homage to before devouring its flavored ice.

"Bye, Mr. Stone," the boys yelled in unison; except for Marvin, who yelled, "Bye, Cousin Abe," as they all rushed out of the door. Marvin ran into Earl Farmer. To maneuver around Earl's immense paunch, Marvin stepped back. Marvin sheepishly told Earl he was sorry before he dashed off to catch up to his friends.

The cowbells clamored when the door slammed shut from its own weight. Abe watched the boys head toward Banneker Elementary School. They were nicknamed The Three Musketeers. You rarely saw one without the other two. Marvin ate his Popsicle as they ran. It caused him to lag behind the others. When he was too far behind, the others waited. He caught up, only to lag behind again. Abe watched until they turned out of sight onto Euclid Street.

"Need some Crisco, Abe." Earl bellied up to the counter. "Where you keeping it these days?"

"Same place as always: third aisle on your right, top shelf. You can't miss it."

"Going to need a pound of bologna, pound of ham, about twenty links of beef sausage, and five pieces of kielbasa." Abe walked over to his butcher section. He lifted his white apron from a wooden peg near the door that led to the back storeroom. The door was open. Abe closed it before washing his hands in the sink next to it and then, after drying his hands with paper towels, he tossed the towels into a round metal trash can near the sink.

"How's Arthel?"

"Good; going to see her grandkids this afternoon."

"In this weather?"

"Arthel wrote the book on 'stubborn'. Think she'll change her mind shortly, though. Expecting another three to five inches by tonight."

From the refrigerated display case, Abe choose a fresh log of bologna. In one deft motion he lopped off one of the sealed ends with a meat cleaver, dropping the cleaver into the left side of a stainless steel sink filled with hot, sudsy water.

"How you want your bologna sliced?"

"Usual."

That meant thin.

"Ham the same way?"

"Yep. You got any wax paper?"

"First aisle, all the way back, lower right shelf."

The cowbells clanged. "Good morning, Abe. Earl." Earl waved his heavy arm in the air in recognition as he sauntered toward Aisle One. His weight and retirement only afforded him one speed—slow.

"Be right with you, Ron."

"No rush."

Ronald Hightower was the youngest of a family of five. He'd graduated college with a degree in Business Finance and moved from Harrisburg to Pittsburgh to help his middle sister and her husband with their department store, situated in the northeast section of Pittsburgh known as the Hill District; a community of locally-owned businesses only a few blocks from centrally-located Downtown. A year later, his sister and her husband sold the store and returned to Harrisburg with her family. Ron accepted a job as a loan officer at Morgan Finance Company, the city's only black-owned financial institution. Shortly thereafter, he moved from the Hill District to East Liberty. Ron was normally at work by this time. That and the fact that Ron was casually dressed made Abe correctly presume Ron was staying home.

"How are you?" Abe asked Ron.

"As well as can be expected on a day like this. Didn't I see Theresa come out of here, a minute ago?"

"Yep."

"Hope she plans on changing before she goes to work."

"Which job you referring to?"

"Don't make any difference. Looking like that, she bound to scare customers away."

"I hear you."

"Penn Hills got sixteen inches of snow last night."

"Four more inches than we got."

Earl waited at the counter with a large can of Crisco and a box of wax paper. Abe worked swiftly and efficiently with first the food slicer, then the meat cleaver. He wrapped each order of meat separately in brown butcher's paper, secured the packages with brown tape, and marked them clearly with a grease pencil.

"Anything else, Earl?"

"Nope."

Abe washed and dried his hands again before hanging his apron back on its peg. He joined Earl at the front counter, bagged his groceries, and gave him change from a ten-dollar bill. There was no cash register. Cash was kept in a wooden drawer to the right of the counter. Abe did all math in his head. If a customer wanted an itemized receipt, Abe would write one. That typically happened when a parent sent one of their kids to the store, to make certain the child did not pocket their change or purchase something for themselves on account; a lesson learned from experience. Anthony, Perry and Dog were notorious for such attempts. Abe made certain they failed.

"Tell Arthel I said hello—and stay home. Her grandchildren will be there when the snow melts."

"Will do. See you later. Later, Ron."

"Bye, Earl."

"What can I get you, Ron?"

"Pound of butter, half a pint of whipping cream, a dozen eggs, flour—bleached—and some vanilla extract."

Abe went around the store, gathered all of the items, and placed them on the counter. Ron rarely got anything himself. If he did, he was in an extreme hurry. Ron's right leg had been broken when he was a child during a freak snow-sledding accident. It never healed properly, leaving him with a permanent limp.

Abe had never heard Ron complain about his leg. From that circumstantial evidence, Abe assumed that Ron suffered little or no discomfort. Either that, or he had learned to bear his pain in silence; although Abe noticed that Ron would automatically shift most of his weight to his left leg when standing, as he did now.

"Anything else?" Abe asked.

"That should do it."

"Plan on doing a little baking?"

"Going to try. Never had much luck with baking." Ron was modest. He was an excellent cook. Abe had sampled enough of his efforts at church socials to confirm it.

"Need any yeast?"

"No, I'm good."

"That'll be $2.28." Ron handed him a twenty-dollar bill.

"You're doing better than me. Only baking I do these days comes out of a box."

"Nothing like scratch."

"Can't tell Dwight that; he's been weaned on Betty Crocker. Probably turn up his nose at a good scratch cake." Ron smiled. Abe found his smile bashful; almost feminine. "See you later."

"Right."

The morning rush was over. Abe walked to the front of the store. On the right corner was a table with a tower of Styrofoam cups, a gallon urn of fresh brewed Maxwell House coffee, a Dixie Cup filled with sugar cubes, a package of plastic teaspoons, and a small plastic pitcher of cream lodged between ice cubes in the center of a green plastic mixing bowl.

Abe wiped and reorganized the table. Two customers had helped themselves to free coffee that morning. Both had rushed off with their coffee still steaming. Bad weather encouraged haste. Snow and bad weather were synonymous, to Abe.

After a quick look down each aisle and a glance at the convex mirror in the farthest corner, Abe got himself a cup of coffee and took his post behind the front counter. He procured his reading glasses from his sweater vest pocket. Abe was a tall man with honey skin and dark brown eyes. Above his slim lips was a polished mustache. A proud nose, handsome eyebrows, square chin, and narrow cheeks filled out the remainder of his face. Abe was a former Army sergeant; a Graduate of Alabama A and M. He believed in God and deemed God believed in him. Before him, he unfolded the *Pittsburgh Courier* he had taken from his mini-newsstand and laid it flat on the counter. He would read it from the first to the last page. Customers scurried in, exchanged pleasantries, helped themselves to coffee, purchased goods, made brief small talk, and then left Abe to his morning reading.

"Abraham Jacob Stone." Abe once overheard his grandfather describe Tennessee sipping whiskey as "velvet for the tongue". The voice Abe heard speak his name could be as soft and smooth and intoxicating to his ears as sipping whiskey was to his grandfather's tongue, if he allowed it to be.

Abe had finished reading *The Courier* and was immersed in a *Time* magazine article featuring a bust of General Westmoreland on the cover when he looked up and saw her. She had eased the door open and shut it without disturbing the bells. Abe looked at Virginia Lovejoy over the tops of his reading glasses and gave her a look that would cause most people to straighten, clear their throats, and humbly declare their intentions.

"When you going dump that old broad and marry me?"

"First of all, she's not a broad, old or otherwise. Second, she's two years younger than you are. And finally, why don't you find a man who's not married and marry him?"

"Only men worth marrying are the ones already married."

"You don't say?" Abe said, looking as annoyed as he sounded.

Virginia leaned in close. Her coat was open. Abe could see past her pearl necklace down the cleavage of her velvet dress. He could also smell gin on her breath. Her smooth skin was creamy ginger. If she wore makeup, he could not tell. Pearl earrings matched her necklace, complemented by her skin. He watched, mesmerized for an instant as her brandy eyes held him captive.

"Don't you think it's a little early to be drinking?"

"I haven't been home yet, sweetie. Have you ever been to Kelsey's?"

Abe raised his eyebrows.

"Silly question," Virginia said with a quick roll of her eyes. "They're open all night. Anyway, Neville Carter just dropped me off."

"You can do better than Neville."

"Don't be silly. The man gave me a ride. I didn't ride him." Virginia smiled. "You're not getting jealous, are you, Abe?"

"Hardly."

"Could've fooled me." Virginia stepped back and, in one sweeping motion, removed her cashmere coat and draped it across her slender arm.

"Like my dress?" Virginia pirouetted. She wore a mauve, tea-length dress with matching high heels. It complemented her hourglass curves.

"Looks fine."

"That's all you can say? 'Looks fine?'"

"Yeah."

Virginia walked toward Abe. Her eyes fixed on his. When she reached for his face, he recoiled. "Did you come in here to buy something or are you just fooling around?"

"The fooling around part sounds good."

"You know what I mean."

"Maybe I do. Maybe I don't."

"I'm not in the mood for your nonsense, Virginia."

"Aren't we snippy? I can see you're not going to be any fun this morning."

Abe removed his glasses and laid them on *Time*. His jaw tightened. His eyes had a touch of wariness. Virginia asked for a package of Doublemint gum. Abe leaned forward. As he reached for it in the display case, Virginia touched his other hand. At her touch, Abe stepped backward and stood erect, hands at his sides. Virginia plucked a silk change purse from one of her coat pockets. Abe noted how it appeared new, as did the diamond-studded bracelet dangling from her left wrist. Gifts from one of her many male friends, he guessed. She dropped a quarter on the glass counter. It sounded like a discharged starter pistol when it struck the glass, spinning in place.

"Gum's a nickel."

"I know. Keep the change. I'll collect some other time, in some other way." Virginia was clearly amused. She had leaned in close. Abe recognized the brand of gin as Tanqueray.

"You know, Abe, if you keep turning me down, I may have to turn my attention to that gorgeous son of yours."

"Don't you think he's a little young?"

"When I'm through with him, he might be able to teach you a thing or two." The thought of Virginia and Dwight becoming involved did not trouble Abe. He knew it would never happen. Whatever people said about Virginia, one thing could be agreed upon: she was not a pedophile. What struck Abe as most strange was that he believed Dwight could teach *her* a thing or two about love.

Virginia laughed softly as she switched out of the door, her coat still draped over her arm. Abe watched her cross the street, enjoying the rhythm of her base drum behind. Virginia passed Felton Dobbs, who was standing near the corner. She steered wide of him, looking away. Felton took measured steps to the curb's edge. A wool scarf wrapped several times around his pencil neck, its tousled ends puffing his double-breasted pea coat. Corduroy pants outlined his skinny legs against the wind. Slush clung to his combat boots. Green earmuffs were clamped in place, their steel band buried within black woolen curls combed back away from his forehead. With his hands shoved deep in his pockets, Felton stared straight ahead.

The first time Abe encountered Felton Dobbs, Felton was about forty pounds heavier. He was an oddly-dressed man in mismatched clothes and shoes. Only half his face was shaven. His hair was cut short, but uneven, and his behavior was—to put it in polite vernacular—peculiar.

Felton had entered the store demanding to see Ralph Lingle. His peculiar behavior did not trouble Abe. He had seen far worse during his enlisted days. Had they not been alone in the store, Abe would have made short work of the mildly deranged man. Instead, patience was his momentary mood.

"I'm the new owner," Abe calmly informed Felton.

Felton stood there for a minute as if Abe's words meant nothing to him, his fingers tightly interwoven in front of him, head askew, glaring at Abe as if trying to burn a hole through him with his bloodshot eyes.

"Can I help you?"

After a few moments of silence, Felton asked, "Willie's Market?"

Abe nodded.

Felton paused as if he required time to digest a difficult concept. More glaring and silence ensued.

"I kept the name because of its good reputation throughout the community," Abe said in an effort to draw out whatever remaining sanity Felton might have.

Felton's bloodshot eyes darted back and forth.

"Do you think that was a good idea?" Abe asked nonchalantly.

Felton nodded deliberately, then slowly shrugged his shoulders. A few uneasy heartbeats passed. Felton watched Abe like an animal eyeing its prey.

"Ralph here?" Felton asked.

Abe tried again to get through to Felton, without success. Out of apparent frustration, Felton stormed out of the store, only to repeat his performance a day or two later, until one day he disappeared.

It had been nearly two years since Abe had seen that quirky runt of a man. Lines now dropped, widened, and creased his owlish face. The glow in his huge eyes had dimmed to glimmers. Felton had a penchant for observing things: people, trees, architecture, traffic lights, dust on his shoes, beetles and moths, slanted rain slicing the atmosphere. Children called him Bubblehead, Turtle Man, Retard, and Space Cadet. On the surface, adults were more tolerant. Only among themselves did they discuss Felton's perceived insanity. To Abe, he was a breathing enigma he had only heard utter a few words.

Abe had encountered an assortment of mental maladies brought on by combat stress during his Korean War tour of duty. "Zombie" was what Abe called it when a soldier aimlessly walked about, residing in our world while existing elsewhere. Many would disagree, but Abe believed that Felton was not a zombie. He seemed aware of himself and his surroundings—even during times when he stared into space, wiped inexplicable tears from his eyes, or had a crazed smile on his face.

Virginia was out of sight when Felton savagely shook his head, followed by an expression of bugged-eyed lust as he gazed after Virginia. Abe returned to reading his *Time* magazine, dismissing Felton as weird. He didn't notice when Felton crossed the street, glared at him, then disappeared around the corner.

CHAPTER THREE

"I can't believe you asked her that," David Hickman said to Dwight.

David was sometimes called Peanut because of the size and shape of his head. His small physique made him an occasional target for additional insults such as pygmy, pee wee, stubby, runt, and small fry. Dwight could relate. He'd received similar treatment, at times. His insults were from a few jealous neighbors who considered him wealthy, since his family owned the corner market. Except, Dwight couldn't care less.

"As long as no one puts their hands on you," his father had told him, "let them say what they like." Sometimes Dwight forgot that principle and verbally lashed back. David had never accepted it; not due to his lack of fear, but David simply could not keep his mouth shut. His responses often caused him to write checks his behind could not cash, which was one of the reasons Dwight liked David. He was tougher than people gave him credit for. Another reason Dwight and David were friends was because David was smart.

Dwight looked down at David and nonchalantly answered, "Mrs. Gergich? She didn't have a problem with it."

"You don't think so?"

"She answered it."

"Only because everybody in class was waiting to hear what she had to say."

"Didn't you ever wonder how somebody could discover something when somebody else was already there?"

"Nope."

"You, Kevin?" Kevin Bankhead was the antithesis of David. Dwight's cousin was bigger, stronger and, in large part, feared by many of his classmates. His temper and bad attitude were legendary throughout Banneker School. Only upper level classmates picked on Kevin, and even though some of them registered caution when they did. Kevin always fought back. Sometimes he won; other times he didn't.

What seemed important to Kevin was the confrontation. He enjoyed them. The outcome was incidental. His only self-imposed rule was no fist fighting in school; not because Kevin feared suspension or the principal's wooden paddle, but because of his father's wrath. Mr. Bankhead would give Kevin a man-sized beating if he did anything to disrupt his education. Everyone was aware of that, including Kevin's teachers. The threat of telling his father was how they controlled him. It was also his biggest shame amongst his peers.

"All I do is read the stuff so I can feed it back to her in class," Kevin said. "A week later and I couldn't even tell you who Columbus was."

"I can't do that," Dwight said. "If somebody tells me that a dude named Columbus discovered America, I want to know how that's possible. To me, it's the same as—remember Tyrone?"

"Ty Sumner?"

Dwight nodded.

"Yeah, I remember him," Kevin answered.

"Me too," David said.

"He got caught stealing a car," Dwight said.

"Which was dumb," David said.

"He can't even drive," Kevin said.

"Why couldn't he say he discovered it?" Dwight interjected. "There wasn't anybody in it when he took it. What's the difference between him and Columbus? Didn't he steal from the Indians the way Ty took that car?"

David shrugged. "You got me, man."

"What makes you think of this stuff?" Kevin asked.

"Things have to make sense to me," Dwight said.

"You keep trying to make sense out of Mrs. Gergich's class and you going be repeating it this summer."

"You must have my grades confused with yours, Kevin."

Kevin looked down at the snow. He was tempted to grab a fistful and throw it in Dwight's face, but the urge soon passed. His unprotected hands were numb from their snowball battle. Their coats, caps, and pants shimmered as if covered in diamond dust. Their faces glistened from a mix of cold and sweat. David checked his Timex watch, a hand-me-down from his older brother.

"We might still make it before the late bell," David said.

"We wouldn't be late if it weren't for Dwight."

"Nobody told you to wait for me, Kevin. I know my way."

"If you didn't, your daddy would show you," David teased.

"You know he would," Kevin added. Kevin stole a sly glance at Dwight. He saw no change in his expression.

A sharp east wind kicked up enough snow to blind the boys. Felton turned a corner one short block away. He stopped and narrowed his eyes as he watched them. With bounding strides, he passed behind them. By the time they regained sight, Felton had squatted behind a snow-covered LeSabre. He rubbed a small section of the rear bumper clear of snow with his jacket sleeve. Transparent ice coated it. Felton blew on the icy surface several times. He sprinkled snow onto it. Snowflakes that had fallen, drifted, or floated on invisible winds dissolved from concrete touches of reality. He grinned, gleefully watching the snow melt. When he was done, he stuck out his grinning head and watched the boys walking toward school.

"What's going on after school?" Dwight asked.

"Homework," Kevin answered.

"Me too," David said.

"After that?"

"I'm grounded," Kevin said.

"What for this time?" Dwight asked.

"Got a D on my history test. Until I can bring home no less than a C, my Dad says. When I finish my homework, he's going to quiz me on my history assignment 'til he's satisfied I got it."

"Maybe you should ask more questions in class."

"What I need in Mrs. Gergich's class is coffee. She puts me to sleep." Kevin feigned a yawn. "I don't know how you stay awake in there."

"I like history."

"I can't stand it. You like history, David?"

"The only thing I like about school is science," David said. "What about you?"

David and Dwight looked at Kevin, awaiting an answer. Kevin thought for a moment. "Recess," he said. They all laughed.

"Recess ain't the only thing Kevin likes about school."

"What you talking about, David?" Kevin asked.

"Marsha Jenkins."

"Ooooo! Kevin's got a girlfriend," Dwight teased.

"Get outta here; don't nobody like no Marsha."

"Dwight, did you see how Kevin looked when Marsha walked by him at lunch yesterday?"

"Un-huh. 'Hi Kevin, hi Marsha.' Then they looked at each other like those people on TV, with stars in their eyes."

"You all are silly." Dwight and David sang in unison, "Kevin's got a girlfriend. Kevin's got a girlfriend."

"Better leave me alone." The singing continued, becoming louder with each chorus. Kevin scooped up two handfuls of snow and threw one at Dwight, the other at David. The boys waged another snowball war. It lasted two blocks. When they finished, they continued their conversation as if nothing had happened.

"Got a new Louis Armstrong album; anybody want to come over tonight and check it out?" Dwight asked.

"Sorry, man." David paused to brush snow off his book bag. "Church meeting tonight. Promised my Mom I'd help with dinner."

"Why you got to help with dinner? What's wrong with your sister?"

"Probably wants to impress some girl with how well he can cook," David said. Kevin reached across Dwight and waved his fingers in front of David's face.

"Like Marsha?" Kevin glared at David. David realized what that look meant. Dwight lived closest to school, so he would be first to leave the pack. When he did, Kevin would seek revenge. It was another block and a half from Dwight's home to his. He would have no problem outrunning Kevin on dry ground, but in snow, wearing galoshes and all his winter garments, it was going to be a close race. If Kevin caught him, he would make him eat snow and apologize about everything he had said about him and Marsha.

Dwight and Kevin brushed snow off each other's backside, as they had previously done for David. Kevin had grimaced when Dwight slapped his lower back to dislodge a stubborn clump of snow. David and Dwight both noticed.

"What's wrong?" they asked Kevin.

"Nothing," Kevin said.

"Then what's with that face?" Dwight asked.

"I said it was nothing!" David and Dwight looked quizzically at each other. Kevin had become prone to uncharacteristic temperamental outbursts or unpredictable periods of deep withdrawal. Dwight changed the subject.

"How're your hands?" Dwight asked Kevin. David and Dwight both wore gloves.

"Can't feel my fingers."

"Got an extra pair of gloves at home," Dwight said. "You can have 'em if you want."

"I'll be all right."

"What happened to your gloves?" David asked.

"Lost 'em."

"Bet your old man loved that."

"He don't know yet."

"What?" David and Dwight said simultaneously.

"I had 'em when I left the house. Must've lost 'em on my way over to David's."

"How many's that?" Dwight asked.

"Three. My Dad said those'll be the last pair I'll see this winter."

"That's messed up."

"Dwight, why you like Louie Armstrong so much?" Kevin asked.

"Cause he's good—and his name is Louis."

"My folks call him Louie."

"Mine, too," David said.

"Sometimes they call him 'Satchmo'," Kevin said.

"Satchmo was supposed to be Satchel Mouth. Some British dude named Percy Brooks messed up when he wrote about him; called him Satchmo. I don't like that nickname. If I ever meet him, he'll be Mr. Armstrong to me."

"You crazy, man," David said.

"So why you like him so much?" Kevin asked. "I could see if you played the trumpet or something." Kevin grimaced as he flexed his fingers inside his coat pockets.

"His music—something about it…I don't know. I can't explain it. You all coming over tonight?"

"Not me," Kevin said. "You know my Dad. When he says grounded, he means grounded."

"I might be able to get out of cooking," David said. "Wait, I can't. I promised my Dad I'd clean my room."

"In one day?" Dwight held back a grin.

"Why not?"

"I've seen your room. It would take the three of us a week to clean that sucker."

"Funny, Dwight."

"Ain't that The Three Musketeers?" Kevin nodded in the direction of a scattering of children converging upon the front entrance of Banneker Elementary School.

"So?" Dwight said.

"Let's get 'em," Kevin said.

"What for?" Dwight asked.

"No reason."

"Why you want 'em then?"

"It'd be fun."

"You sound like a bully."

"I ain't no bully, Dwight."

"Count me out," David said. David gazed at the displayed pastries in the window of Brahms' Bakery as they passed. Felton stealthily moved four cars forward, squatting behind a Galaxie 500/XL.

Dwight switched his book bag from his left shoulder to his right shoulder, adjusting the shoulder strap across his chest until it was comfortable. "I don't get you, man," he said. "Marvin's your little brother."

"That's just it," Kevin said. "At home, my parents are always yelling at me: 'Don't touch Marvin. He's your baby brother. You shouldn't treat him like that. Leave him alone.' Even when I'm not hassling him, I get in trouble. All Marvin has to do is tell my folks I was messing with him and they come down on me. Nobody to yell at me now. Come on, let's get 'em. It'll be fun!"

"You were having all kinds of fun yesterday when those two sixth graders tried to heist your milk money."

"I handled it."

"With our help." Dwight slapped David five.

"Forget it. You two sissies ain't up to it."

"We ain't sissies."

"Could've fooled me."

"That don't take much."

"Should be wearing a dress, like your Mama," Dwight squared off with Kevin.

"You going need more than a school nurse when I finish whipping up on you, Dwight."

"Nothin' to it but to do it."

David checked his Timex. "One minute before late bell," he announced. They all took off running.

"You're lucky, Dwight."

Dwight glanced over at Kevin while they ran. "Yeah, right," he said in Kevin's ear.

They arrived at the salted stone steps of Banneker Elementary School just as the late bell sounded.

CHAPTER FOUR

It was a day set in dusk. Cars plowed through muddy-brown slush, feeling their way along like a blind person down an unfamiliar street. Bare-knuckled trees hovered over white lawns. Snowflakes fluttered from a bleak sky through swaggering winds. Icicles and gelid stalactites formed where water once dripped. Shoveled and salted sidewalks shined with a clear icy film. From morning until evening, dusk remained.

Snow had become a nasty nuisance after Christmas. Winter had worn out its calm mystery; its subdued charm. Children who delighted in its crystal wetness became anxious for spring. Only those with commitments and urgent errands ventured out. For most, it was work, school, and home—no bar stops or perusing of East Liberty stores. Telephone lines hummed with the conversations of teenagers with best friends and romantic interests. Adults discussed weather, family, domestic news, sports, world events, and local gossip. As an endeared relative can sometimes do, frigid, irritable, sloppy winter overstayed its welcome.

The widow Powell stared through the clear front glass of Willie's Market at a blue and white three-story house across the street, spellbound by the house standing proud through the pall of day. It had an ample porch and a large front yard that sloped toward the sidewalk. From where she stood, she could see only a corner of its back yard. In her mind, she pictured how it had looked for many summers past. Its docile beauty was fenced in by eight-foot-high cedar planks covered in morning glories. There were splendid oaks that broadened and stretched higher every year, with grass as green as a country meadow. It appeared every bit as regal as when she, her husband, and their five children had occupied it. Sounds and smells and memories of her family were present in the walls, carpeted floors, draped windows, and furnished rooms.

When her husband died and, one by one, her children departed to cultivate their own families, it became too large to manage. She sold her past and bought a quaint, two-story future on Alder. It was modern and comfortable and within her meager means.

Yesterday would have been her sixty-fifth wedding anniversary. To her, it was a day painted with all the grays and browns of a somber tapestry. She survived it. That night, she prayed for souls departed and present; then slept until morning nudged her awake.

The Browns were good people: forthright Christians who worked hard. They took exquisite care of her home (as she still imagined it to be). On paper, it was theirs. In her heart, it would forever be hers.

Mrs. Powell meandered midway to Aisle Three, where she examined a small box of Tide.

"Abe?"

"Mrs. Powell?" Abe responded without looking up from an article on the Supreme Court that held his interest. He had finished his copy of *Time* magazine and was now reading *The Post-Gazette*.

"How much for this box of detergent?"

Abe peered over his reading glasses at the convex mirror. He could see Mrs. Powell, but her back was to the mirror.

"Hold it up so I can see it." She did so with both hands. "Seventy-eight cents."

"Hmm," she said, drawing the wrinkles in her ashen brown face into her sagging jowls. She always asked the price of things, despite the fact they were clearly marked on the package. Abe didn't mind. All but one of her children lived out of town. She was lonely. Any minute she could spend with another human being seemed a comfort to her, and he knew it.

"I don't know if I can afford that. I'll have to shop around the store for something a little less expensive." Mrs. Powell smiled with all the pleasantness of a warm cup of cocoa. Abe returned her smile and then resumed reading.

Abe looked up when the cowbells clanged. "Good afternoon, Darius," he said. A dark brown, clean-shaven, stout man of average height, wearing black leather gloves, a black fedora, white scarf, black dress coat, black two-piece suit, white shirt, and black bow tie returned his greeting as "As-Salaam-Alaikum," followed by, "How's Mrs. Stone?" Darius's voice often had a threatening edge. Abe imagined it was unintentional. It was his way of sounding authoritative.

"Good," Abe answered in response to his question.

"Dwight?"

"Good."

"I had hoped we would have seen you and yours over at the Temple by now."

"Thanks, but no thanks."

"Have you read the latest issue of Muhammad Speaks?"

"Not yet."

"There's an article in there on how the black man has allowed himself to fall prey to the white devil's temptations. Read it carefully. I think you'll find it most enlightening."

"I'm sure I will."

Mrs. Powell appeared at the end of Aisle Three, eyeing a box of Brillo Pads. Darius turned to notice her. "Good afternoon, Mrs. Powell."

"Oh, hello, Eddie." Abe smiled. Darius ignored him. "My name is Darius now."

"Are you still Muslim?"

"Yes, ma'am. I'm a minister at Temple 21. I'll be speaking on the subject of respect for our elders tonight. If you would care to come, we'd be happy to have you join us."

"That's nice, honey." Abe suppressed a snort of laughter. "Maybe some other time." Darius adjusted his bow tie and vanished at the back end of Aisle One. Mrs. Powell made her way down Aisle Two.

"Mercy, it's cold out there." The cowbells clamored as Wallace Hickman burst through the door.

"Good afternoon, Wallace," Abe said.

"Mind if I help myself to a cup of coffee?" Wallace asked Abe, ignoring the quizzical expression on Abe's face brought on by Wallace's brusque entrance.

"That's what it's there for."

"You read what the *Courier* wrote about Malcolm X?"

"Sure did."

Wallace poured himself a cup of coffee and held it between his huge hands. "What'd you think?"

"It was good; short but sweet."

Wallace took a quick sip of coffee. Steam rose from an invisible source between his palms. "Only thing bothered me about him was his religion. I don't go in for all that Arab stuff. Know what I mean?"

"No, Wallace, I don't." Wallace held the coffee in his left hand. With his free hand, he wiped his forehead. There was nothing to brush away. It was a habit; one Wallace had since Abe had known him. Abe deduced Wallace developed it from years of working in the sweltering environment of a steel mill. Sweating constantly, it had become a reflex for him to wipe his forehead periodically to dry his brow.

"It just seems silly. I hated that he got murdered, but I like Dr. King better."

"Suppose you couldn't like them both."

"That's because you're not enlightened, my brother," a deep voice interjected.

Wallace looked to his right. "I didn't know you were here, Darius." Darius held two cans of green beans in one hand and a small box of Salada tea in the other. "When can I expect to see you at the Temple for a little spiritual enrichment?"

"Hello, Wallace," Ruth Powell said. Wallace took another sip of coffee as he leaned forward to glance down Aisle Two.

"Good afternoon, Mrs. Powell."

"Thought you weren't going to speak for a minute."

"Nothing like that, ma'am, I didn't see you."

"How's the family?"

"Good. Debbie told me to invite you over for Sunday dinner. If you're free, that is."

"I'll be there."

"How about it, Wallace? When are you going to return your mind, spirit and body to almighty Allah?"

"Not today, Darius." Darius followed Wallace to the counter where Darius deposited his goods. Wallace turned to look down on him. Wallace's bald head shone in the washed-out winter light. Darius stared almost straight up. Wallace worked in the smelting plant at Allegheny Ludlum. All hair had been singed from his face. When Wallace raised his eyes, as if to indicate an end to the discussion, the absence of eyebrows made this effect more dramatic and more menacing. Darius took the hint and continued his shopping.

Wallace leaned forward on the counter. Abe stared at him over the top of his reading glasses. Wallace sipped his coffee. "What's wrong?" Wallace asked in response to Abe staring at him.

"Did you want something?"

"No," Wallace coolly answered. Abe picked up his reading where he left off. Abe knew his best friend. If Wallace had something to say, he would have said it. This was his way of prodding Abe into opening a dialogue. Abe decided not to play along.

"I'd better not stay long. Debbie needs a few things for her dumplings tonight."

"Am I stopping you?"

Wallace put his coffee on the table near the urn, then took a note out of his coat pocket and walked down Aisle Two.

Jesse Wilkerson, a tall, lanky man who moved with contented ease, ambled in, said a casual hello, and went right to shopping.

The door opened with a faint clang. In walked a dirty little boy wearing grubby clothes one size too large. A one-time friend had informed the boy his sister was living with his aunt in their old neighborhood. He'd even supplied Darren with an address. It had taken him all morning to make his way across town to investigate. Nena did not live there. The old man who did sent him running when he refused to open his door, called him names, and threatened to call the police if he did not leave immediately.

Walking to prevent from freezing and in search of a bus stop, Darren happened upon Willie's Market, a place to warm himself for a moment. He glanced toward the counter. The last time he had been in Willie's Market, the Lingles owned the store. Not recognizing anyone Darren saw standing near the counter, he decided not to ask about his sister.

Jesse, Wallace and Darius had made their purchases. They and Abe were standing around discussing philosophical distinctions between the Quran and the Bible. Mrs. Powell browsed Aisle One. Other customers had filtered in to do their grocery shopping. At the back freezer, a young woman in a gray coat puzzled over which flavor of ice cream to purchase. An elderly couple conferred in soft voices near the butcher's section, periodically pointing at different meats through the display glass. No one seemed to notice the child. He furtively vanished down an aisle lined with canned goods.

He looked left, then right. Sardines enticed him. He fingered two gold-colored cans before he grabbed them and shoved them into his coat pocket. They dropped through a hole in his pocket, landing in the thinning lining of his coat. Potted meat, Vienna sausages and Spam went the same way. Someone approached. He seized a can of Pork 'n Beans from a shelf and pretended to read the label. Mrs. Powell sauntered by with a gracious smile and a nod. Darren watched her disappear before he put the can back.

He became reckless. The fact he would eat well tonight made him abandon caution. A ring of stolen goods swelled the bottom of his coat.

"I don't know much about gods," Jesse Wilkerson said, while cleaning his fingernails with his pocketknife, "whether they're named God, Allah, Yahweh, Jehovah, Zeus, Isis, Osiris or one of many titles man bestows upon supreme deities. In our effort to rationalize our lives, we seek a logical, higher purpose. Most religions satisfy that aspect of our needs through doctrines that dictate to us what, supposedly, these universal rulers have decreed as warrants for enlistment in their legions of righteous souls. We are thereby reduced to abiding by another's ethics of living. There are some problems with thinking this way. We all know these lessons of life are often taught through parables. As with laws, parables are open for interpretation by any and all who so choose. To communicate anything with absolute clarity, words alone are difficult.

"Each of us here could stare at the same sunrise. If asked to describe it, we would in all likelihood compose unique descriptions. So much so, that if an individual who knew nothing of our shared experience read our compositions, they would not realize we were describing the same event. Faith filled teachings as vague as allegories, fables, myths and legends are nearly impossible to decipher with infallible certainty. How can any religion—which, literally translated, means 'a way of life'—honestly be more than philosophy?"

"Jesse, I didn't ask you all that," Wallace replied, wiping his forehead. "Do you, or do you not, believe in God?"

"Not in the manner you're suggesting."

"*Aww man*. Getting a straight answer out of this dude is impossible."

"Hear the brother out. His rationale is correct, even if his direction is a bit askew," Darren said.

"Abe, you believe in God, don't you?" Wallace asked. Mark Brown lived in the blue and white house across the street. He was a clean cut, roan-skinned, medium-built man with large round eyes. He had entered the store shortly after the woman who was still puzzling over ice cream. Mark always knew what he wanted. Abe helped him place an armload of goods onto the counter before answering Wallace's question. "Of course."

"Darius?"

"My Lord is Allah, but yes."

"See, Jesse, it's that simple: yes or no."

"How can you disavow the Holy Scriptures?" Mark said to Jesse.

"That's the difference between us," Jesse said. "I believe in God. You believe in the Bible."

"He finally said it," Wallace said with a triumphant expression. Jesse ignored him.

"The Bible is the teachings of God through his prophets. 'Before the world was created, the Word already existed; he was with God, and he was the same as God,'" Mark said in a conscientious voice.

"The Bible is a book on Christianity," Jesse responded with equal commitment, "once again a religion; a set of principles and beliefs. What some might define as a creed. Or, as I stated previously, a way of life."

"God's way."

"In part, you are correct."

"That'll be $7.58," Abe interrupted.

"His principles have been proven through the ages to work for all of us," Mark said, reaching for his wallet.

"Lives are diverse and complex," Jesse responded, putting away his pocketknife.

"We all follow the same path." Mark scooped up his bag of groceries after pocketing his change.

"Life is not a line, but a circle. All religions possess some supreme deity who is said to originate our seed. This assertion centers our lives and gives us purpose, identifying a higher being responsible for all things beyond our control."

"But you can control what happens in your life." Darius saw his opening and he took it. "That is one of the many gifts you will receive if you open your heart and mind to the teachings of the Honorable Elijah Muhammad. How about giving him a chance, Wallace?"

"Never."

"Jesse?"

"Religion is all relative."

"Brother Abe?"

"My answer's the same as always, Darius. Thanks, but no thanks."

Darius looked at Mark. From his expression, he knew better than to ask. "One day, brothers, you will see the light. Allah will show all of you the path to true salvation."

Wallace opened the door for Mark, who needed both hands to carry his bag.

"If you brothers are in search of true spiritual awareness, come by our church Bible study some evening." They stared blankly at Mark before he left. Each man knew they would not be there.

Abe had noticed the child when he entered. He knew a thief when he saw one. Could smell them like skunk spray. He had continued his conversation with his friends all along, eyeing the boy in the convex mirror. Abe excused himself and rushed to the rear of Aisle Three where Darren fingered a box of cherry Jell-O, looking suspiciously around. Abe peered around the corner. No sign of the child. He eased over to Aisle Two, the frozen foods section, and Aisle One. The child had vanished.

"Hold it!" Abe darted to the front of the store. Wallace had secured the child by his coat collar. Darren struggled, his face red with anger.

"What's going on?"

"Caught this little man leaving a few pounds heavier than when he got here," Wallace said.

"Are you stealing from me, son?" The child stopped struggling.

"Who the hell are you?"

"I own this store."

The child's throat collapsed. Nothing came out. Abe stepped up to him and looked down as if he stood on a mountain. "Well?"

The child shook his head. Phlegm dripped from his nose onto his crusted upper lip. Abe noticed smeared drippings on his coat. "I-I was just leaving."

"Mind if I search you first?"

"You got a search warrant?"

"These two hands are the only search warrant I need."

The child made desperate efforts to maneuver out of Wallace's grasp. Wallace settled him down with one hard jerk.

"If you put your hands on me, I'll scream for the police!"

"Go ahead." Before Darren could respond, Abe had him upside down, shaking him. His bony ankles were chaffed and grimy. Abe noticed the holes in his shoe bottoms. Wallace helped by holding Darren's coat seams. The dull sounds of cans hitting the floor mixed with pleas to be let down. Everyone in the market had gathered around when they heard the commotion.

"Help! Police! Police!" Darren's eyes bounced around in their sockets. The smell of urine wafted up the legs of his pants. Abe turned his head to one side to lessen its nauseous effect. Wallace and Darius chuckled. Abe dropped Darren on his back.

"What do you think the police would say if I told them what I found in your thieving pockets? Do you think they'd ask if I had a search warrant?"

Darren groggily got to his feet. He felt queasy. His eyes were cloudy. "I was goin' pay, soon as this money—." Before he could finish, Darren convulsed. Phlegm had rolled down his throat into his empty stomach. A mixture of mucus, stomach acid and blood came up. Abe recognized it. He had seen the condition before among destitute people in Korea and in this country. It was as an early indication of starvation.

All but Abe backed away from the child. Wallace and Darius appeared ashamed. Others were openly appalled at the sight of his vomit. If the child had asked for help, Abe would have given it to him. Stealing was unpardonable in his book, just below murder and rape.

Felton Dobbs rushed in. He quickly passed in front of Darren, marched to the corner nearest the coffee urn, pivoted, stood at attention, saluted Abe, then settled into a position of parade rest, glaring at the child. Aside from Darren, everyone dismissed his presence.

Abe followed Felton's line of sight back to the woozy child. Wallace had slipped in behind to hold Darren up. Abe grabbed a shopping bag from behind the front counter and filled it a quarter of the way with various items about the store, beginning with goods that had fallen out of the child's coat. Everyone watched in silence, their attention straying from Abe to Felton to Darren.

Abe handed Darren the bag. Darren looked confused. "Take it," Abe commanded. Wallace nudged Darren in his back. The child cautiously reached for the bag, all the while staring at the stern face of Abe Stone.

"I don't take charity."

"You're not too proud to steal, but you're too proud to take it when it's given to you? Get your little butt out of my store before I stuff you in that bag and toss you out."

Shame swept across Darren's face. "I'm goin' pay you back, mister."

Abe crossed his arms over his chest. "You can repay me by never setting foot in my store again." Darren opened his mouth as if to speak. He wanted to ask about his sister. The people staring at him kept him silent, especially Felton, whom he regarded as strange and possibly dangerous.

Wallace opened the door. Darren nearly collapsed from the weight of the bag. Wallace bent forward to help, and then straightened as if he changed his mind.

After Darren left, everyone returned to shopping. Mumbles and murmurs came from almost every segment. Felton stood still, fixated on the spot where Darren had been.

Abe went to the window. He watched the child disappear. Darius had followed Darren out of the door. Darius said something to Darren that the child frowned upon, then they went in opposite directions. Jesse left shortly afterwards with only a brief glance and timid goodbye. Wallace followed, hurrying groceries home to his wife. Mrs. Powell settled in beside Abe. Placing her palms on the small of her arched back, her face uplifted toward the ceiling, she stretched with an audible "Ooooo," followed by, "my God, that felt good." Abe quietly took notice. She wrapped her ancient arms around his waist.

"That was a nice thing you did, Abe." They looked into each other's eyes. Both pairs registered sympathy. Abe draped an arm over Mrs. Powell's slumping shoulders. As hard as her old muscles would allow, she squeezed his waist.

"What kind of parents would allow their child to live like that?" Ruth Powell asked.

"He's a street orphan, Ruth. Hustling, running numbers, stealing—whatever it takes to get by, that's what he'll do. When he gets old enough, he'll probably take to dealing drugs or robbing people. Or maybe he'll remain a thief."

They had both seen kids like Darren. You could find them in any city, but it had never hit this close to home. Never settled into their lap of comfortable existence and said with a frail, soiled body and desperate eyes, "I am a child who needs help."

Felton Dobbs had become only as much as a common table or chair; a physical object that existed, not to be noticed, commented on, studied but to be recognized and then mentally discarded—stepped over or around as a puddle in the street, a drunk comatose on a sidewalk, or a relic host of mourners' sons, daughters, fathers, mothers, aunts, uncles, cousins and friends. A kinship with emphasis on 'kin', sanity required distancing oneself from the ship.

Felton rushed out as abruptly as he came. Abe cleaned up the vomit. Mrs. Powell resumed shopping, along with other patrons. Word circulated about what had transpired in Willie's Market. The remainder of the day, Abe checked out each customer with an earnest "Thank you." Each remarked positively on the incident they had either witnessed or heard about.

None of their comments placed Abe at ease or erased the image of that child. Between customers, he stared out of his front window. He watched cars slide up to one of the three stop signs he could see at the four-way intersection. *Temperature's dropping*, he thought. *Roads look slick.* Again, he thought of the child.

"Abe, how much for these prunes?" Ruth Powell had returned before the dinner hour for her last social visit of the day.

"Nineteen cents, Mrs. Powell," Abe said.

"How much?"

"Nineteen cents!"

"Hmm, sounds a bit much."

Abe imagined that at one time Ruth Powell was very beautiful. Traces of it still lingered in her radiant eyes. That boy's eyes were scared. Surviving: that's all he was attempting to do. Make it to the next meal, the next day, hour, minute, second of life.

"Abe, are you all right?" Mrs. Powell stood across the counter from him with a can of prunes in her hands.

"Yes, ma'am."

"Thinking about that boy?" Abe looked at her and nodded. "You did what you could do. The rest is in the Lord's hands." Abe thought about how full those hands must be by now, with all sorts of souls in need.

"I think I'll take these prunes after all. Could you put them on my account?"

"Yes, ma'am."

"Thank you, honey. Goodnight. Tell Winona and Dwight I said hi."

"I will. Goodnight."

Street lamps flirted with impending darkness. Their shuddering light hovered like a giant lightening bug above Willie's Market. Abe stepped out into the whispering night. He looked around, closing the door behind him. Someone was out there. He sensed it. Abe turned on his combat instincts, surveying the area. The north wind bit his face. He saw no one. The store was dark. Abe stared through the caged front door at its blackness. It had been a good day despite bad weather. He took solace in that thought as he walked home. From the deep shadow of the Brown's porch, Felton stepped forward into the light and smiled.

CHAPTER FIVE

"Winona called."

"Is there more, Roberta?"

"I'm just telling you."

"What she want?"

"Nothin' special."

"Humph." Curtiss turned a page of *The Pittsburgh Press* and scanned it before deciding to read an article about the Civil Rights Act. Roberta grabbed the last sheet from the white heap she had been ironing for the past three hours. They were for a woman in Squirrel Hill. The woman's husband would arrive at seven a.m. sharp to pick them up before he went to work. Three other Squirrel Hill residents would follow him. Another five hours of ironing due at eight, eight-thirty and nine, respectively. She would have to finish it all tonight, which meant she would be forced to leave her church group meeting early. Her legs ached. She stretched upward with her thin arms, attempting to ease the tightness in her lower back. The alcohol buzz she had earlier had evaporated. She felt sluggish and heavy. When she slowly rolled her neck around, Curtiss glanced up from his reading chair across the room.

He noticed how she had aged twenty years over the last ten; not with elegance, but in hammer and chisel fashion. Age engraved into her forehead, about her neck, under her eyes, and on her hands. Gray hair sprouted enough to be noticed. Fatigue was her constant state.

Roberta turned up a Billy Eckstine song on the radio. Curtiss fidgeted in his chair. She had been a sprite, beautiful young woman when they met, the lead vocalist for the blues band Butterbean. Stars in her eyes and her voice, she alone compared to Billie Holiday. He wondered: had her deterioration been his doing? Had he and their children reduced her to this person? Taking in white folk's laundry, active only in the church, becoming better friends with Jim Beam than anyone else in her life—she deserved more. Could he deliver whatever she needed to boomerang her back to the Roberta he loved?

Part of the reason for Roberta's current state could be traced back to the year the Stone family arrived, 1958. Abe Stone had written aunts, uncles and cousins all over the northern part of the country. He had heard good things about the north from his communications with black relatives and friends who had migrated north; less racism and better opportunities being on the top of that list. He knew it was worth a try.

Most said they could stay a week or two. Two offered a month. Curtiss barely knew his cousins. It did not prevent him from extending an absolute welcome. Roberta was not as hospitable. She protested to Curtiss in private, but was polite to the people she referred to as houseguests. Curtiss helped Abe and Winona find jobs and cared for Dwight as if he were his own. Roberta became jealous when she believed Curtiss showed Dwight a favoritism he denied his own sons. This created friction between Winona and Roberta. Sometimes brief skirmishes broke out when one or the other perceived bias; skirmishes that resulted in bad feelings that could last for days.

After Abe and Winona found a place of their own, Roberta and Winona found a safe zone. A level of tolerance emerged that bloomed into courteous friendship.

One day, Mr. Lingle mentioned to Abe that he wanted to sell Willie's Market. It had become difficult for him to manage the store after his wife's death. His three sons, including the store's namesake William, showed no interest in continuing his legacy. Abe and Winona had been saving for such an opportunity. He talked it over with Winona and they decided to make an offer. Through Ron Hightower, they were able to acquire what Abe and Winona believed to be a substantial loan. They offered that, along with all of their savings, to Ralph Lingle. He turned them down. When Mr. Lingle told them what was acceptable, the deal seemed doomed. Abe mentioned his predicament to Curtiss, who loaned him the additional funds.

Once Roberta learned of their plans from Curtiss, her behavior toward the Stones changed. She would visit bearing gifts of pies and cakes and advice about anything she believed might interest Winona. They were seen shopping together and taking lunch, arms interlinked like conjoined twins as they went to church and participated in community projects. She became a second mother to Dwight and encouraged Curtiss to spend more time with Abe.

Curtiss was unaware of his wife's intentions. His only motivation in loaning his cousins the money was the sole fact that they were family who needed help. To Roberta, there were implicit terms of repayment that exceeded formal agreements and transcended subliminal promises. It did not matter to Roberta that they reimbursed them for the time they lived in their home and paid back everything they borrowed.

Roberta invited Abe and Winona over for dinner. The ploy was that it would give them an opportunity to catch up, since everyone had been too busy to see much of each other. Roberta had literally set the table for her impending proposal with a down-home feast: simple, homemade dishes, when done right, made your mouth water and your palate praise the Lord.

Curtiss eyed the spread on the dining room table of buttered mashed potatoes, rolls and cornbread, vegetable soup, turnip and mustard greens, potato salad, macaroni and cheese, red beans and rice, and honey-baked, hickory-smoked ham while Roberta freshened up. He sampled the sweet tea and lemonade that he made to assure they were acceptable refreshments to accompany the meal. They were. He questioned if anyone would have room for Roberta's legendary peach cobbler, still warm in the kitchen.

Abe and Winona could smell the ham when they walked in. Roberta made a big show of their arrival before she escorted their guests into the dining room.

The children weren't a bother. Roberta arranged for Kevin, Marvin and Dwight to spend the weekend with Tina Russell. Tina owed Roberta a favor. Tina was also in on the ruse.

The dinner conversation was light and festive. Roberta was a gracious and hospitable host throughout. When time came for dessert, everyone begged off for the moment. *Hogs fattened for the slaughter,* Roberta thought of Abe and Winona as she cleared the table.

Everyone retired to the living room. They had switched from lemonade or sweet tea to wine. The couples made themselves comfortable. Abe sat next to Winona on the couch. Roberta put a stack of 45s on the record player and then joined Curtiss, who had taken a seat in his favorite chair. Roberta dropped down on the armrest beside her husband, draping an arm around his shoulders.

"Roberta, thank you for doing this," Winona said.

"No problem; anytime," Roberta said.

"It feels good to spend time with family," Winona said.

"That's for sure," Abe added.

"Like my baby said, anytime." Curtiss placed an arm across Roberta's legs. "You know, we should make this a regular thing."

"I'm up for that as long as you plan on doing your part in the kitchen next time," Roberta said. Everyone laughed.

"I will, but that's not what I mean. It doesn't have to be all out, all of the time."

"I understand," Abe said. "A regularly-scheduled break from the routine."

"Like movies or the theater," Winona said.

"Or dancing," Roberta added. The women smiled at each other.

"Or–," Abe said, being interrupted by Curtiss.

"Game night!" Curtiss and Abe said simultaneously.

"*Exactly*," Curtiss said. "Dominoes, cards, Scrabble, Pokeno— whatever we're in the mood for."

The women stopped smiling. Their demeanors went from happy to dismay. They both knew why their husbands were not keen on their ideas. Abe was a mediocre dancer who thought everyone made fun of him when he danced. Curtiss was as fidgety as a hopped-up child on sweets when he and Roberta went to a film or play.

"That's also an idea," Winona said about the game night suggestion, not veiling her annoyance.

"Yes, it is," Roberta said, matching Winona's tenor. The men noticed the tone in their wives' voices as well as the expressions on their faces.

"Maybe we could do both," Curtiss said.

"Yeah, kind of mix it up," Abe said.

"Next time we can have this get together at our place," Winona said.

"Or a dance club," Roberta said.

The men smiled and nodded. Winona and Roberta laughed.

They agreed on two weeks from the day to meet at the Stones' house for dinner and dominoes. Dancing and movie dates were to be planned for later. In either case, no children were allowed.

Once that was settled, the music had a chance to sink in. Roberta snapped her fingers and swayed in time to Fontella Bass singing *Rescue Me*.

"I like this song," Winona said. Abe agreed.

"Oh yeah," Curtiss said.

"The way Fontella sings this is like soft butter on hot biscuits. Her voice melts in your ears." Everyone but Roberta laughed at her metaphor. She was too locked into the music.

"Have you ever heard of Butterbean?" Roberta asked Winona and Abe.

"The food?" Abe said.

"No, the music group," Roberta said.

"I've heard of them," Abe said. "Never heard any of their music."

"I used to sing lead," Roberta said.

"You mentioned that to me before," Winona said.

"We were mostly a blues band. We'd mix it up with a little jazz, soul, and R & B. Even throw in a little pop and country now and then."

"My baby can sing," Curtiss said.

Curtiss was right. Roberta harmonized with Fontella Bass in perfect pitch. The song faded, but Roberta's voice rang on clear and true.

"What happened to Butterbean?" Winona asked.

"Time, adult responsibilities taking precedence over childish dreams— the usual. You know what that's like," Roberta said to Winona and Abe.

Abe and Winona nodded. Abe took Winona's hand. They glanced at each other. The suspicion passed between them that Roberta might be referring to the realization of their dream: to own a store. Abe detected a hint of resentment in Roberta's voice. He wondered if Winona sensed the same.

"Refill?" Curtiss asked. Everyone's glass was near empty. The consensus was yes. Curtiss did the honors as The Miracles sang *The Tracks of My Tears*. Roberta again was in perfect harmony with the lead singer.

"Did Butterbean ever make any recordings?" Winona asked once Curtiss was settled back into his seat.

"Unfortunately, no," Roberta said. "We'd get close; but for one reason or another we'd fall short. Opportunities and money; that's the name of the game. They drive everything in business, whether it's janitorial services, grocery stores, or music. They all dance to the same tune."

Curtiss sensed that Roberta was falling into one of her melancholy moods. She often did that when she was drinking and reminisced about Butterbean.

"Well, that's water under the bridge now," Curtiss said. He gave Roberta a couple of reassuring pats on her legs. He noticed something in the way his wife stared at Abe and Winona. Curtiss did not like the look in her eyes. He knew his wife well enough to know that she was up to something.

"I spoke to Melon the other day," Roberta said.

"Who's Melon?" Abe asked.

"He's the drummer and former manager of Butterbean," Curtiss said.

"He's getting the group back together," Roberta said.

"Why is this the first time I'm hearing about this?" Curtiss asked.

"I was going to tell you, honey, as soon as I made a decision."

"A decision to do what?" Curtiss asked.

"I want to go back to the band," Roberta said.

Junior Walker and The All Stars filled the room with *Shotgun*.

"Melon says he found someone who will record us an album on the cheap without cutting corners on quality," Roberta said.

No one said anything. They sipped their wine.

"All he needs is ten thousand dollars to make it happen."

"Honey, don't do this," Curtiss said.

"Now, hear me out. I've spoken to Melon and the rest of the band. We're ready to make this happen. All we need is a little help."

"Are you asking us to back Butterbean?" Abe asked.

"She's not doing any such thing," Curtiss said.

"We're good. Butterbean is an excellent band. With me as the lead singer, there would be no telling how far we could go."

"We can't help you, Roberta," Winona said.

"All we're asking for is a loan to get us going. We'll pay you back in no time."

"We don't know anything about the music business," Abe said, looking for a way out.

"You don't have to. Leave that to Melon and me. We'll handle everything. All we need is a little seed money from you and Winona, and we'll take it from there."

"We can't do that, Roberta," Abe said.

"Why not?"

"All of our money is tied up in the store."

"Are you two telling me Willie's Market ain't making you good money? Everything on that table came from your store. Just about everything in our cupboards too."

"We're doing all right, but we're not pulling down the kind of money you're talking about."

"All it would take is ten thousand dollars to make this happen. Like I said, seed money: we'd get it back to you before you know it."

"Roberta—," Curtiss said.

"Let me finish, Curtiss."

"I think you've already said enough," Curtiss said.

"Maybe you're right. Abe, Winona—what do you say? Are you willing to loan us the cash?

"Roberta, we don't have the money to loan to you," Abe said.

"You mean, you *won't* loan us the money."

"He means," Winona said, "that we don't have that kind of money to spare. Most of what we make goes right back into the store."

"We're solvent, but our average profit margin is less than a quarter of what you're asking," Abe said. "To give you the money you need, we'd have to take out a loan."

"I see," Roberta said.

"Roberta, honey," Curtiss said.

"Don't 'Roberta, honey' me. So that's how it is."

"How what is?" Abe said.

"We take in you poor, backwoods, sorry bumpkin asses—"

"Now, wait a minute, Roberta—," Abe said.

"Feed you, clothe you, welcome you into our home, and you can't even show a little reciprocation when one of us is in need."

"They don't owe us anything," Curtiss said.

"*This ain't about us*," Roberta screamed at Curtiss. "This is about me. This about the music career I've always dreamed of having. The music career that I deserve."

"I think we should leave," Abe said, more to Curtiss than to Roberta.

"Get the hell out," Roberta said. "Get the hell out of my house!"

The music had stopped. Abe and Winona got up and made their way to the front door. Roberta blocked their way.

Bitterness like Curtiss had never before heard from his wife spewed into the faces of his cousins. The pity Abe had felt earlier for Roberta dissolved into anger. Winona wept with apologies as Roberta cursed and slashed their characters. Curtiss could see the fury in his cousin's face. Abe would have knocked her flat if Roberta were a man; not as much for what Roberta said to him, but for having made Winona cry. Abe led his wife away without a parting word; only a dissenting look that told Curtiss that while Abe appreciated what they had done, things between them had reached a continental divide—a breach only an epic earthquake could unite.

Curtiss and Roberta argued for hours about her behavior after Abe and Winona left. Almost five years had passed since that time and still her anger burned red.

Roberta flexed her right wrist several times. She sprinkled water from an aqua-colored water shaker onto the white sheet, then set the hot electric iron in motion, smoothing out wrinkles.

"You gotta work tonight?" Roberta asked.

"Yep."

"When's Melon coming back?"

"Next week."

"You the boss; why you got to be the one to make up his time?"

"Because I'm the boss."

"Don't seem right."

"Right or wrong, that's the way it is. That reminds me. Kevin!"

"What you bothering that boy for?"

"Kevin! Get down here! Did he do his reading today?"

"I don't remember."

"How can you not remember, Roberta? We have to stay on this boy. Kevin!"

"Yeah," Kevin shouted down from the upstairs hall.

"Yeah? Bring your butt down here!"

"Why you so hard on the child?"

"Roberta, hard on him ain't hardly what I am. All I want is an education for our son."

"You doing all right without one."

"Educated men doing better."

"Like Abe Stone?"

"Like Abe Stone."

"He got lucky."

"Yeah, Dad?"

"That man's smart and ambitious—did you do your reading?" Curtiss's eyes moved from his wife to level on his son's face.

"Yeah."

"Sit down." Kevin sat in the chair to the left of his father. "Teach me something."

"What'd you want to know?"

"Tell me something about what you read."

Roberta looked at her son. He seemed perplexed. With an earnest nod from his mother, Kevin returned his father's stare. Curtiss patiently waited for his son to speak.

"In 1773," Kevin began, "some American colonialists—I mean colonists—dressed up like Indians and threw some tea into Boston Harbor. They called it The Boston Tea Party."

"Why'd they do that?"

"Because they were mad."

"About what?"

"What the British did to 'em."

"What'd they do?"

"I don't know."

"Think." Curtiss tapped Kevin's forehead with his forefinger.

"They were helping some tea company."

"What was their name?"

"Whose?"

"The tea company's?"

"Give him a chance, Curtiss." Curtiss ignored Roberta. He continued to press Kevin for an answer with his stare.

"East something, ah…East Indian…East In-dee-ah, East India Company; they were a private company. The British wanted to help 'em not go broke. They figured a way to make money and that made the colonists mad, because they were making less money. That's why they dressed up like Indians and got on those ships and threw their tea overboard."

Curtiss nodded his approval. Mother and son smiled.

"That didn't hurt any, did it?"

"No, sir."

Curtiss leaned in close to his oldest child. "When you study something, Kevin, you need to know it backward and forward, inside and out. Make it yours. That way, no matter what the teacher asks, you're ready. That's what education's all about: preparation, same as life. The more knowledge you get, the better prepared you are, the more you can achieve."

"That's right, baby," Roberta chimed in.

"When you apply yourself there's nothing you can't do."

"Yes, sir."

"That's all the questions I have tonight."

"Did you get your clothes ready for school?" Roberta asked.

"Yes, ma'am. Can I go over to Dwight's house after school tomorrow?" Roberta's face soured. She rested the iron on its heel.

"You still on punishment," Curtiss answered. "If you keep up the good work we might cut it short." Roberta glared at her husband.

"Tomorrow's out of the question," Roberta said. Kevin hung his head.

"What's Marvin doing upstairs?" Roberta asked.

"Nothing."

"I can't hear you with your head down."

"Leave the boy alone, Roberta."

"I'm not talking to you, Curtiss."

"Marvin not doing nothing, mama; reading some comic book."

"What were you doing before your daddy interrupted you?" Curtiss glared at Roberta.

"Studying," Kevin answered. Curtiss sucked his teeth, something he only did when angry or in deep thought.

"Go on back upstairs," Curtiss said. "We'll talk later."

Roberta waited until she heard Kevin shut his bedroom door before she spoke. "I don't like Kevin hanging out with Abraham Stone's boy."

"Dwight's a good influence on Kevin."

"He's just like his daddy."

"There's nothing wrong with the Stones."

"How can you say that after the way they treated us, after all the hospitality we showed them?"

"They owe us nothing. They're family. And let me remind you, Abe's a big reason I'm boss. They wanted to give him the job, remember? He talked the owner into making me supervisor."

"Big deal."

"You used to think it was."

"They can do a lot more."

"We're comfortable."

"Not as comfortable as the Stones."

"They earned it."

"Why you so protective of them?"

"I'm finished with this conversation. And what's this I hear about you and Mabel and Tina not goin' pay what you owe Abe Stone?"

"I don't know what you're talking 'bout." Roberta stared down at her ironing.

"Mark Brown overheard Mabel talking to Tina Russell at Bible study about some stupid plan you three have cooked up not to pay your grocery bills."

"What if we did? It'd serve him right."

"Forget it, Roberta."

"We should be getting our groceries free."

"If I find out you're not sending the money 'round to the store to pay our grocery bill, I'll start paying it myself."

"You do that and you'd better find yourself another wife."

Curtiss stood, folded his newspaper, and placed it under his right arm.

"One more thing, Roberta. Kevin's been getting a little accident prone lately. I walked past the boys' room Sunday just after he'd taken off his shirt. There were bruises on his back. He said he got them playing football. Is that true?"

Roberta lifted the iron and made a couple of deft passes over the sheet. "If that's what he said."

"They didn't look like football bruises to me. Seemed more like somebody took a strap to our son's bare back." Curtiss waited for Roberta to respond. Roberta continued ironing.

"Make no mistake. I love you, but if I find out you're abusing our kids, my sons and me are gettin' the hell out of here. Understand?"

Roberta and Curtiss unflinchingly stared at one another.

"Bye," Roberta said, holding the hot iron above the sheet.

Roberta assumed Curtiss would go into either the living room or upstairs bedroom to finish his newspaper. Nancy Wilson crooned *Gentle Is My Love* on the radio. Roberta did not hear the closet door open and close or the front door gently snap shut. She pressed the hot iron harder on the final sheet, steaming away spots of water and an occasional tear.

CHAPTER SIX

Dinner was on the table when Abe walked in the front door. He disposed of his coat, sweater, scarf, and gloves, washed his hands, and joined his waiting family in the dining room. Fried pork steaks, collard greens cooked with salt pork, mashed potatoes, homemade brown gravy, buttermilk biscuits and a pitcher of iced tea were neatly arranged near the center of the table. Abe sat at his customary spot at the head of the dining room table. To his left sat his wife; to his right sat his son. Each person unfolded their cloth napkins and spread them in their laps.

They grasped hands. Steam from the mashed potatoes dampened the underside of Dwight's bare forearm. Abe led them in a brief prayer before they ate. The prayer referenced God, his family, their friends, and the food they were about to eat. Little was said during most of the meal. Everyone filled their hungry bellies before they recollected their mouths served another function called talking.

"How was school?" Abe asked Dwight.

"All right."

"Did you see Eli?

"Yeah."

"So what happened?"

"Nothing. He looked at me. I looked at him. Then we kept going to class or whatever."

"I don't like this, Abe."

"Neither do I, Winona. But Eli's got to learn that anytime he messes with Dwight, he's going pay the price."

"After the last whopping I gave him, he won't be back. If he's dumb enough to try me again, I'm ready."

"I suppose what Reverend Wilshire said last Sunday about turning the other cheek didn't mean anything to you, Dwight?"

Abe frowned.

"Don't matter what cheek Eli turns my way. I'm going bop him on it."

"That's not what the Reverend meant and you know it."

"Your mother's right. There's a big difference between self-defense and fighting. I only asked because I know Eli hangs out with that Pillars boy. Thought they might try something."

"Can we change the subject?"

"Got a new Louis Armstrong album," Dwight boasted.

"From where?" Abe asked.

"Bill's Record Mart. Still sealed and everything."

"Which one did you get?"

"The Greatest Concert."

"Heard it, son."

"So have I."

"Every time I get a Louis Armstrong record, you two have heard it."

"Your Mom and I are big fans of Satchmo."

Dwight cringed. "I don't like it when people call him Satchmo. His name is Louis Daniel Armstrong. Why can't people respect that?"

"How do you know he didn't prefer being called Satchmo?" Abe asked.

"I don't." Dwight paused. "Where are all the records?"

Abe and Winona looked at each other. Abe raised and dropped his shoulders. Winona's eyebrows did the same. They both looked at Dwight. "Pardon?" Abe asked.

"If you've heard all his music, where are all the records?"

"Back when we were growing up, records and record players were expensive. Most of the music we heard was on the radio."

"Or at socials."

"Or jook joints." Winona glared at Abe who mischievously grinned, pretending to ignore her. She did not speak again until after she had eaten her last forkful of greens.

"You certainly have a feel for Louis Armstrong," Winona said.

"I'm doing my next school report on him."

"Don't mean to change the subject, but, Winona, do you remember a woman by the name of Marcia Reed?"

"Husband left? Used to live way over on Polk Street?"

"That's her."

"Haven't seen her in years."

"She was murdered down in The Projects."

"Abe." Winona rolled her eyes toward Dwight.

"Sorry. Didn't she have two kids?"

"Can I be excused?"

They both glanced at Dwight's plate. It had nothing but thin brown smears where he had sopped up gravy with his biscuits. Abe nodded. "Get started on the dishes before you turn on that TV," Abe told him. Dwight took his plate, silverware, and drinking glass into the kitchen.

"I believe so," Winona responded to the question. "One girl. Her name was Nena, or something like that. She had a little boy, too. Pretty children."

"I could've sworn I saw a boy in the store today who looked like her son."

"Really?"

"What happened to her kids after she passed?"

"Last I heard, they were sent to an aunt on the Southside."

"I swear that boy is her son."

"Why didn't you ask him?"

Abe cut his eyes toward the kitchen. Dwight came in and scooped up as many serving dishes as he could carry back to the kitchen. "I'll tell you about it later."

Winona got the hint and moved the conversation along. "Our Sisterhood meeting's tonight. So I expect you two to clean up."

Dwight had returned for another load. "I'm doing my part," Dwight said as he worked his way around his parents. Winona suppressed a laugh. Abe stared at Dwight, who pretended to ignore his father, carting as many dishes as he could carry into the kitchen.

"Why's the meeting tonight instead of Thursday?" Abe asked.

"Elise has to leave town this week. We thought we'd have it earlier so she wouldn't miss anything."

"Her father?"

"I still can't believe it."

"Neither can I, baby."

"All over some stupid segregated water fountain."

"If he would've left Alabama when we did, maybe he'd still be alive."

"You can get shot for being a Negro in Pennsylvania just as easily as in Alabama."

"Not likely, and haven't you heard? We're Black now."

"Bullets don't care what you call yourself."

Abe and Winona helped Dwight clear away the few remaining dishes. Dwight stayed in the kitchen by the sink. Abe and Winona returned to the dining room to sit at the table.

"I called Roberta today," Winona said.

Dwight turned on the water.

"What for?" Abe asked.

"To see how she's doing."

"Is she still a bitch?" Winona playfully slapped Abe's forearm, but her face was stern. "How's she doing?"

"About the same; still upset about that Blues thing."

"That woman will take that to her grave."

"I feel sorry for her."

"I feel sorry for Curtiss and those kids."

"She's drinking more, these days. One of her regulars stopped having her do her laundry because Roberta scorched a couple of her silk blouses."

Dwight turned off the water. What followed were sounds of hand-agitated water and dishes being roughly submerged.

"She won't set foot in the store," Abe said.

"I know."

"Always sends Curtiss or one of the boys."

"Did you hear anything more about those delinquent accounts?"

"Yep, last week I talked to Louis and Mark about 'em." Abe took a sip from a glass of iced tea he had brought with him from the kitchen. Winona rested her elbows on the table and put her fist beneath her chin. Abe silently appreciated her delicate beauty before he continued. "They're all paid up. Mabel and Tina don't know anything about it. Curtiss told me to keep him posted. If Roberta didn't pay by the end of this week, he'd pay it himself."

"I'm thinking about inviting them for dinner next week."

"Curtiss and the kids will come. Roberta? Good luck."

"I'll ask her tonight."

Abe turned sideways in his chair to get closer to Winona. "Is she going be at the meeting?" Abe gently rubbed her forearm.

"I'm sure she will."

"She's not hostile to you?"

"No. Not in an overt way. Reverend Wilshire wouldn't stand for any nonsense in his church."

"You believe what they're saying about the Reverend and Virginia?" Winona recalled a rumor she'd recently heard about Abe and Virginia.

"She's an attractive woman. He's a man. It's possible." Abe tried to determine what Winona meant by that comment. She smiled and winked at him. His apprehension dissolved.

"I've also heard rumors about him and some of the prostitutes he's supposed to be counseling," Abe said.

"Since when has Abraham Jacob Stone been interested in ugly rumors?"

"I guarantee most of his congregation doesn't think they're just rumors."

"Do you?"

"Only the ones that can be substantiated; then they're ugly facts."

"He tries," Winona said with a sympathetic tone.

"Trying's not enough. A spiritual leader should abide by a higher moral code."

"If it's God's will."

"God's got nothing to do with lust."

Winona disliked the way Abe spoke of Reverend Wilshire, as if he were simply another man, not divine or holy, likening his soul to those of a sailor or drug dealer or butcher. To her it exhibited indignation; a sacred lack of respect. She stretched her arms out over the table and changed the subject.

"Did Eva come in the store today?"

"No."

"I'll probably see her at tonight's meeting. What you going do this evening?"

"I need to go over the books for the store. Since I won't have the pleasure of your company tonight, I may as well do that."

"I'll be back as soon as I can."

"Won't be soon enough."

"When I get back, we need to talk about Dwight."

"No problem."

They smiled at each other. Winona pinched Abe's forearm, then glanced over her shoulder. Dwight was out of sight. He could be heard sloshing water over what sounded like silverware, rinsing it, and then dropping it in the wire dish rack.

"Are you still having those headaches?" Abe asked.

"Not as bad," Winona answered.

"Want to see a doctor?"

"They'll go away. With all that's happening these days, I can't seem to relax."

"It's for the better. Change always involves growing pains."

"I know. It still frightens me. Riots, protest marches, people threatening to murder each other over this issue or that."

"We can't go back. No more than we could go back to Alabama. Our people have to continue to move forward. No matter what happens. It's like Dr. King said, 'One day historians will record this movement as one of the most significant epics of our heritage.' It's up to us to make those words prophecy."

Dwight made more dishwashing noises. It sounded as though he had moved on to the pots. Winona squeezed her husband's hand. Their eyes searched the soul of the other. A passionate kiss happened. Winona realized she had better douse the spark before it became a flame. "I'd better go," she said.

"You sure that's the only thing bothering you?" Abe asked.

She kissed Abe. "I'm over that now."

"Think you might need counseling again?"

Winona did not answer. She put on her scarf and heavy wool coat over her plain brown dress. She had taken time to dress after cooking dinner, knowing she would be in a rush to leave. She went into the kitchen to "get her hug," as she put it and say goodnight to Dwight. Abe saw his wife to the door. They hugged, and then kissed. He checked to make certain she was bundled up.

"What about your gloves?"

Winona took them out of her coat pocket and put them on. Abe kissed her gloved hand; the one with the wedding band.

"Be careful," he said.

She wondered what he meant by that. Bethlehem Temple was three short blocks away. Whatever was on his mind, it was too late to pursue the matter.

"You want me to come around and get you when the meeting's over?"

With her gloved hands, she touched his face. "I won't need an escort, honey, but thank you."

"I'll be here when you get back." Abe kissed her before she left.

Abe sat for a minute on the living room couch. He too had overheard rumors involving Winona and Reverend Wilshire. Winona had come to believe she would never bear children, despite hospital tests that proved her and Abe both capable. The doctor encouraged them to keep trying. Winona could think of nothing else but the eleven years they had been trying with no success. Her mood had grown dark. Depression ruled her existence. One day, concerned, Abe closed the store at lunchtime to check on her. She had been in her worst depression that morning. When he got home, he found her lying on their bed, wearing her wedding dress, a Gideon Bible clutched to her bosom. An empty bottle of sleeping pills lay on the floor on his side of the bed. He got her to her feet and forced her downstairs into the kitchen where he made her drink milk, then coffee. After she vomited, he rushed her to Mercy Hospital.

When she returned home, her depressed state returned with her. Shortly afterwards she began private counseling sessions with Reverend Wilshire at Reverend Wilshire's suggestion.

The once-a-week sessions seemed to help. Her mood brightened. She became less concerned about children and more focused on living a full, contented life. Then suddenly, after three months of therapy, Winona became withdrawn. She stayed up late reading her bible, asking Abe for time to herself. Abe became concerned she was having a relapse. He was hesitant to leave her alone, but did as she asked.

That's when the rumors surfaced about Winona and the Reverend. At first, he dismissed them as ridiculous. They persisted, although they were never told directly to Abe. He overheard snippets of information at the barbershop and around the store.

Had they had an affair? If perfidy had occurred, Abe preferred ignorance to divulgence, especially in her delicate state. Nothing was more important to him than his wife's welfare.

"Dwight."

"Yeah, Dad."

"Done yet?"

"Just about."

"Keep washing and I'll dry."

He joined Dwight in the kitchen. A strainer spoon and a knife were all that remained.

"Is your homework done?"

"Yes, sir."

Abe looked at Dwight and wondered if he even suspected he was not their natural child.

"When we're finished, why don't we have some of your mom's blackberry pie and listen to a little bit of your new Louis Armstrong album?" Dwight gave his approval with a smile.

CHAPTER SEVEN

White fluorescent light filled the church basement. Central gas heat kept it warm. An eight-foot-high, hand crafted ceiling reached wood paneled walls. Tan indoor/outdoor carpeting covered a concrete foundation as long as a bowling alley and as wide as a two-lane street. At the farthest wall from the stairs, leading up to the pulpit, hung a crucifix. From the remotest point in the basement, one could see tears of blood tracing the pearly face of Jesus. Under the crucifix was an eight-foot-long foldup table. On the table were cups and saucers, silverware, chocolate, and angel food and pound cake randomly placed on either side of a silver coffee urn filled with hot tea (since most members of Sisterhood disliked coffee). Along the wall opposite the stairs were three doors. Two were open, and the center one was closed. A bronze plague mounted on the closed door read "Pastor Embry Wilshire." He was inside.

Thirteen padded chairs had been neatly arranged about the circumference of a round table near the middle of the room. No one was seated. Chapter Seven of Sisterhood drank tea and nibbled cake in divided, affiliated camps. Roberta, Mabel Brown and Tina Russell found an area near the crucifix; Winona, Eva Hearn, Debbie Hickman and Mrs. Powell huddled near the left of the round table; Lisa Palmer, Elise Kale and Arthel Farmer stood near the stairs. Each knew where they belonged and none, except Mrs. Powell, ventured into another's territory without invitation.

Mrs. Powell, her black patent leather purse slung over her shoulder, had visited Roberta, Mabel and Tina earlier in the evening. Winona had accompanied her. Mrs. Powell was welcomed. Winona was not.

"Good evening, sisters." Winona greeted the three with a nervous smile.

"Winona," Tina said. Mabel nodded her head. Roberta stared.

"It sure is cold out there." Winona tried to sound folksy. She was aware of what Roberta and her friends thought of her behavior. 'Haughty' was the most common word they used to describe it. 'Uppity' and 'arrogant' were others.

"It certainly is," Mrs. Powell responded.

"Usually is this time of year," Mabel said. Mabel's sharp comment made Roberta and Tina grin. Mrs. Powell took Winona's hand. The firmness of her grip surprised Winona.

"I'm really excited about this year's bake sale. Looks like we're going to have plenty of contributors; twice as many as last year."

"That's nice," Eva said. Winona had been elected to organize the bake sale, ending Eva's five-year reign. Winona, realizing her mistake, changed the subject.

"How's Curtiss?" Winona asked Roberta.

"Fine."

"The kids?"

"Fine."

"Yourself?"

"Fine."

"Would you like to come for dinner sometime?"

"No."

"Is that a new dress you're wearing, Roberta?" Mrs. Powell jumped in.

"No, ma'am."

"Girl, it looks good on you. You lost weight?"

"No, ma'am. Gained a little, if anything."

"Doesn't it look like she lost weight, Winona?"

"Sure does."

"Well, I haven't." There was an uneasy pause. All three women stared at Winona as if they wished Winona were nailed to the crucifix on the wall. Mrs. Powell looked toward the group near the stairs.

"I'm going to give my condolences to Elise. Are you coming, Winona?"

"Yes, ma'am."

Winona and Ruth Powell walked away. Mrs. Powell released her hand. The two of them were politely received into Elise's cluster of friends. Elise kindly noted their commiserations. Casual conversation developed. Winona's clique joined Elise's coterie. Roberta's group remained isolated.

The center door opened. Everyone looked in that direction. Conversation stopped. Reverend Wilshire emerged, a lean sand-colored man of average height, sensitive eyes, and an alluring smile. He wore his clerical uniform. A weathered black leather Bible was tucked under his arm, a college graduation gift from his mother. Branded inside its back cover were the words *Embry Wilshire, Minister of Christianity.*

"Good evening, Sisters." The Sisterhood responded in kind. Reverend Wilshire stood behind one of the chairs. He laid his Bible before him. Mrs. Powell took her usual place to his right. From that close, she could see his strawberry-colored birthmark, shaped like a carrot on the underside of his right cheek. To his left stood Roberta. Winona was across from him. Others took their places behind chairs near their cliques. All clasped hands, bowed their heads, and waited.

"Dear Lord," he began. His voice was compelling, unlike his tranquil speaking voice. "Bless this humble gathering here tonight. Give us strength and guidance to help those most in need of our assistance. Arm our spirits in the ceaseless battle against evil we all must endure. Allow the light of your wisdom to cast out our demons of doubt, and lead us into your hallowed halls of redemption."

There was a dramatic pause before he continued.

"Tonight we ask a special request of you, our Lord. One of your loyal servants, Sister Elise, has had her father called home. We pray you forgive any sins he may have committed during his passage through this life. We also beg—Our Savior, Our Guiding Light—that you see fit to welcome him into your divine kingdom. Amen."

A discordant response of amens fell silent as everyone was seated.

"I am so pleased each of you was able to make it tonight. I know it wasn't easy to leave your comfortable homes. Believe me, I considered staying put." Reverend Wilshire smiled. Sisters Mabel, Lisa, Tina and Debbie nodded their heads in agreement. The rest sat still.

"But everyone here has answered the calling. Thank you, Sisters, for mustering the fortitude that makes this chapter of Sisterhood our city's finest."

He panned their faces as he spoke. All but Elise seemed to have appreciated his comments. He unbuttoned his jacket and placed his forearms on the table. "Let's get started, shall we? Sister Ruth, would you read the minutes from our last meeting?"

Mrs. Powell stood and smoothed the front of her gray quilted skirt with both hands. Her white-framed reading glasses, with lenses shaped like the eyes of a Siamese cat, hung from a gold chain around her neck. With meticulous care, she positioned them. They slid down to the tip of her nose. Everyone waited. No one spoke. Ruth Powell had been Secretary since the formation of Sisterhood, Chapter 7, before any of them had heard of such a group. Not one could imagine its existence without her presence. If Reverend Wilshire was the backbone of their organization, Mrs. Powell was its heart and soul.

She had removed a steno notebook from her purse that lay beside her chair and placed it on the table to her right. Ceremoniously, she lifted the notebook and checked its tan cardboard cover. SISTERHOOD, CHAPTER 7, MINUTES had been meticulously printed in blue ink above the first of three thin red lines. With studious care, she leafed through it. Only the dates were not in shorthand. She stopped, cleared her throat, glanced over the group, and then read the minutes, beginning with the date.

Winona only half-listened. Reverend Wilshire dominated her thoughts. His taking over Bethlehem Temple had met with stubborn resistance. Unlike his revered predecessor, Embry Wilshire was young, a bachelor, an outsider, and The Temple was his first assignment. Many elder parishioners objected to such a man leading them in spirit. According to them, he was a baby on the doorstep of corruption. Most of his detractors fled to the nearby Episcopal Church. Younger and more moderate members ignored old attitudes and welcomed Reverend Wilshire. He was dynamic and innovative. Unlike his predecessor, he ventured into indigent communities, persuading many to join his congregation. He ministered out of storefront ministries. Everywhere he preached, people were listening. Converts from iniquity came to accept his teachings of Christianity. Many considered him a blessing. Several of his vacated flock returned.

"Who could not follow a man dedicated to ending suffering?" Jesse Wilkerson once said of him.

Four years after his arrival, rumors began to surface. The first was by a prostitute named Wilma Talis. She claimed to have given the Reverend a "hand job." Then Tenisha Gray, also a prostitute, said she performed fellatio on him. A third prostitute, Crystal Olson, insisted they had sex.

None of them were considered credible; not even by his most ardent doubters. When a cauldron of rumors involving the Reverend and Virginia Lovejoy materialized from a variety of sources, enough were convinced to make matters uncomfortable. Though never confirmed, Virginia's reputation won out. Embry Wilshire fell from grace. He became mortal.

For that reason, Abe had been reluctant to suggest that Winona see Reverend Wilshire. The rumor mill stated that all his clandestine liaisons occurred during private counseling sessions at his home. Her bout with suicide left him no choice. Winona had made it clear that it would be her spiritual leader or no one at all.

In many ways, Embry Wilshire helped Winona through her painful depression. He gave sound advice. He listened to her concerns and fears with acute attentiveness. The first time they made love was accidental. She cried. He held her, as he had several times before. As he wiped tears from her cheeks, they kissed. Little was said, in the end. Guilt and excitement were twin emotions to the act. He wept in her lap and pleaded with her and God to forgive him.

When Winona returned home, she feverishly read her King James Bible as Reverend Wilshire had suggested. All night she poured over Psalms and Books of Prophets, Apostles and Kings in hope that it would quell her tormented spirit. Exhaustion claimed her shortly after dawn. She awoke in her bed. Abe had left a red rose and a gold heart-shaped locket on the pillow beside her. Inside the locket was a small emerald Winona had thought lost: a stone worked loose from a friendship ring Abe had bought for her shortly after they met.

Winona and the Reverend had sex once more, after that. Embry Wilshire instigated the act. He had prayed on what they had done and had concluded it had been the will of God. Within the same speech, he stated what was done in private should remain private. What they would do was for God's eyes alone. Out of weak confusion, Winona conceded. There was no passion to what they did. Amazingly, she felt reborn when it was over. Spiritually cleansed from the adulterous act that had tortured her. Roberta began the rumor about Winona and Reverend Wilshire. She had no proof and no witnesses; merely the soiled reputation of a tarnished saint and her own malice toward Winona. Truth was not essential.

The meeting went along at a smooth pace. There were reports by the Treasurer, Special Events Committee, Chairperson, and Chief Fund Raiser. Old news was addressed, new issues surfaced. Debates arose—

heated, sincere, and diverse—which prompted a reading by Reverend Wilshire of the Sisterhood Purpose Statement. It had little effect. Whatever stance Winona held, Roberta opposed. Winona had learned that lesson some time ago. Any time she required support from Roberta, she would abstain from saying anything. Not able to determine which side of the fence Winona was on, Roberta would usually side with the majority. Roberta never saw past her own simmering wrath to make a decision by any other means.

Roberta left about three-quarters of the way through. When the meeting ended, all that had been decided was when the next meeting would be held. Everyone stood, bowed their heads, and held hands. Reverend Wilshire said a parting prayer.

Winona covertly glanced at Reverend Wilshire as she put on her coat. He stood sideways, talking to Elise, holding her hand between his. He glanced her way. There was an instant of recognition. Abe stood beside him in her mind. She compared their bodies, countenance, and style. Copulation with Reverend Wilshire was a mistake evolved from weakness. Her love for Abe was genuine, as was her love for God and her respect for Reverend Wilshire. It was late. She would go home to her husband. Winona turned and walked away. Only Mrs. Powell noticed that Winona had gone.

CHAPTER EIGHT

It was the worst winter in over two decades. Pessimistic prophets had pronounced it as the Second Ice Age. Snow dulled the sun for four continuous days, with local weather predicting at least another two days of the same. Christmas was white, musical, and memorable not only for its flourishing of gifts, songs, decorations, joy and goodwill, but for its record low temperatures, advancing homelessness, and civil unrest.

Darren was not thinking of Christmas as he plodded along snow-shrouded streets. Clammy insulation, provided by stolen newspaper packed into his old tennis shoes, covered the breaches in Darren's soles. His tattered underwear, coat, pants, and two shirts each had unintended holes. Only the new pair of kid's gloves that he found after he exited Willie's Market provided a notion of winter relief.

From age nine, Darren had survived on his ingenuity. Nothing escaped his perception. His eyes panned places and observed people and conditions, recording details with the detachment of a movie camera that remaining keenly aware of particular elements: the situation, whom it involved, and routes of escape. Of these matters, Darren had compulsory knowledge. Before his slip in Willie's Market, he had never been caught stealing. Fred was his defense, when cornered: a straight razor, his superhero. He would have used it on the big man who grabbed him in the store if it were not buried underneath his contraband.

Darren had made his way to a nearby bus stop. Theresa Peoples—the part-time stripper and full-time hair stylist—had seen the boy struggling with his shopping bag.

"Hold on!" Theresa yelled at him from half a block away. If she were not so oddly dressed, Darren would have tried to flee.

"Have you seen Anthony?"

"Who?"

"My son, Anthony."

"Ma'am, I don't know any Anthony."

"I didn't ask you if you know him. I *asked you* if you've seen him."

Theresa described her son to Darren.

"No ma'am, I haven't seen anybody who looks like that."

"Are you sure?"

"Positive."

Theresa sighed, crossed her arms, and then, as if a spotlight struck Darren, she realized his predicament. He could not understand why she was not cold, dressed as she was.

"You're not from 'round here, are you?" she asked. Darren shook his head. She asked if he went to Banneker School. Darren told her he had to get going. She offered to help. He refused. She ordered him not to move.

Theresa lived in a quaint, conservative, two-story red brick house with a small front yard and porch. It seemed a dwarf between its two three-story neighbors. Her porch light was on; a faint white glow amid the dispersion of daylight. He waited. The bottom of his shopping bag had become damp from his having to drag it more than carry it, as well as putting it down to rest. Theresa returned with a plastic garbage bag. She made him hold the garbage bag open while she deposited his shopping bag inside. She warned him not to drag his bags if at all possible because he could tear a hole in the bottom and lose everything. When he turned to leave, she handed him three crumpled dollar bills. He thanked her. She resisted an urge to question him about his parents, his home, and his life.

"What's your name?" she asked. Without a reply, Darren slung his parcel over his shoulder and staggered away under its weight. Theresa watched him for a minute before she went inside. As she closed the door, it struck her. She hadn't found Anthony.

At the bus stop, Darren ate half a pack of Premium Saltine Crackers. The salty crackers tasted wonderful and settled the gnawing in his nauseous stomach.

He boarded the 82 Lincoln, paying his fare from change Jesse Wilkerson had given him when he tracked Darren down shortly after he left Willie's Market. At the back of the bus, he settled into one of the corner seats. Not counting the bus driver, seven people shared this ride with him. Huddled with his bounty, he stared out at the world. It was quiet and cozy on his side of the misty windows. Without invitation, sleep visited for a time.

***

"Wake up, Darren!"

Darren heard the husky voice of his mother as he came out of a dead man's sleep. A tall, rangy woman whose being seemed to fill his room looked down upon him. Her narrow brown eyes were the second things he saw—first was the implacable expression on her face; a face his father had described, when he lived with them, as that of the true Queen of the Nile.

"Get up!"

"I'm up, I'm up," he groggily said, the back of his head impressed in the green pillow. His mother's presence warded off slumber demons lingering just behind his half-opened eyelids.

"I mean it," his mother said, leaving the room. "If you're late for school again this morning, I'm going whip your butt."

A doleful sigh broke the silence. His eyes closed for a few moments, and then crept open. He grinned at a spider strolling along the brocade ceiling. One of his black Chuck Taylor All-Stars was within reach beside his bed. Darren grabbed it, then sprung to his feet. The bed squeaked under his vertical weight. The spider stopped, a shadowy insect with spindly legs and a body no larger than a pea.

They waited. Darren willed it to move. The spider did not oblige. Fragments of plaster rained onto the bed from the impact. His mother's voice careened into his room from her own, as clear as a thundering waterfall: "Darren, what are you doing?"

"*Nothing, Mom,*" he answered. Darren examined the bottom of his tennis shoe. A creamy film was all he saw. He inspected the ceiling. A small dark dot pressed into the white finish verified his kill. He leaped onto the floor wearing only his pajamas, dropped his shoe, and walked barefoot to the bathroom.

The bathroom door was closed. Darren heard the sound of running water coming from inside. Thin clouds of steam escaped from under the door. He knocked. The water stopped. Nena cracked open the door and peeked out at him.

"You want in here?" she asked, her clean, glowing face feigning surprise. Darren noticed how much she resembled their mother before he answered, "Yeah."

"Where's your robe?"

"None of your business."

Nena looked down at his feet. "And your slippers?"

"That's none of your business, either."

"If Mom sees you ain't wearing 'em, she going tear your behind."

"So."

"So? Mr. Big Man ain't afraid of nobody."

"That's right."

"Well, tough guy, I'm almost done."

"I got to get ready for school, too."

"Try studying."

"Come on, Nena."

"Wait a minute." Nena eased the door shut.

"Mom!"

"What?"

"Nena's hogging the bathroom!"

"Nena, get out of that bathroom, now!"

Nena jerked opened the door, wearing only her bathrobe and slippers. She leaned against the wooden doorframe, blocking his way. Her hair was pulled back in a tight shiny ponytail that flowed away from her round face. Darren had overheard his Aunt say to his mother that "Nena had gotten a cute little figure."

Darren disliked his Aunt and therefore discounted much of what she said. But he had noticed differences in his sister. She did not want to play games that dirtied her hair or nails or made her appear unfeminine. She spent more time with her girlfriends, who did not want him hanging around. Dresses replaced blue jeans and T-shirts. When he eavesdropped, he heard names: Jeffrey, Scottie, Bruce, Eric and Chucky. They were described as cute, funny, smart, and strong. His sister and her friends planned ways to get their attention. Older boys; mean boys who picked on Darren while they courted his sister. Darren did not understand why Nena suddenly found boys so appealing. He did not like those boys. They made him angry. It made him angrier that she did not want him around when they talked to her.

Darren tried entering the bathroom. "Crybaby," she said as he attempted to force his way through.

"I ain't no crybaby."

Nena grabbed him in a headlock. Darren did not resist. She smelled like Ivory Soap.

"Guess you think you done something," Darren said.

"Get out of this one, crybaby."

"You don't want me to body slam you again."

"Try it, crybaby."

"Nena, you ready yet?" their mother yelled.

"Almost!"

"How do you expect to get ready, hassling your brother?"

"Yes, ma'am!"

Nena let go. Darren smiled at Nena, pointing a finger in her face. Nena snapped at it with her teeth and then laughed. Darren went into the bathroom and closed the door behind him.

***

When he screamed Nena's name out in his sleep, Darren lurched forward. "What's going on back there?" the bus driver yelled, looking in the rearview mirror. Eight people had boarded since Darren had dozed. None of the previous seven had disembarked. Everyone stared at Darren; most for a brief moment. Low-key comments were made. One caused two people to snicker. Darren looked down. His goods were securely lodged between his dangling feet, both gloved hands gripping the closed mouth of the plastic bag.

When Darren's father lost his job of thirteen years with Jones & Laughlin Steel, he desperately sought work of any kind. Word came from a cousin in Memphis that Memphis Steel was hiring. Creighton Reed packed one suitcase and left his family with promises of a quick reunion.

Days passed without word. His cousin had not seen or heard from Creighton. Marcia Reed put out an all-points bulletin on the family wire about her missing husband. After six weeks of absence, the police were notified. Her only sister asserted he'd deserted his family. Marcia did not believe her. Another three months passed without a sign. Marcia found work as a waitress. Her sister contributed what little she could afford. Darren and Nena shined shoes, sold newspapers, washed cars, cut grass, shoveled snow, and sold Christmas cards and magazine subscriptions. Any odd job they could find to supplement their mother's limited income, they did. It was not enough. The family savings were exhausted eight months after Creighton Reed's disappearance. They were forced to move into a low rent, high-rise apartment community known as The Projects.

Darren and Nena hated their little three-bedroom apartment. They resented the garbage and filth, urine-stained walls, roaches, rats, drug dealers, pimps, prostitutes, and the residents, who, in their estimation, allowed these things to happen. Only a handful of their neighbors did they come to know as mates wading their way through the muck in search of a better life—the life Marcia Reed promised her children they would return to one day.

On a crisp November morning, Nena and Darren had breakfast with their mother. She rushed them along as usual, serving as hostess, guidance counselor and referee.

Down the hall from them lived a prostitute—not much older than Darren's fifteen-year-old cousin, was what his mother had told her sister. Neither knew her name, and their mother wanted it kept that way.

In front of her apartment, a flamboyantly dressed black man stood very close to the girl. He was stocky and dark and rubbed his forefinger across his nostrils a lot when he spoke. The door behind her was closed. Daddy Mack was his name. Every person old enough to walk in The Projects either knew or knew of him. Daddy Mack was a pimp renowned for his silky lures and ruthless discipline tactics. He looked angry. The woman he had cornered seemed frightened. Her heavily made-up face twitched as he spoke. The two of them saw Darren and Nena after Darren closed their door behind him. Darren's eyes met those of Daddy Mack's. Darren saw bristling coals.

Nena tugged on Darren's coat sleeve. They made their way to the stairs at the opposite end of the hall from where Daddy Mack and the young prostitute stood.

On their way down the stairs, Nena warned Darren, "*Don't you ever do anything that stupid again.* In The Projects, people mind their own business."

"Did Chucky or Scottie tell you that?" Darren said with a smirk.

"It's common sense."

"I'm not afraid of Daddy Mack."

"There's a difference between fear and foolishness, little brother. Going up against Daddy Mack is just plain stupid."

"I'm not stupid."

Nena halted their escape in the lobby. She firmly turned Darren by his shoulders to face her until their faces were only a whisper apart.

"I love you, Darren. I don't want to see anything bad happen to you. Getting in the business of someone like Daddy Mack is nothing but trouble...serious, serious trouble. Do you understand me?"

"If you mess with Daddy Mack, you could end up dead."

Nena took her brother's face in her hands. She nodded.

"I'm still not afraid of Daddy Mack, but I'll do it for you, sis."

Nena and Darren hugged like loving family who had not seen each other in years.

"You're my favorite brother, knucklehead."

"I'm your only brother."

"Let's keep it that way. One of you is enough."

"You need to talk to Mom about that."

"True."

"I love you, sis."

"How could you not."

By the time they arrived at school, the Daddy Mack incident had become a cautionary tale.

Marcia Reed left after her children had already settled in for their first morning class. She entered the hall to find Daddy Mack kicking the unknown prostitute.

Marcia stood frozen in her tracks. The young woman had hunkered down against her own apartment door, trying to protect herself. She bled from her mouth and nose. Marcia noticed red marks around her neighbor's neck, as if someone had recently choked her.

"Help me! Please, help me!" The woman pleaded with Marcia. "He's going to kill me!"

"Shut up, you stupid bitch," Daddy Mack snarled at his victim. "If I wanted to kill you, you'd be dead already."

Daddy Mack glared at Marcia. "You got a problem?"

"Leave her alone or I'll call the police!" Marcia yelled at him, struggling to contain her fear.

Daddy Mack ran at her. Marcia rushed back into her apartment. She tried to close the door. Daddy Mack slammed his shoulder into it knocking her to the floor. He kicked her in her side before she could get to her feet, and then shut the door behind him. A violent struggle ensued.

When Daddy Mack left Marcia's apartment, the unknown prostitute was gone.

Darren and Nena were summoned out of class to the Principal's office that morning. The police escorted them home. Their anxious queries garnered one response: "All of your questions will be answered very soon."

Outside of their building, police, neighbors and the coroner waited. Darren and Nena became hysterical when they saw the battered woman on the stretcher with her throat slashed. It was their mother. No one claimed to have seen or heard anything. No one was ever brought to trial.

***

Darren glanced at the window. It was fogged over. He rubbed his coat sleeve across it until he could see outside. They passed old apartment buildings, an anonymous record store, Bean's Gas Station, Hartsburger's, the Post Office, Hick's Store, Taylor's Bar, Jack Henry's, Parker's, Gordon's Shoe Store, Irene Kaufmann Center, Center Grill, Bill's Barber Shop, Shelton's Pharmacy, Rebba's Ribs, New Granada, Roosevelt Theater and the No. 2 Police Station.

Darren knew the area. Centre Avenue in The Hill District—a place of coexistence. Hill District patrons filled the shops and markets, smiling and laughing, cursing and arguing. It brought back aching memories for Darren. He and his family had once been participants in that vibrant scene of patrons and commerce. He had spent many a Saturday afternoon shopping there with his mother and sister. He looked out the window, barely subduing a grieving sorrow that threatened to overtake him.

They were three blocks from downtown. Darren had slept for most of the trip. He would transfer to a bus that would transport him across the Sixth Street Bridge to the Northside. From there, he could walk to Mexican War Street. Amongst the abandoned, dilapidated homes, he would find winter shelter. He would be safe.

CHAPTER NINE

"What are you doing?"

"If you have to ask, I must be doing it wrong." Abe kissed Winona along the length of her neck.

"Stop it."

"Why?" Abe continued kissing.

"Dwight might hear us."

"I've been meaning to teach him about the birds and the bees."

"Keep doing what you're doing and he won't need an explanation."

"All the better." Abe kissed Winona just below one ear, then the other.

"What are we going to do about Dwight?"

"Nothing."

"What if he finds out?"

"Who's going tell? Only people back home know."

"Keeping it from him scares me." Abe nibbled on Winona's ear. "We really should tell him."

"All in good time; meanwhile, a little sugar will take your mind off Dwight and put it on me, where it should be about now."

"Abe."

"Dwight's asleep, honey."

"How do you know?" Winona set what remained of her glass of wine on the dining room table. Abe had finished his.

"Trust me."

Winona turned within Abe's arms to face him. Each kiss roused their passion more than the one before. Abe unbuttoned Winona's dress, kissing her body at each spot he uncovered. Winona did the same when she unbuttoned Abe's shirt.

Upstairs, Dwight tossed in bed. His legs churned to escape a subconscious beast. He awakened, arms flailing, heart pounding, gasping for air, the smell of his own fear filling his lungs.

There was no spectrum. That was all that remained of a nightmare that had incinerated as rice paper into flames. Dwight had no idea what it meant. One world replaced another. Dwight throttled back his fear and used his blanket to wipe his face clean of sweat and tears. The pounding of his own heartbeat resounded in his ears, making him oblivious to what his parents were doing downstairs.

Across town, Darren stepped off a streetcar onto Allegheny Avenue. Clouds surrounded a full moon like a chorus of angels. Stars, sparse, twinkled. Darren passed homes still decorated in colorful Christmas lights. They blinked, danced, and glared into the cold night. Darren saw, but did not notice them. His only thought—his only motivation to take another step—was food.

Darren disliked Christmas. It symbolized every lie he could conceive regarding peace and goodwill. A handout was a gesture driven more by guilt than benevolence. Christmas propagated that premise. What Abe had done was not charity, according to Darren. It was an act of penance to appease his God and his conscious. That was why it was important to Darren to pay Abe for his groceries. Someone else would have to serve as his redeemer.

***

Dwight crawled onto the floor. From beneath his bed, he pulled out a reel-to-reel tape recorder given to him by his parents for Christmas. He plugged in the earphone and turned the silver dial to PLAY. Every song Dwight taped, he made by holding the wire microphone close to one console stereo speaker. Dwight experimented with volumes, balance, bass, timbre, and microphone distances. Nothing sounded as good as it did when played on the stereo. Still, most songs were clear enough that he could enjoy them. He turned up the volume. The Four Tops were into the second verse of *I Can't Help Myself*. Dwight stared at a life-size poster of Roberto Clemente thumbtacked to the back of his bedroom door, as if expecting it to sing. Clemente had finished what appeared to be a home run swing. He was watching the baseball in flight, a glint of satisfaction in his dark eyes.

Dwight wondered why the song made such a big deal out of girls. He noticed older boys talking to girls all the time, saying stupid things to make them smile or laugh or giggle like Kevin did with Marsha Jenkins. The whole thing made him nauseous. *Boyfriend and girlfriend stuff, they can keep that,* Dwight thought.

He fast-forwarded the tape. Louis Armstrong's *Hello Dolly* crackled through the earphone. Dwight wrapped himself in his blanket, listened, embraced calm, and returned to himself.

***

Darren trudged up a rusted fire escape, his footsteps crackling on the snow. He slipped unseen through a glassless window of an abandoned third-floor apartment building. It was dark inside. He instinctively moved through shadowy debris and rubble toward the closed door of a small, windowless bedroom. Inside, it was clean and organized. A twin mattress sat atop a wooden pallet on the floor, two folded blankets and pillows at its head. Darren turned on a flashlight he had stolen. It illuminated the room in a pale light. He removed his coat and left it on a metal crate to his right. Setting the flashlight on his coat, he removed his shoes and socks and left them near the front door.

Darren had not eaten anything since late afternoon. Abe had supplied Darren with enough food to last for weeks, if he ate one meal per day. Money from working at Turley's paper stand, giving shoe shines in the lobby of the Frick Building, and whatever odd job or hustles he could find, kept him afloat. When he found Nena, everything would be all right, even if it meant living with his mother's alcoholic sister again. This time he would not run away. Not until he was old enough to get a job. Then he would leave and take Nena with him. East Liberty was a false lead, but Aunt Pam was out there. And he was going to find her.

The cold had numbed his hands and feet. He clothed himself in donations he'd received from the local St. Vincent DePaul: a pair of blue fuzzy slippers and an oversized flannel robe. He sat on a wooden crate near the head of his bed, sifting through Abe's gift bag. He ate potted meat on Ritz Crackers. His mouth salivated and his nose ran. He could feel the knot in his stomach unwinding. Darren forced himself to eat slowly, so not to make himself ill. The food gained flavor and texture in his mouth. Before, it had tasted like sand.

***

Dwight had listened to *That Old Feeling* followed by *I Got A Right To Sing The Blues, Learnin' The Blues,* and *Body And Soul.* The silky notes of Louis Armstrong's music massaged their way into Dwight's fading consciousness. Every measure inched him closer to sleep. His eyes found the moonlight backlighting his winter curtains. He made a mental note to put a variety of artists on his next tape. *Home* pulled down the shade over his thoughts.

***

One of winter's blessings was that Darren did not have to share his living quarters with the ants and flies that plagued him during warmer seasons. Rats were not a problem. They preferred the basement this time of year. Roaches could still be a bother if he was not tidy. He folded the paper towel he had in his lap to catch crumbs and ate them. Darren topped off his meal with a bottle of Pepsi he had bought yesterday. It was cold and flat, but had maintained its syrupy sweetness. He prepared his bed and climbed in wearing his robe and slippers. The bed was cold and rigid. So were the pillows. He made himself as comfortable as possible before turning off his flashlight. The whistling north wind lulled him to sleep.

***

Abe looked in on Dwight, as he did every morning before he left for Willie's Market. His son was curled up on the floor, wrapped in a blanket, earphone sticking out of his ear, tape recorder stopped at the end of a tape. Abe placed the tape recorder and earphone on top of Dwight's dresser. He deposited Dwight back into his bed, tucking him in as he had last done when Dwight was six. Dwight stirred but did not awaken. Abe kissed his forehead, then left for work about the time Darren again dreamed of his mother.

CHAPTER TEN

On her first day as a married woman, inside a rustic three-room house surrounded by nature, Winona sat upright in their feather bed. Her brown eyes remained closed. She drew her smooth knees to her breasts and squeezed them within the gentle halo of her arms, mind sedate, body calm. Traces of last night lingered in the air and on her skin. She was wearing Abe's flannel long johns that were roomy enough for two of her: a warm, comfortable, flannel conservator of their first honeymoon night memories and their first time not just having sex but making love—being loved, shameless, innocent, remorse-free, giving kisses, caresses, touches, hugs, rubs, squeezes, pinches, nibbles and tweaks. Passion in all its singe and sizzle had enveloped her, lifted her, and carried her atop Mount Ecstasy where she trembled, panted, squealed, moaned, writhed, and finally sighed in content.

The patchwork quilt her mother had given them covered her sinewy legs and flowed across her tight torso, spreading itself over her crescent hips as if it were a multicolored, incongruous Phoenix at rest. Abe knew Winona was not a virgin before their wedding night. Neither was he, he had told her when she declared her previous experience after their engagement. "Virginity is overrated," he went on to say. "To become lovers takes practice and patience. I'm very much in love with you. For me, that's all that matters—that and your happiness."

Winona had thought about those words which Abe had earnestly spoken. They had caused a flurry of honest confessions: shared, silly, sullied, and sometimes embarrassing secrets, painful events, and wanton deeds. One secret Winona did not share with Abe was her first sexual experience. Abe had shared his. He explained in comic detail how he and

Anna Mae Tuckett stole away to a small clearing in the woods and attempted to mimic procreating pigs they had seen in his father's trough. Winona laughed so hard she cried. When her turn came to submit her first encounter, she declined—a clumsy and uncomfortable event she would rather forget was her concluding statement; a conclusion that was far from the truth.

It was a Sunday, brilliant in sunlight and absent of birds in flight and animals scavenging for food. Slight breezes were languid ripples of sweltering air, cursed with thick humidity. Warm water droplets deposited on hot bodies already burdened by sweat, suffocating smells, and smothering sounds. Above the stilled green center of Jackson Pond, dragonflies danced with gnats and mosquitoes. For Winona and Andrew, time was an inert presence dangling from a light blue sky.

They sat shoulder to shoulder on the grassy bank of their secluded hideaway. A slick layer of milky sweat pasted their clothes to their bodies. Dreamily, they stared across the tranquil pond. Searing waves of heat distorted their perception of trees and sky and bushes. Winona had considered resting her head on Andrew's narrow shoulder. His body told her then, as it had many times in the past, that Andrew would have enjoyed the gesture. *It's too hot,* she had thought. *Too hot to be alive.*

She was sixteen. Andrew was almost sixteen, a devout Baptist boy who only went as far as closed-mouth kissing. Winona desired more. Hers were the hands that strayed into sensitive areas. A gentle squeeze here, a teasing rub there. An occasional attempt to force her tongue between Andrew's tightly pressed lips. Andrew scolded her when she did such things. Explained to her that copulation outside of marriage was a sin. Gave her pithy sermons about how bowing to temptation led to damnation in the fire and brimstone of Hell. On that day, Andrew remained pure in the eyes of his Lord. Winona took a decadent step with Satan.

Andrew hugged Winona before he left for home, his face showing concern that she had insisted on staying. Winona watched him vanish through a stubborn thicket of green bushes west of where she sat. A breeze sauntered through. She closed her eyes, laid back, and fell asleep.

When she awoke, the sun had angled further west. Cleavon Waters quietly fished beside her. It was too hot to be startled. He stared out over the pond. His eyes were as dreamy as Andrew's and hers had been. Barefooted and bare-chested, a loose-fitting pair of overalls were his only clothing. Cleavon was a brawny man from head to toe, cut sharp and deep from long hours of arduous toil.

She was still woozy when she said hi. Cleavon Waters responded, "Hello, Winnie." Only her family and Cleavon ever called her Winnie. People she cared for deeply. Her family for obvious reasons; Cleavon, in a way Andrew would have claimed was reserved for husband and wife.

She was fourteen when she started looking past boys and noticing men: how different men were, the pitch and cadences of their voices. How they walked, stooped, stood, labored, interacted, and loved. She was drawn to them; particularly Cleavon, her father's best friend. She preferred their company to girls, seeking their attention and flirting in her immature way. She argued when her older brothers were allowed to stay while she was shooed away by her father when she loitered in the vicinity of his male company. "That's different, they're boys," her father used to say. "You should hang around women. It's healthier for a girl your age."

A low fire had settled in her abdomen. The more she was forbidden to be in her father's male company, the hotter the fire burned, working its way down to her stomach and sweeping through her thighs. It made her restless and shrewd. She would serve refreshments and find ways to linger; become a part of their conversation. Catch Cleavon's eye. So adroit had she become at loitering in their company that her father was fooled to the point her mother would have to fetch her.

It happened when he was teaching her how to fish; in the isolated company of Cleavon Waters. Winona was seated between his legs at his request, holding his fishing pole in the manner he had instructed her. Her back rested against his chest. Cleavon's arms encircled her—mighty brown arms, powerful enough to reel in a shark. She felt his breath on her cheek; even waves of warm air. He pressed himself against her. His chest rose and fell with ease. Her body rode its rhythm.

Looking into her eyes, he explained to her the need for patience. She listened. Did what he said. As he emphasized the necessity for silence, she kissed him. Her kiss gave Cleavon the motivation he needed to press forward. Before she knew it, callused hands explored her body. Private secrets were forced open to him. He pulled her sundress over her head, kissed and massaged her breasts, stroked her back and thighs, and squeezed her hips. He slipped out of his overalls. Winona became afraid, aroused, and confused. Cleavon took considerable time to build her excitement before he entered Winona. A deep, penetrating thrust caused

Winona to cry out and squirm beneath his weight. New sensations rattled her body, sending her into a tailspin of muddled feelings.

When lust ended, they lay panting beside one another, sweaty and winded. Cleavon jumped to his feet. "May God forgive me," she heard him mumble as he hastily buttoned his pants, nervously looking around. After he grabbed his tackle box, he gave Winona a long, shamefaced look before he ran off. His abandoned rod lay on its side where he left it.

Winona looked at the crumpled pile of her dress. She reached for it, and then changed her mind. It felt hotter now than before she and Cleavon had had sex. The air was a thick, oppressive mass of latent humidity enveloping her body and saturating her lungs.

She looked out over the pond. Tiny ripples lapped the fishing line submerged near its center. "That is where the fish will be," Cleavon Waters had told Winona. "Deep down near the center, where it's coolest."

Winona sprang to her feet and ran into the velvety warm water, following the fishing line out to where it disappeared below the surface. Ignoring her body's soreness, Winona dove repeatedly for the better part of an hour in search of fish; any fish. Gnats and mosquitoes bit her each time she surfaced. Not one fish did she see.

In the days that followed, Walter Perkins and Cleavon Waters had a brutal fistfight that left both men battered and emotionally bruised. Winona's father forbad Cleavon ever to enter their home or walk their land. To violate his decrees was punishable by a blast from his double-barrel shotgun. No one in the Perkins household would discuss the situation with Winona. Even local gossip channels denied her access. While she felt certain everyone knew about her and Cleavon, not one person would admit it in her presence.

When Winona inquired of her father as to why he suddenly despised his best friend, Walter became angry and threatened to beat her if she did not drop the subject. Dorothy Perkins reacted quite the opposite when asked about Cleavon. She'd stare at her daughter as if she were a pitiable stranger requesting aid she was powerless to provide before she'd walk away, leaving Winona alone and perplexed.

Walter and Dorothy forbad Winona ever to see Cleavon again; a difficult expectation since his farm was next to theirs. Stubborn and determined, every day Winona snuck away from her chores to spend a few solitary moments with Cleavon. At first he was polite—almost apologetic.

He explained to Winona that while what they had done was beautiful, they could never do it again.

Each surprise visit from Winona nudged Cleavon to a higher level of discontent. He allowed himself to be hugged and kissed on the lips without responding in kind. After one week, the kisses were stopped, and then the hugs. He implored Winona to stop pursuing him. Begged her—for the sake of both their families—to forget what had happened and move on with their lives. Winona could no more do what Cleavon asked than she could tell her soul to repudiate his touch. There came a time when Cleavon stared blankly at Winona, not allowing her within arms' length of him. She would talk, become emotional, and attempt to convince him of their destined love. Nothing worked.

Six weeks from the time Winona began stealing away to see him, Cleavon became enraged with her. He grabbed her by the throat with the hands that had caressed her body and threatened to kill her if she did not leave him alone. She did not recognize him. His face was that of a lunatic. His words were tainted with bitterness and disgust. When Cleavon released her, Winona fled. She dared not go home to face her parents' wrath for having defied them. Dazed and confounded, she ran through a thin line of Southern pines to an open field behind the Waters' farm.

Niobe was the youngest of the Waters clan. She was seven years younger than Winona. Niobe came across Winona, where Winona had found a place to lay down with her sorrow. Lying on her back, Winona stared at the sky, a blurry vision of blue with wispy white clouds streaked across its canvas. The weather had cooled considerably by then. Winona was wearing the same dress she had worn on the day she relinquished her virginity. Neither Niobe nor Winona had sisters. They had adopted one another in that sense. In all of that time, Winona had not once given thought to Niobe. She had not considered any of Cleavon's family, as he had implored her to.

Somehow, Niobe got Winona to talk. They discussed things from dresses to horseback riding. Winona stood to show Niobe how to hold a pair of imaginary reins. Niobe squealed with delight as they skipped along, pretending to be on horseback. Winona chased Niobe around the field. Niobe giggled as she tried to get away. Winona caught her and tickled her into a laughing frenzy. It shocked Winona when Niobe hugged her. Winona held Niobe until she quieted down, before they both stretched out on nature's floor to talk.

Winona did not tell Niobe why she was crying. She never told anyone about her and Cleavon Waters, which seemed satisfactory to all parties concerned. On that day, with her adopted baby sister by her side, she tamed lust and began to discover love.

Winona avoided the men whose company she once sought, despite the fact that Cleavon Waters was no longer amongst them. Andrew and Winona parted company after her rendezvous with Cleavon. His constant preaching ignited furious rebuttals by Winona which she could not control. An eighteen-year-old named Jeremiah became her lover. He believed himself the first, and Winona found no reason to deprive him of that notion.

It was after her third clandestine affair that she met Abe. She was at Marion Junction's Feed and Seed Store with her two older brothers when Abe walked in wearing a two-piece suit. It was Sunday. Abe and Winona eyed each other. Winona passed near enough to show her interest without seeming forward. Abe took it from there. They dated for fourteen months before he went off to war. She knew she loved him. No one else had made her feel anything like what she felt for Abe. When he left for Korea, he promised he would marry her when he returned. She faithfully waited. He kept his promise.

Winona turned her head and rested it on her knees. Daylight played on her skin. When she opened her eyes, she saw their backyard, a half-acre clearing framed by a wall of Cypress trees. In the distance, the skyline was dusty gray. Dawn had broken. Winter was in the air.

Abe stood near a stump. He had neatly stacked a small group of previously-cut logs to his right. Winona watched him grab one with his bare hand and place it in the center of a large tree stump, axe perched on his shoulder. He stared at the log. In an instant the axe rose high above his head and steadied for a second before it plummeted straight down. Thwack! The log split in half. He reached behind him for another, placed it on the stump, and performed the same ritual. Thwack! It, too, split in half.

Beneath his winter army jacket and baggy khaki pants, she could envision his honed muscles stretching and tightening, as he drove his axe through the center of each log—her husband, his wife. Winona became serene, filled with warm sweater thoughts that could erupt into thousands of fireworks without harming one thread of the fabric of their commitment. Thwack!

What was their future? She had pondered that question on their wedding day. At that instant, she didn't care at all about their future. Only that particle of time for her to love and be loved had any importance. Thwack! She closed her eyes, stretched out, and laid her head upon her pillow. With the quilt pulled beneath her chin, she enjoyed that peaceful morning, enriched by an occasional sound of her man splitting wood.

CHAPTER ELEVEN

People are non-communal during the solitary season. Introverted bundles, they hurry along, holding fast to warm thoughts and constructing and reconstructing themselves as a puzzle with infinite outcomes, condensed into a place with only enough space for one life to ferment; one soul to kneel at the tranquil altar of prayer. In this time, before the warm spring rains awaken a hibernating kingdom, dreams become a state of existence rather than an escape from reality.

Abe enjoyed the internal solitude of winter; the gentle sting of icy wind on his face and its ghostly moan. It provided an opportunity to pause and ponder matters from the celestial universe, from Winona's wedding anniversary present to the intricacies of man. All these, and more, his mind negotiated through stipples of reasoning during his ten-minute walk to Blade's Barbershop.

Dwight often accompanied Abe to the barbershop. It gave them an opportunity to talk man-to-man. But politics had become a powerful force in the Stone house. For the past six weeks, Dwight had gone with Kevin and David to the barbershop on Friday after school for his once-a-week haircut. Abe and Winona had attended political agenda rallies and conventions, encouraging others in their neighborhood to do the same. Abe studied the political histories of local, state, and nationally-elected officials and relayed his findings to all who would listen. Winona realized what importance the right to vote had meant to millions of struggling minorities; but to her it was simply an exciting development. Dwight took a mild interest. Abe became obsessed.

Snow had vanished from the streets and sidewalks. Sub-teen temperatures thwarted any threat of snow's return. There were few people about on that late Saturday morning. Those who passed Abe said a brisk hello as they rushed to their destinations.

Abe entered Blade's Barbershop to a scattering of greetings. It was cozy inside Blade's. A hodgepodge of hair tonics, colognes, aftershaves, and a hint of talcum powder scents vibrated throughout the barbershop. W-A-M-O could faintly be heard playing "It's A Man's World" from a dusty Philco radio perched on a small wooden ledge above the back room doorway.

Abe removed his fur-lined leather gloves and stuffed them in the right pocket of his chestnut cashmere coat. With casual ease, he unfastened the buttons. Abe claimed an available hook on the oak coat stand amongst the legion of overcoats near the door, draping his woolen scarf over the suede collar so it hung like gossamer wings about his coat sleeves.

Jesse Wilkerson, Darius X, and Ron Hightower were seated in vinyl-covered chairs along the east wall facing the barbers' chairs. A few feet behind each barber's chair were chest-high marble mantels displaying a variety of supplies and tools of the trade. Underneath each mantel were two small, elegantly stained oak drawers with polished brass handles. One long twin was beneath each couplet and a triplet cabinet reached down to the brown and white-checkered linoleum covering every inch of the barbershop floor. Above each mantel, a mirror spanned its length. It extended upward, midway between the cream-colored ceiling and west wall.

Of the six barbers' chairs, only the three furthest from the front door were being used. Compact, dark, middle-aged Frank Turner sculpted Earl Farmer's short hair with a long pair of stainless steel scissors as Earl and Jesse argued the destined fate of the Pirates. Maxwell Jenkins, the senior member of the group, worked next to Frank. 'Blade' was what his oldest friends called Maxwell. Abe never asked why. Swaybacked, bald on top, thick eyeglasses and forearms, quick tongued, and smart alecky were his prominent traits. Blade's hair clippers made swift passes through Mark Brown's dense growth. Hair fell back away from his face. No jerk or twist of his head was necessary. Blade repositioned himself as needed, not disturbing Mark, who was reading his Bible.

Skillfully shaving a supine customer next to Blade was Avery Parker, the youngest member of the shop, cocky, with a thick black beard, intense brown eyes, and a narrow disposition. Whatever he did not know, he never admitted. Calling him 'Junior' usually angered him into silence.

"There he is!" Frank shouted when Abe walked in. His scissors poised over Earl's hair. "'Bout time you showed up. Man gets a little involved in politics and forgets to take care of himself. Look at that head."

"Where's Flea and Drake?"

"Out with the flu," Blade answered.

"Flea was more an' likely out late chasing pussy last night, you ask me," said Avery.

"Shut up, Junior, ain't nobody ask you shit." Darius and Frank chuckled at what Blade said. Avery lowered his large head and pretended to concentrate on his work. Abe sat next to Jesse. Abe ignored what Frank had said to him until he could make himself comfortable. "If you don't get involved early, Frank, it'll be too late come election time."

"That's a ways away," replied Ron.

"You should already know who you want in office by now—gotten to know them, studied their histories."

Earl asked, "You planning on voting?" Everyone except Jesse laughed.

"Yes," Abe replied. The laughter died. Blade, Avery and Earl shook their heads in disbelief.

"Who do you want for president?" Ron asked Abe.

Felton passed by the barbershop. A few people noticed. No one commented.

"I'd like to see Dr. King running things, myself," Jesse answered. Everyone agreed with that ticket; even Darius, who added, "As long as the Honorable Elijah Muhammad is his V.P."

"Ain't never going happen," Blade said. Ron asked him: "Why not?"

"They's the wrong color. Ain't no colored man ever going be president of anything more than a janitor's union."

"If that," Earl added.

Abe's face looked determined. His voice was resolved, as were those of Ron and Jesse. When he listened to Avery, Blade, and Earl, he heard what he termed a defeated mentality from those who had accepted less and believed themselves worthy of nothing more.

"Earl, you keep thinking that way and it won't ever happen."

"It ain't my thinking. It's the white man's thinking keeping us down."

"I don't see any white man," said Darius. "Does anybody see a white man in here?" The consensus was no. "Sounds like the only one doing all the keeping down in here is you, Earl. And unless I miss my guess, you're still Black."

"Negro, thank you."

"That's your slave label. What the white man wants you to call yourself. When you become a free man, you'll realize that you're descended from great people: Egyptian, Mandinka, Zulu, Yoruba, Hausa, Bantu, Herero, Ashanti, Nuba, Fulani, Maasai, Igbo, Agau, Galla, Tuareg, Berbers, Hottentot—African people; people of color."

"I hope they got more sense than you got," Blade said. "Blabbing about Africa this and Elijah Muhammad that. If you knew half as much as you claim, you'd be a genius 'stead of a fool."

Darius dismissed Blade with a wave of his hand. Earl frowned at Darius, then directed his comment at Abe and Jesse. "No matter what you—or Mr. Bean Pie—say, Abe, presidents are elected out there; not in here."

"Presidents are elected by people, Earl, American citizens who vote. We have become a part of that process."

"I hear you, man," Jesse said.

"We'll see come next election." Abe could tell from the tone in Earl's voice that he was not convinced.

"Hasn't anyone in here ever heard of the Egyptians?" Jesse asked.

"Educate them, Brother Jesse," Darius said.

"Cleopatra and shit, so what?" Avery felt it was safe to reenter the conversation.

Jesse took out his pocketknife to clean his fingernails. He encapsulated an explanation about Egypt being the cradle of civilization. He explicated how the Greeks fashioned their democracy after the Egyptian government. He was neither animated nor aloof. He spoke as if everything he said were matter-of-fact.

"Wake up, Jesse. We ain't in Egypt now. This here is America, land of the brave, home of the free." Frank winked at Blade, who smiled back.

"Frank...I swear sometimes you don't get enough air in that brain to make it work," Jesse said. Abe, Darius, Avery and Ron laughed.

"Yeah, well, your 'do is overdo too, Jesse. Look at that head. Next thing you know you'll be wearing one of them Afros. Running with one of them subversive groups—whatcha call 'em?"

"The Black Panthers," Darius answered.

"Yeah, talking 'bout 'kill whitey' and all that nonsense."

"Ain't nobody said nothin' 'bout killin' whitey," Daruis said. "All the brothers are saying is: protect yourself from the racist cowards that believe they have the right to murder us anytime they have a beef about something in their lives they're too weak to handle. Nothing wrong with that." Jesse looked at Abe. Quietly, both agreed it would be useless to continue. Jesse silently surrendered, feigning concentration on his fingernail cleaning.

"When you vote, let me know how it works," Blade said, as if he had not noticed.

"I'll do better than that," Abe said. "I'll pick you up and take you there so I can personally demonstrate how it works."

"My, my; will there be a quiz afterwards?"

"Election results will tell you if you passed."

Theresa Peoples walked into the barbershop wearing a pink and white pant uniform underneath her light gray overcoat. Her hair was covered with an opaque printed scarf. Framing her creamy chocolate face was a delicate lattice of shiny black curls. She stood near the door, looked around the barbershop, then walked over to Jesse.

"Ain't no work for you in here, Theresa. Men get haircuts here. Not fofo'd or fefe'd, like you do it."

"It's called hair styling, Avery. And I'll have you know that more men are getting their hair styled today than them tired haircuts you be giving."

"Not in here, they ain't."

"Did you want something, Theresa?" Blade asked.

"Just wanted to give Jesse back his wallet; is that all right with you?" Theresa sarcastically asked. Blade grunted. All the men stared at Jesse. "It ain't nothing like that. Tell 'em, Jesse."

"I must've left it at the club."

"You did."

"Sure he did," Blade said with a smirk.

"Blade, you should keep your mouth shut. It's not like I ain't seen your squirrel-ly ass at the club back there in the corner peeking at me when I'm dancing."

"Peeking ain't what he's doing back in that corner, Theresa." Everyone laughed at what Abe had to say except Blade.

"Thanks, Theresa," Jesse said.

"No problem baby. Maybe I'll see you later — at the club this weekend?" Theresa smiled in the direction of Abe and Jesse. Jesse smiled back. Abe looked away.

Theresa walked toward the front door. All eyes watched her graceful strides; the erect way she held her head and squared her shoulders. Each had seen her dance nude. Only two had been her lover.

"Take it easy," she said to no one in particular as she reached for the door.

"Honey, I'll take it any way you want to give it to me," Avery said.

"In your dreams."

"I ain't had a dream that good in a long time." Avery shivered as if he had a chill. Theresa left, leaving all the men staring after her, lost in their own fantasies.

"Beg your pardon, Reverend," Avery said to the supine customer he was shaving. "But that woman does something fierce to me."

"That's quite all right." Avery wiped the Reverend's face with a moist, hot towel.

"She does something fierce to all of us," Frank said.

"Speak for yourself, Frank," Mark said.

"When you going join us at the club?" Blade asked Abe. "They got a new dancer name Lolita. Put Theresa to shame."

"Winona won't let him," Frank answered.

"I'm not interested."

"Check his pulse," Avery said. "I believe the man's dead."

"I understand where you're coming from, Brother Abe," Reverend Wilshire said.

"Do you, Reverend?"

"Indeed."

"And just where might that be?"

"Women like Theresa are vexations to the soul. They're placed on this earth to test our fortitude; our might for right."

"Do tell," Abe said. Avery adjusted his barber's chair so the Reverend sat upright.

"God needs to know each and every man's true self. We must resist that which He has deemed sinful. We rise or fall based upon our earthly principles."

"Preach on, Reverend," Mark chimed in.

"It's the Devil who carries out those acts of temptation."

"Amen."

"But God allows it."

"I hear you, Reverend."

"Follow the steps of the godly instead, and stay on the right path; for only good men enjoy life to the full. Evil men lose the good things they might have had, and they themselves shall be destroyed."

"Proverbs 2:20," Mark said with a grin.

"Believers are they only whose hearts thrill with fear," Darius chimed in, "when God is named, and whose faith increaseth at each recital of His signs, and who put their trust in their Lord." Reverend Wilshire nodded in agreement with Darius's words.

"Truths are beliefs we accept in our lives. They don't actually exist," said Jesse, putting away his pocketknife.

"Do you believe in God, Abraham?" The radio disc jockey made a comment about the record he had just played. Abe had only half-listened to what Reverend Wilshire said.

"I do."

"Didn't see you at service last Sunday."

"True enough, Reverend. Or the Sunday before that, or the Sunday before that."

"Feeling okay? I mean, is your health in good order?"

"Excellent. Yourself?"

"Couldn't feel better. The Lord is looking out for me." Reverend Wilshire stood, straightened his knit sweater, then checked his appearance in the mirror behind Avery. He held his leather-bound Bible in his left hand, close to his heart.

"So I hear."

"Abe's got a store to run, Reverend," Frank said as he continued to work on Earl's hair with his back to the Reverend. Embry Wilshire looked at Abe's reflection in the mirror. Aside from Frank, all eyes were on the Reverend. Jesse crossed his legs and angled himself toward the Reverend. Darius leaned forward. Embry had the floor.

"Willie's Market—a fine store, fine store. But doesn't God deserve a couple of hours of your time on His holy day?"

"You saw my wife and son there?"

"They honored us with their presence."

"They take with them my prayers and offer them to our Creator for me."

"I see."

"Would God object to that, Reverend?" Abe asked.

"Possibly not, if theirs—and yours—are sincere offerings?"

"I know no other way to offer myself."

"I heard that," Darius remarked.

Abe looked through the clear glass front of the barbershop. Cars and people silently passed. Virginia Lovejoy walked by, holding the arm of plump, well-dressed Neville Carter. A boy sprinted past them in the opposite direction. Abe believed it was the ragged child he had caught stealing in his store not long ago. Only Abe seemed to notice.

A man they did not know came inside the barbershop and attempted to sell them jewelry. After a series of cold shoulders and brusque comments about his wares, he left.

"Do you ever counsel men, Reverend?"

The question silenced the barbershop. Even the radio hushed. All eyes fell upon Abe, then flowed back to the Reverend. Embry Wilshire had stepped toward the mirror for a closer inspection of his face. He turned at the waist, allowing his instinct to gather what mood prevailed. He returned to the mirror. With his right hand, he adjusted his shirt collar so it rested precisely the way he wanted on the neck of his sweater.

"I counsel any and all who need my services."

"What about your needs? When you have a problem, who counsels you?"

Without hesitation the Reverend answered, "God."

"And you accept his word? Do as he suggest?"

"God does not suggest. His word is law. I abide by that as much as humanly possible."

"A lot of room for error in that human area, Reverend." Embry rubbed his hand over the shaved area of his face. He tucked his Bible under his arm, then helped himself to a bottle of green aftershave.

"No one is more aware of that than I, Abraham."

"And God."

"Most certainly," the Reverend paused. "In times of trouble, who do you consult, Brother Abraham?"

"My family, friends, God."

"You're always welcome in the House of the Lord. We're all family there."

"The Lord's house is everywhere, Reverend."

"Amen to that," Blade said.

"Yes, sir," Mark said with a lilt.

"There's not a space in this universe where man can venture without residing in the Lord's house."

"Amen," Mark said.

"You, me, Jesse, everyone in here—out there—everywhere is under God's watchful eyes."

"You missed your calling, Brother Abraham. You should have been a preacher." Embry said.

"Like you?"

"That wouldn't be so bad. Now, would it?"

"It depends."

The Reverend's eyes narrowed. He turned and faced Abe, "On what?"

"Your definition of bad: does it correspond with God's? If by bad, you mean sin."

"It does."

"Then being a man such as you would not be such a terrible thing," Abe said in a sarcastic tone. Embry and Abe stared into the soul of each other. Satan would have enjoyed the swift spark of mutual animosity that had pricked their hearts.

Reverend Wilshire paid Avery, who diffidently thanked him. Embry retrieved his coat from the coat stand. In one sweeping look, he conveyed his blessings upon everyone. Mark reminded the Reverend he would see him at Bible study on Wednesday. Aside from Abe, Jesse, and Darius, everyone mentioned they would see Reverend Wilshire on Sunday. The Reverend calmly departed with his coat open.

Darius took the seat vacated by Reverend Wilshire. Through the back doorway, Wallace emerged, preceded by the sound of a toilet flushing. He carried in his left hand the latest issue of *Jet Magazine*. A few people kidded him about the malodorous state he had probably left the bathroom in. He waved them off and sat next to Abe.

"Who's minding the store?" Wallace asked Abe.

CHAPTER TWELVE

"Where's Abe?"

"The barbershop," Winona answered Virginia as she pressed firmly on a green receipt pad with a ballpoint pen.

"It's about time he got a haircut; can't have a good-looking man like Abe not taking care of himself." Winona stopped writing and looked up.

"Are you suggesting I don't take care of my man?"

"Not at all." Virginia winked at the person behind her. Arthel Farmer chuckled, her hefty arms cradling an irregular heap of canned goods. Winona and Virginia helped Arthel unload them onto the counter.

"Then what are you saying?"

"I said what I said, nothing more."

"Un-huh," Virginia made no secret of wanting Abe, but she was not the type of woman who would steal a man. Instead, she would entice a man to come to her. Winona trusted Abe. That was the only thing preventing her from ripping Virginia's throat out.

"Dwight!" Winona yelled as she took more cans from Arthel's arms.

"Ma'am." Dwight answered his mother from the frozen food section, where he rummaged through one of the freezers.

"Come here."

"Thank you," Arthel said as the ladies helped ease her load. "They were starting to get heavy."

"How'd you managed to get all of those cans piled in your arms like that?"

Mrs. Farmer turned her thick brown body to answer Debbie Hickman, who stood behind her. In detail, Arthel explained to Debbie how she came to be in that predicament. A red fishnet bag of Spanish onions dangled from Debbie's right hand. Cradled in her left arm was a ten-pound bag of Idaho potatoes. The strain of each would seem too much for a woman of her diminutive stature, but no sign of tension showed in her wistful eyes.

"We're out of Fudgesicles," Dwight said, standing next to his Mom.

"You're here to work, not eat Fudgesicles. Now help Mrs. Farmer with her cans."

Dwight unburdened Arthel Farmer of the remainder of her cans. Winona handed Virginia her receipt and change. Neville Carter had waited until the moment he was needed. Virginia stepped to the side. Neville stepped forward and lifted the large brown bag filled with groceries. Mrs. Farmer pulled a quarter out of a small beaded change purse she kept in her patent leather purse. Winona eyed her son. Dwight respectfully declined the tip that Arthel urged him to take. Neville held the bag of groceries in one hand while he opened the door for Virginia with the other.

"Tell Abe I'll see him later," Virginia said. Neville grimaced.

Winona ignored any inference when she replied, "Will do." Virginia left, mischievous eyes twinkling, with Neville close behind.

A sharp cold rush violated Willie's Market each time the front door opened. Inside, warm air harbored faint scents of onions, garlic, and fresh-cut meats. Winter frost glazed the store's glass front. Instead of inhibiting daylight, it seemed to magnify its luminance, making Willie's Market bright with natural light.

Dwight returned from having answered Mrs. Powell's question on the price of Del Monte Cream-Style Corn to rejoin his mother behind the counter. Mrs. Farmer looked on as Winona mentally calculated her cost. In every aisle, there was customer activity. Ron Hightower studied the selections of meat in the butcher's section. Everyone in the store knew everyone else. Conversation about church, school, children, husbands and wives, and then some buzzed throughout. It was a typical late Saturday morning crowd.

Ron made his choice. He summoned Dwight with a gesture of his hand. Dwight left his mother's side to help him. His father's apron was big on him. Winona had knotted the neck string so the loop could still fit over his head, and its chest portion fell somewhere in that vicinity on her son. Like his father, he washed and dried his hands, then put on disposable plastic gloves before he touched the meat.

"Winona, where's the peanut butter?"

"Aisle Three." Mabel made a beeline for Aisle Three. She said hello to Theresa and Lisa on her way. Mrs. Powell nabbed her right after she got her peanut butter for what became an extended and pleasant chat.

"Four thirty-nine." Winona folded the carbon paper back on the receipt book. "Do you want a receipt, Arthel?"

"No, honey, I don't need a receipt."

"Shopping bag?"

"Yes! I couldn't carry all these cans any other way."

"I don't know. You seemed to be doing all right without one," Debbie said. Mrs. Farmer smiled. Winona hoped to have a smile as glowing, when she had grandchildren as old as Dwight.

"Where's Earl?" Debbie asked.

"Out jitneying." Debbie nodded her head as if to give his absence legitimacy.

"I'll double the bags to make sure they won't rip."

"I appreciate it, dear."

"Dwight can carry these home for you, if you'd like?"

"That won't be necessary, honey. This old lady could use the exercise."

"Next time you get this many things, grab a few and put them on the counter. There's no need for you to haul all of these cans around like that."

"I didn't plan on it. Next thing I know, my arms got so full, it took all I had to keep them cans from spilling on the floor."

"I know what you mean," Debbie Hickman chimed in, her jittery soprano a half-octave higher than Arthel's satiny contralto. "Seems like every time I come in here, I always leave with more than I expect."

"What's wrong with that?" Winona smiled. They laughed. "Long as we eat it, ain't nothing wrong with it, I suppose," Arthel said.

Ron joined the women in line, shifting the majority of his weight to his left leg. Everyone traded pleasantries. Debbie chidingly asked Ron what he had bought.

"Steak."

"Oh!" Debbie replied. The women all looked at each other as if he had revealed a juicy secret. "A lot of paper to hold one steak."

Dwight had hung the apron on its peg and joined his mother at the front counter.

"Dwight. How much paper did you use to wrap that steak for Mr. Hightower?" Winona asked. Dwight appeared puzzled when he answered, "Enough to hold two steaks."

"Two," Debbie and Arthel said in unison.

"T-bones?" Winona asked.

"Yes, ma'am."

Ron feigned ignorance to their inferences.

"Ron," Arthel Farmer stepped around Debbie and stood close to Ron, "you look fit. I'm just not sure you can eat two T-bone steaks by yourself."

Fighting a grin, Ron replied: "Only one is for me."

"*Really*?" Arthel said.

"Pray tell, who is the other for?" Debbie asked. Winona watched, amused. Mrs. Powell stopped browsing long enough to enjoy the moment.

"A friend."

"Do we know this friend?"

"No—it's nothing like that. This is just business."

"Just business." Winona winked at Debbie and Arthel. "What sort of business?"

"Funny business," Debbie said.

"Business."

"Is she pretty?" Arthel asked.

"Yes, but that's not why we're having dinner."

Winona finished placing the cans inside the doubled shopping bags for Arthel. Debbie and Arthel stood on each side of Ron. He blushed from the attention. Winona moved next to Dwight, who was between her and the end of the counter where Ron stood.

The women had discussed Ron amongst themselves. None were certain about his gender preference of intimate partners. All admitted they hoped he was straight. They believed Ron Hightower would make any woman a good husband. It was their self-appointed duty to encourage him into a marrying frame of mind.

"Can I please get these steaks home before they spoil?"

"Those steaks will keep," Arthel said.

"Hold on." Debbie stepped up to the counter. "I'm before you, sweetie." Arthel nudged him. Ron turned his smiling face away. "Don't let me hear about no wedding bells before I get a chance to meet this girl."

"Mrs. Farmer, I do believe I have a mother."

"Yes, you do, baby! But she ain't here, so I'm looking out for her. Do you have a problem with that?"

"No, ma'am."

"Then we understand each other?"

"Yes, ma'am. Now can I go?" Winona took care of Debbie while Debbie and Arthel flirted with Ron. He seemed relieved when Arthel and Debbie left together. Winona did not tease him any further. She wished him luck. When he asked her why, she told him, after a few seconds thought, "No one can have too much luck." He was still blushing when he left.

Mabel Brown returned with a jar of peanut butter, a loaf of bread, and a jar of grape jelly. Winona had not seen her since the last Sisterhood meeting. Dwight handled the transaction while Winona explored the back storage room for a case of red tomatoes and a case of Spanish onions for the store's former owner, Ralph Lingle, who had surprised them with a visit. Ralph made mention he was visiting friends in the neighborhood, although he never said who. He complimented Winona on the condition of the store and asked about Abe, business, and the neighborhood. Ralph took time to chat with everyone in the store.

There was awkwardness when Ralph talked to his former customers and friends. Mrs. Powell offered the warmest and most sincere response to his presence. Each inquired about his family and his retirement. But they were like strangers at a bus stop groping for familiar interest. He had been one of them once; a staunch member of the community. Welcomed as he was, the feeling of kinship was lacking.

Many believed the Watts riot frightened him more than he cared to admit; more than his wife's death. Fear undermined the trust he once had for his East Liberty neighbors and eroded a decade of comfort forged on common ground. The Stones had taken the Lingles' place in the hearts of his former patrons. While not expressed in words, many felt deserted when Ralph Lingle retired to upper class Fox Chapel. The prevailing mood was that was where he now belonged. East Liberty was no longer his home.

Ralph Lingle wandered Willie's Market, making casual comments on what had changed and what remained the same. It was quiet as he walked about. Everyone watched him: an invader, an outsider. He seemed very concerned about Felton Dobbs. When all anyone could do was confirm information he already had, he was clearly distressed. Winona noticed, and found his reaction peculiar. She could only presume they were closer friends than she had imagined. Ralph paid for his cases of vegetables and left to a chorus of courteous goodbyes. Dwight held the door open for him.

When Darren walked in, only Dwight was behind the counter. Dwight asked if he could help him. Darren said nothing at first, but stared at Dwight. His nose wasn't running. He wore the same coat as before. Underneath, he had donned a hooded sweatshirt, beneath which was an oversized dress shirt and two off-white T-shirts, a wrinkled pair of khaki pants, and clean boxer shorts; all stolen from the Northside Goodwill. His new sweat socks and tennis shoes were stolen from McCrory's. He wore the gloves he'd found on the day Abe had given him groceries.

"Where's the owner?" Dwight frowned at Darren's tone of voice.

"I'm the owner," Dwight answered.

"You're not the owner."

"My parents are. What'd you want with 'em?"

"None of your business."

Winona had answered a question for Mrs. Powell and now joined Dwight at the front counter.

"Can I help you?" Winona asked Darren.

"I'm looking for the owner."

"I'm the owner."

"I mean the man owner."

Abe had been right, Winona thought. *Older, taller, dingier; but definitely Marcia Reed's child.*

"Is there something he can do for you that I can't?"

"No ma'am—I mean, it's between me and him."

"I see. He's not here right now."

"When will he be back?"

"This afternoon. You can wait for him if you like."

Darren and Dwight exchanged glances before Darren half-heartedly thanked Winona and left. Dwight looked after him. He disliked Darren—this much he knew. But he didn't know why.

Mrs. Powell called Winona to ask another price question. Winona went to her side. They searched for a can of black olives which was price stamped. Winona examined every can on the shelf for the same thing. She found them all unmarked. To her best recollection, she told Mrs. Powell, they were nineteen cents. Mrs. Powell thanked Winona, then proceeded to confide in her that Darren was the boy Abe had helped after he caught him stealing.

"I thought that was him," Winona told her.

"Does Dwight know?" Mrs. Powell asked.

"We didn't think he needed to."

"You're probably right. Thanks again." Mrs. Powell touched Winona on the shoulder before Winona returned to the front of the store and ordered Dwight to price stamp the cans of black olives.

Roberta Bankhead walked in. Winona was stunned, as was Mrs. Powell, who was the second to notice Roberta. A nervous quiet permeated throughout Willie's Market as more people realized Roberta was there. Shoppers muttered under their breath to those close to them. Roberta journeyed around the store, scowling, picking up an item here and there and examining it, only to put it back with a disapproving expression. Even purchases she decided upon were clearly choices made by default. Roberta's neighbors said a hasty greeting, then immediately distanced themselves when she happened near. Winona cautiously watched.

Dwight had manned the butcher's section to help an impish man he had heard his father call Flea, when the front door burst open. The clamor from the cowbells alarmed everyone. Oblivious to his disturbance, David Hickman walked over to the meat section without a worry. Dwight remained focused on his task, ignoring his friend.

"Hi, Mr. Arvind." Flea stared at David, due to David's obliviousness to his abrupt entrance. Flea shook his head in disbelief before he said, "Morning."

"Hey, Dwight."

"Hey."

"What's up?"

"Take a guess?"

David stepped behind the meat counter. He watched Dwight slice bologna with the electric food slicer. To this, David said, "Oh," then proceeded to tell Dwight why he came.

"I'm heading up to Mellon to play football. You interested?"

"Who's all going?"

"The fellows."

"I have to ask my mom."

"The answer's no," Winona said.

"Morning, Mrs. Stone." Winona stared down at David for a long moment before he realized why. Shamefaced, he stepped backward from behind the counter.

"Dwight is helping me this morning. He can't play with you boys right now."

"Mom!"

"Don't start, Dwight. If I have to argue with you about this, you'll be grounded for the rest of this century. So stop while you still have your freedom."

Dwight pouted. A raised eyebrow from his mother served to adjust his attitude. David turned to leave. Over his shoulder, he told Dwight they'd probably be playing for a while, so come up, if he had a chance.

"All right," Dwight said as he handed Flea his order. Roberta Bankhead unloaded her groceries onto the front counter moments after Flea left. Winona warned Dwight about sulking before she helped Roberta.

"Was that Ralph Lingle I saw leaving here, a minute ago?" Roberta asked. Winona smelled whiskey on Roberta's breath.

"Yes, it was. He stopped by to say hello. Said he was visiting friends in the neighborhood."

"Right," Roberta said with a smirk. "I hear his youngest boy's hooked on drugs." Winona stared blankly at Roberta. She decided it would be best to allow Roberta her say.

"Will that be all, Roberta?" Winona asked when she thought Roberta had finished.

"He was never no good, anyway."

"Will that be all, Roberta?"

"Always into something he shouldn't ah-been."

"Will that be all, Roberta?"

"Yeah."

Winona tallied up her groceries. "Would you like a receipt?"

"Yeah, and put it on my account."

Winona wrote down each item and how much it cost on the green receipt slip.

Dwight walked over to his mother. "Is there anything else I can do, Mom?"

"Nothing at the moment," Winona said.

Dwight realized he still wore the butcher's apron, and grinned in Roberta's direction.

"What you grinning at, fool?" Roberta yelled.

Winona stopped writing and placed her pen down on the counter. With care, she turned and cupped her son's chin in her hand.

"There *is* something you can do for me, Dwight. Go back to the storage room and count how many cases of canned peaches we have left."

Dwight did as instructed without hesitation, accepting a kiss on his forehead from Winona before he left.

A hushed tension filled the store. Winona walked around the counter. Roberta stood her ground.

"It's one thing when you silly wenches fuck with me. But when you take out your problems on my child, you have stepped over the line. If you ever so much as think about treating my son in the manner you just did again, I will give you a good old-fashioned Alabama ass-whooping from here all the way up to Lincoln Avenue and back. Do you understand me, bitch?"

No one in the store had ever heard Winona swear. Roberta stepped backward. Winona took up the slack.

"I've had enough of you crusty, tired-ass, broke-back, boil weevil, toe-jam sucking hussies. If the three of you want a piece of me, then come and get it. My family and I have swallowed enough of your bullshit. I'm fed up having to feel guilty for a dream we've been fortunate enough to realize. *Members of Sisterhood my ass.* If you were any kind of real sisters, you'd strive to accomplish something for yourselves instead of wasting time trying to tear down what someone else has worked so hard to build."

The cowbells clamored. In walked Reverend Wilshire. Winona returned behind the counter and finished writing Roberta's receipt.

"Did I interrupt something?" the Reverend asked. Mrs. Powell motioned for the Reverend to join her at the front of Aisle Two. Roberta waited, clutching her bagged groceries to her body. In one fluid motion, Winona tore off the receipt and handed it to her. Roberta snatched it from Winona and left.

"Mom, we got two cases of canned peaches. We're probably going need another two cases by next week." Winona thanked Dwight and told him to write it down on the supply log they kept on the back of the storage room door. Reverend Wilshire stepped up to the counter.

"Sister Ruth told me what transpired here. Are you all right?"

"I'm fine, Reverend."

"Would you like me to have a talk with Sister Roberta? Maybe I can help quell these torrid flames of jealousy before they erupt into a hurtful inferno."

"Thank you, Reverend. It's under control."

"If you find a need to consult with someone about this matter, my door is always open to you, Sister."

The Reverend touched Winona's downturned hand. Winona's hand recoiled as if coming in to contact with fire. Dwight returned and stood beside his mother.

"Can I get you anything, Reverend?" Winona asked.

"As a matter of fact, yes. I'd like a box of tea bags."

"First aisle, midway, to your right," Dwight answered.

The Reverend thanked Dwight, found the tea bags, and paid for them without any further discourse.

CHAPTER THIRTEEN

Abe first saw Winona at the Tri-County Baptist Church Summit in Sumter County. It was the premier social gathering of the combined Hale, Chilton and Perry County congregations. It was held on a Sunday in the heart of summer, but blessed with soothing breezes and dry eighty-degree temperatures. Lucinda Gray was his date that day. Love was not in his heart, though marriage was on his mind. She was a good woman: graceful and witty and charming in a quaint country manner. Everyone who knew them told them they made the perfect couple.

While he and Lucinda held hands and walked amongst their congregation, Abe noticed, from a distance, a woman wearing a white sundress. Washed-out sunlight had found her naked shoulders through an overcast sky. In bare feet, she walked along like a butterfly skimming over the prickly grass. Abe veered in her direction. Lucinda retained a firm grip on his hand, smiling and commenting on something he did not hear. Friends and neighbors, acquaintances, and sisters and brothers of the church at play in the fields of the Lord stopped them, each interruption a mounting hindrance. A young man joined the mystery woman. Abe watched as they played discreet lovers' games. Lucinda chatted, drawing Abe into the conversation whenever possible. Abe's distraction became more obvious. A sense of destiny took charge.

Abe excused himself from a conversation with Reverend Parsons and his wife. Lucinda was startled when Abe jerked free of her hand. Abe politely waded through the maze of people toward the mystery woman. Her back was to him, now. She crested a small hill with a group of people she clearly knew. Abe started to yell for her to stop when his younger brother, Clay, grabbed his arm, panting, telling Abe their father needed his help to unload their truck. Abe turned to look at where the woman had been. She was gone. He assumed his chance would come later that day. It did not. Winona and her family left early to visit cousins they had not seen in years in nearby Perrysville.

"I don't love Lucinda," Abe said to his mother.

"What you know 'bout love?"

"It's true, Mama."

"Six years you two have been together. All of a sudden that doesn't matter?"

"No, ma'am. It's not at all like that. I've never loved Lucinda. I like her, sure enough. I think she's beautiful and bright and sweet. Without love, what is there? Is there any other reason to get married?"

"Abe." Joseph stepped around his wife, who stood with her arms folded across her chest between him and their son. "Are you sure about this?"

"Yes, sir."

Renata Stone put her arms around her husband's round waist. They stopped walking in the open field behind their house. Abe looked up. Afternoon clouds had moved on. A warm breeze swirled about their feet. Stars twinkled against a blue velvet sky. Joseph sighed. The weight of his wife's head on his chest was negligible.

"You've told Lucinda?" Joseph encircled his wife's plump figure with his beefy arms.

"Yes, sir."

Abe reflected briefly on that moment. When the picnic was over, Abe drove Lucinda home in his second-hand pickup truck. Lucinda did most of the talking on the way. Abe tossed over in his mind how to end their relationship. They pulled up to the dirt path leading to her front steps. Her family had arrived only moments before them. Lucinda's father and brother were unloading their truck by the storage shed a stone's throw from the back of the house.

Lucinda asked him to set with her for a while. He declined. Said he didn't feel well. She leaned over and kissed him on the lips. He halfheartedly kissed her back. He said it before she closed the door, slowly, distinctly; as if he were rehearsing to himself.

"It's over between us, Lucinda."

"What?"

"I hope you understand."

"Understand? What are you talking about?"

"I'm not in love with you. If you want to know the truth, I don't think you love me, either."

"Don't tell me how I feel," Lucinda yelled at him. Her father and brother stopped what they were doing. They looked toward Abe's truck.

"This is about that girl, ain't it? You got an itch for her. I saw you staring at her like she was some kind of honey-dipped spare rib."

Abe looked past Lucinda and saw her father and brother jogging their way. Her mother and sisters had emerged from the house onto the front porch. He made out a faint voice as Lucinda's mother asked, "What's going on?"

A tearful rage overtook Lucinda. The calm, soft-spoken woman he cared for cursed at him in a manner he had heard only in gin joints, climaxing when her spent body collapsed in tearful convulsions.

Abe wanted to lift her by her shoulders. Tell her about her beauty, personality, and intelligence. Explain that any man would be honored to have her choose him for her husband. For him, those qualities were not essential. All he required was love. He believed he had found it. Truly, he knew, one day, she would too.

"What's going on?" This time it was Lucinda's father. Her grief was too debilitating for her to answer. Nolan kneeled next to his daughter, who had collapsed on her knees. Her brother stepped toward Abe. A glare from a bigger, stronger Abe stopped him from advancing any further. Her father ordered Abe off his property.

Abe reached over and closed the truck door. Through the open window he said, "I'm sorry."

Lucinda screamed at him as he drove away. "Not as sorry as you're going to be! If it's the last thing I do, Abraham Jacob Stone, I'll get you for this! I hate you!"

"There's more." Abe broke the silence. His parents looked on.

"At the picnic there was this girl—a woman, really. Her name is Winona Perkins. I think I'm in love with her."

"Dear God," his mother gasped. "A girl you just met?"

"I haven't exactly met her, Mama. She left before I got a chance."

"Are you kidding? Since you've been going to college, I've had a hard time telling when you're serious and when you're making a joke," his father said.

"I'm serious, Papa."

"You're telling us you're in love with some girl you don't know nothin' 'bout? That's the reason you broke off your relationship with Lucinda?"

"Yes, sir."

"That's madness, Joseph. I'm going back to the house. Maybe you can talk some sense into your son." Renata touched Abe on the arm and shook her head. "Baby, I sure hope you know what you're doing."

Abe hugged his mother. He and his father watched her amble back to their home. The silence was broken when she closed the door behind her.

"How do you know her name if you didn't meet her?"

"A person from her congregation told me."

"You went looking for this girl?"

"Yes, sir."

"I don't know about this, Abe. Could be you wanting to sample a different fruit?"

"Didn't you tell me the first time you saw Mama, you knew she was the woman you wanted to spend the rest of your life with?"

"I wasn't involved with somebody for six years when I met your mother. When I met her, it was face-to-face. Not some specter from across a field."

"I know she's the one, Papa." They paused. Joseph glanced at the sky.

"What're you going do about it?"

"Going over to her place tomorrow and ask her out."

"She got a boyfriend?"

"Been told that. I saw her with somebody. Makes me believe it's true."

"Risky; could be a roughneck—you might get jumped."

"I'll take that chance."

"Maybe we can work something out." Joseph put his hands in his pocket. Abe looked on.

"How 'bout a chance meeting?"

"What'd you mean?"

"A place where you two can coincidentally be at the same time."

"Why?"

"Subtlety. Trust me. Women like to be swooned, not bull rushed."

"Chance meeting, huh? How?"

"Leave that to me." There was another moment of silence.

"I won't wait long."

"I promise you won't have to. Are you sure about the feelings you have for this girl?"

"Yes, sir. What about Mama? She seems pretty upset."

"She'll come around. All your Mama wants is for you to be happy. If this Winona's the one, then so be it. What about Lucinda?"

"Long as I don't give her a clear shot at me for a while, I suspect she'll be okay." Abe paused. "Lucinda doesn't love me, Papa."

Abe and his father looked at one another. Joseph Stone saw a child who could not walk or talk or tie his own shoes, all grown up, wondering when he'd leapt from infancy into manhood. Abe saw a man full with the harvest of age, deserving of his devotion and love and utmost respect. "There's worse things in this world than marrying someone who doesn't love you, son." Joseph paused for a moment. He resisted an impulse to hug his son and folded his arms across his chest instead. "But I expect you're right about Lucinda. I only hope your heart isn't wrong about this Winona."

CHAPTER FOURTEEN

Light spring rain dampened East Liberty throughout morning into early afternoon. Weather excluded, it was a typical Sunday. Willie's Market opened at seven and closed at one. Abe, alone, minded the store. Winona and Dwight attended morning service, returned home, changed out of their Sunday clothes, and went their separate ways inside the house.

When Abe arrived, dinner preparations were well underway. Aromas of fried chicken, collard greens, macaroni and cheese, candied yams, and sweet yellow cornbread greeted him at the front door. Dwight did not notice his father when he entered. He was belly down, mesmerized by a blue uniformed Cavalry chasing loincloth-wearing Indians, whooping across the western plains of their black-and-white console television. Abe followed his nose to the kitchen.

In the kitchen, Winona returned his hug and added a kiss. They talked briefly about their respective day. Shortly thereafter, Winona shooed Abe out of her kitchen after he sampled a steaming candied yam.

Abe returned to the living room.

"Dwight, turn down that television!"

"I can hardly hear it!"

"Just do it!"

"*Man, I can't even—*"

"If you give me any more lip about that TV, I'm sending you to your room!"

Dwight did as ordered, stifling his grumbling behind a pout that extended into his body language.

"That's better," Abe said. "You had that darn thing up so loud, you can hardly hear yourself think."

Dwight responded by sulking. Abe settled on the couch and read portions of the Sunday paper until Winona declared it time to eat.

Dinner conversation opened as it had for the past few weeks. Abe dove into politics. There was an article he saw in the Sunday paper that posed the question: "Would President-elect Johnson show the type of dedication the late President Kennedy did in the battle for Civil Rights?" Two minutes into his analysis, Winona brusquely stated, "Abraham Stone." With calm precision, Winona told him how weary she had grown of the topic and suggested he not speak of politics again unless someone else opened the subject. Stunned into silence, Abe agreed.

"Thank God," Dwight mumbled under his breath, which drew a glare from Abe.

Other subjects were discussed: school, friends, enemies, church, upcoming events, gossip, and neighborhood concerns. By the time Winona mentioned she had been elected to organize the Young People's Carnival for Sisterhood, Abe had emerged from his sullen state.

Abe and Dwight cleared and did cleanup detail after dinner while Winona treated herself to a soothing bath. Dwight was permitted to play outside with his friends when they were done. Abe stepped out back.

Outdoors, he was allowed to indulge in an old vice that occasionally craved his attention. Under the largest maple tree, the one Dwight called his "smoking tree," Abe inhaled smoke from a fresh-rolled cigarette. It bit his tongue, swirled down his throat, and filled his lungs with exhilarating sparks. On his fingers, he smelled the abrasive odor of the Brillo pad he had used to scour the metal pots and pans. Damp earth compressed beneath his feet. Young grass and maple leaves and ancient tree bark and soil blended to form a wet, organic odor upon the moist air. He held a wet tin can beneath his cigarette to catch the mounting ashes. He would place the can back at the foot of his smoking tree when done.

Abe thought about his political obsession. It had strong ties to the society in which he lived. If he were to write an essay on the subject, he would have titled it 'Obsession Born of Necessity'. For him, an American future hinged on people he never met. Television images assured justice and opportunities for all. Optimistic promises were made by politicians who had never experienced the cold teeth of ostracism in their flesh. They were propagators instead of regulators or philosophers, testing theories with the lives of him and his loved ones, for all he knew. In their hearts, most of them may have wanted things to stay the same, despite what they said in newspapers or on television.

He needed to believe tomorrow would be worth suffering through today's oppression and that a better world could emerge from the ashes. That Dwight would not have to endure the physical and psychologically maiming effects of overt racism. If honor evades men when politics and power are on the table, then what Blade, Earl and Ron said in the barbershop was correct. Voting doesn't matter.

In front of their house, Dwight played touch football with his friends. Abe did not hear their laughter, cheers, yelling, or loud arguments. He saw Winona wearing a flowered housedress pass by one, then the other, kitchen window. She had a magazine in her hand. Her face was sedate, hair brushed back. Politics became secondary. *Beautiful* was his first thought; *lovely* his next. She poured herself a tall glass of orange juice. She seemed to glide from cupboard to refrigerator to the kitchen table and back to the refrigerator before she vanished from view. No matter what, Abe thought, he would still have Winona. Perfection would be a child of their own. Another dream not yet realized. Tonight could be their immaculate conception.

Abe crushed out his cigarette inside the can. When he entered the living room, Winona was seated on the couch, legs crossed, her dress covering her from neckline to below mid-shin. She looked up from her magazine and watched Abe walk past her to their console stereo.

"What are you doing?" Winona asked.

"You'll see." Abe answered with a deliberate sense of mystery in his voice.

Abe leafed through albums until the jacket of one made him smile. Louis Armstrong's *The Circle of Your Arms* filled the living room.

"Oh yeah, that's the right stuff." Abe said, swaying in time to the music.

Abe turned to face his wife. Winona's resistance was evident in her expression.

"Again I ask: Abraham, what are you doing?"

Abe beckoned her to come to him. Winona watched. Abe danced over to her. Winona put down her magazine on the coffee table near her orange juice and crossed her arms in mock defiance.

"May I have this dance, young lady?" Abe asked, taking both of Winona's hands in his.

Winona stood and walked with him to the center of the living room.

"Dwight is going to be upset with you for playing his albums without his permission."

"His wrath is worth the pleasure of holding you in my arms, my love."

Winona laughed and surrendered to the moment. Abe embraced Winona, coaxing her into following the grinding, circular motion of his hips. Abe moved one of Winona's hands from his waist and placed it, palm down, over his heart. They stared into each other's eyes. The smell of cocoa butter on her skin was intoxicating. Their bodies pressed together in rhythm. The moment stilled. They kissed.

The magic ceased when Dwight interrupted.

"What's for dessert?" he asked his mom.

***

"Give me a drink, Melon."

"You don't need nothing else, Roberta."

"Don't tell me what I do and don't need, man. I bought it."

"Shit, you crazy."

"I did."

"Where'd you get it?"

"The liquor store, fool."

"I bought this whiskey."

"Whatever…get me another drink."

"All right, don't blame me when your big ass gets a hangover tomorrow."

"My hangover ain't your problem."

"Suit yourself."

Melon stumbled out of bed. His skinny body staggered through their disheveled clothes and made its way downstairs to the living room, where he retrieved the remains of a fifth of Jack Daniels Green Label; most of which he had drunk.

Roberta waited for Melon's return, reflecting on the first time they had sex. It was late morning, the Tuesday before Thanksgiving. Kevin and Marvin were at school. Curtiss had been saddled with a surprise double shift and would not be home until six that evening. Roberta had errands to run in the East Liberty Shopping Center, one of which included a stop at the State Liquor Store.

116

While she waited for a clerk wearing the name pin BUDDY to return with her fifth of Jim Beam, someone hugged her from behind. Roberta turned her head to see who it was.

People who knew Jackson Foster called him Melon because his head was shaped like a honeydew. Melon kissed her on the cheek. He worked the night shift with her husband at the U.S. Steel Building. His eyes were red. His coat collar was pulled tight around his neck. Roberta could smell the Jack Daniels on his breath. She smiled in response to his boyish grin.

"How you doing, Songbird?" Melon asked. No one but members of Butterbean ever called her Songbird. Buddy returned with her brandy. Melon released Roberta. "Allow me," he said, showing Buddy two twenty dollar bills, then ordering himself two fifths of Jack Daniel's Green Label. Buddy disappeared down one of six aisles walled with wooden shelves of green, tan, clear and burgundy-colored bottles. Melon and Roberta waited and talked.

Roberta rarely saw Melon in spite of the fact he worked with Curtiss. He lived in Garfield, a neighborhood west of East Liberty; that much she knew. Like many neighboring residents, they shopped at the East Liberty Shopping Center, a place where the closest liquor store could be found.

Roberta offered Melon a ride home. When they entered his place, a proud, shiny drum set was the only thing worth noticing. Slanted across the face of the bass drum skin was the word BUTTERBEAN in cursive, glittering gold letters.

Roberta graciously took the couch seat offered her in an effort to dispel her uneasiness. Melon left and returned with two spotted water glasses, each holding three cloudy ice cubes. He filled his glass with Green Label. She received half as much of the same.

They reminisced. Years and worry became less cumbersome with each fiery sip. Melon played a sultry backbeat from one of Butterbean's original tunes, *Songbird in a Storm*. Melon and Flea, the former bassist for Butterbean, had written it for Roberta. Melon asked her to sing it. Roberta closed her eyes.

In her mind's eye, Roberta saw herself back on stage at the Carlisle Club, wearing a pink satin dress. Blue smoke drifted in and out of the low lights. A murmuring crowd hushed when Roberta stepped into the spotlight. All eyes looked her way, anticipating that first haunting note. The music played. When it felt perfect, she sang. Roberta allowed the notes to float from her soul, slow and moody; the way she always sang that song, reaching into herself to discover caverns of power and passion she would never have imagined. When she finished, Melon wiped the tears from her cheeks with his thumbs. What happened afterwards was foggy. Nothing came clear until Roberta dressed to leave. Melon gave her his telephone number. Roberta rushed home to bathe.

"Ain't but a corner left." Melon sat next to her in bed. He held the clear bottle aloft for Roberta's inspection. Roberta squinted through the dim bedroom light in an effort to see. She reached for it. Melon guzzled the last of the Tennessee sipping whiskey.

"*You bastard.*"

Melon maliciously smiled. Roberta playfully slapped his flat chest.

"Where are my panties?" Roberta sat up, clutching the blanket to her bosom.

"Panties, hell; them's bloomers."

"You seem to have a thing about my butt all of a sudden?"

"I like your butt."

"Damn right you do." There was a dull pause. Roberta searched for her clothes. Melon collapsed on the bed.

"What you going do when he finds out?" Melon asked before she left the bedroom. Roberta stopped and turned. She squinted to see Melon.

"He ain't goin' find out."

Melon belched. "If he don't know already."

Roberta sat at the end of the bed near Melon's feet. She hadn't noticed it earlier, but his bedroom was hot. The saucy smell of after-sex dominated the thick air. She gauged his baby face for clues to his thoughts. His eyes wavered in a glassy-eyed stare.

"You've been talking to Curtiss about us?"

"No, but he ain't stupid."

"Long as you keep your mouth shut, ain't nothing going change." Melon sat bolt upright. His eyes narrowed. Roberta clutched her clothes. Melon reached down and grabbed one of his shoes. He hurled it. Roberta jumped. It struck the opposite wall.

"Got 'em," he said; and in the next breath, "I love you, Roberta. Always have. You could've been another Billie Holiday. Leave Curtiss and come with me. We can still make it happen. I've already talked to the band. They'll do it if you'll do it." Melon paused and looked at Roberta. His breathing became labored. His eyes flickered with one sober thought.

"You still got the pipes."

"Keep your mouth shut, Melon, or you'll never see me again."

Roberta dressed in the living room. Melon fell into an asthmatic sleep.

The children were still asleep when Roberta tiptoed into her home. She took a hot, steaming bath before retiring. If Curtiss smelled booze on her, it wouldn't matter. He had repeatedly told her she reeked like a whiskey still, these days.

***

"Good evening, Reverend." Rebecca Jones, as expected, arrived at Reverend Wilshire's home at precisely seven. The way she was dressed was unexpected. Rebecca wore a crimson dress with a deep V-neck, black stockings, dark red high-heels, and white pearls. She had a medium build and skin as dark and smooth as a black olive. A bright face made of unbroken curves to form its shape framed her large brown eyes.

She walked in with confidence and poise. Reverend Wilshire led Rebecca by the hand to his study, her clicking heels following him down the hall. In front of the small loveseat they stood, holding hands, heads bowed, eyes closed, breathing meditatively. Had someone been capable of seeing through the study drapes, they would have mistaken them for lovers on the verge of an ardent kiss instead of in silent prayer.

"Amen," Reverend Wilshire concluded the prayer. They sat on the loveseat. He held Rebecca's left hand in his right. This was their eighth session together.

"How are you holding up?" Reverend Wilshire asked.

Rebecca sighed. The gesture seemed to lift the weight of the world off her shoulders. She slipped her hand from Reverend Wilshire's, folding her hands in her lap.

"It's been three years since he's been gone," Rebecca began, her voice soft; almost introspective. "I still miss him. Love is like that, I suppose. You carry it with you like some sort of heavy baggage locked away in a vault in your heart. No matter what happens, seems like you can't unload what's in there."

The reverend patted her folded hands as she spoke. Her hands were trembling. He liked her love metaphor, only he would substitute the word "soul" for "heart".

"We never had children. We tried and tried and tried. I guess it just wasn't meant to be. Not having children with the man you love only seems to make his..." Rebecca paused. She took a deep breath to steady herself before she could continue.

"It made his passing even worse. There's nothing to hang onto of him but memories. Sometimes memories are just not enough. Do you know what I mean, Reverend?"

"I do indeed, Rebecca. I do, indeed."

Reverend Wilshire had acknowledged her concerns with a caring nod, a knowing frown, a sympathetic smile. He held onto her folded hands as they sat in silence for the next twenty minutes. The trembling had stopped. In the silence, tears flowed from Rebecca. Embry daubed at her soggy cheeks with his laundered white handkerchief. Rebecca scooted next to him. The reverend placed his free arm around her shoulders. His hand was sandwiched between hers, still resting in her lap.

"I want a family, Reverend. Is that so bad? Is that so bad that I still want a family even though the man I love is gone?"

Reverend Wilshire whispered into her ear, "If it is God's will, all these blessings will be yours."

Her head fell upon his shoulder. A perfume of a light bouquet beckoned like a siren song. He stroked her mink-soft hair. She accepted its soothing pressure. Rebecca moved to her breast the hand she held between hers. They kissed, separated, and then kissed again.

Lightning did not strike them. Condemnation did not rumble down from on high. They grunted, groaned, sighed, and sweated, as had many lovers on that spring Sunday evening under the ubiquitous blue vault of heaven.

Embry Wilshire put on his long, green cotton robe. While Rebecca dressed, Reverend Wilshire reassured her that what they had done was perfectly natural. Rebecca made an appointment for Tuesday for the same time.

"Baptist Ministers can still marry, can't they?" Rebecca asked as she slipped on her shoes.

Embry answered with a cautious, "Yes."

Rebecca kissed his lips. She thanked him with a smile for his kindness and patience and strength to persevere.

After Rebecca left, Embry Wilshire knelt before the wall-mounted crucifix in his study. He feverishly prayed for redemption. His teary eyes aimed at heaven, he asked his Creator for forgiveness. With emotional earnest, he concluded, "I have not seen your blessed eyes since I was a child, when sunlight was my silliest friend and dreams peeked at my life like weeds through cracked asphalt. I pray to you now, Father. Grant penance to this sullied soul who is in desperate need of your benevolence. Dear lenient, compassionate Lord, I beg for mercy."

Sweaty and spent, he lay on the floor. God had once again passed judgment in his favor. It had been His will.

***

Theresa pulled the peach blanket up to her bare waist. Jesse returned from the bathroom to find her dozing. He slipped into bed, easing back the blanket enough to allow him a place beside her. Theresa rolled over. Her head rested on Jesse's chest. Jesse placed one arm around her, embracing Theresa. Together, they worked the blanket up to Theresa's neck; Jesse's chest. Theresa stretched a long leg across Jesse's stomach. Jesse glided a finger up and down her sleek outer thigh.

"Tell me about yourself?" Theresa asked. The gas furnace kicked on with a click, then a loud thud.

"What would you like to know?"

"Everything."

Theresa pushed the blanket down a little. Her leg rested between Jesse's hairy thighs. Jesse continued the movement with his finger.

"To make a short story long, I was born in Cincinnati, Ohio, the only son of a philosopher father and educator mother. Of course, they made their living employed in jobs below their abilities. But in terms of book learnin', they were as versed in academia as any of the highest highbrows in Cincinnati. They instilled that thirst for knowledge in me.

"I left home at eighteen to attend Lincoln University. There I met a young lady—are you certain you want to hear this?"

Theresa yawned. Her eyes closed. She had taken to making small circles with her forefinger over Jesse's right nipple. "Yes," she answered.

Jesse kissed her on top of her head.

"Her name was—actually, her name isn't important. We met when I was a freshman; became acquainted when I was a junior. She was a native of Pittsburgh who talked me into visiting one summer. I liked it; decided to stay—although the truth be known, it was her I liked. The city didn't make an impression on me until much later.

"Anyway, my maternal grandparents had made a fair amount of money with black hair care products. They set up a trust fund for me with the provision that I graduate college. I did so. My father would never accept money from my paternal or maternal grandparents. Gifts, yes; money, no. He believed I should do the same. Men were supposed to earn their way in this world. In his words, 'It builds character when a man labors for his keep.' These factors were supposed to harness dignity and respect and appreciation of what is good in life. That was where my father and I parted company. I took the money. He still has his dignity."

"What happened to her?"

"Who?"

"The girl you moved to Pittsburgh for."

"We had an amicable parting."

"Why?"

"The true test of love is not in its seed. It is in that which grows from it. As we got to know each other better, we discovered that what once was roses had turned to thorns."

"Do you love me?"

"Sometimes I don't understand you."

"No, you don't. But it doesn't matter, as long as you love me."

"That's why I asked you to marry me." Theresa shifted slightly.

"I wonder what kind of flowers our seeds will grow."

"A garden as beautiful as Eden, my love."

Jesse drifted toward sleep during a long silence.

"I'm afraid of what people will say."

Jesse heard himself answer as if he were detached from the voice speaking: "There are no perfect people; merely perfect myths. All I ask of you is your love. Ask nothing more of me and we'll be fine."

Theresa opened her eyes. The fragrance of fresh rain drifted through her cracked, open bedroom window. An occasional sound of automobile tires on wet asphalt in the distance caught her by surprise. Rain patter against the glass lulled her in and out of sleep. She eyed the green fluorescent numbers of her ticking alarm clock on top of the long dresser, squinting, as if seeing them through a patchy fog. 12:01. One minute past midnight. She had not heard Anthony come in. Jesse shifted toward her. She waited for him to settle before she snuggled against his chest.

"What about Anthony?" she asked. Jesse snored.

CHAPTER FIFTEEN

"Here's what I owe you, mister."

Darren shoved a crumpled paper bag across the glass counter. Abe opened the bag and looked inside.

"Where'd you get this money?"

"Earned it."

"How?"

In her sleeveless smock, white sandals, and shorts, Mrs. Powell eyed Darren and Abe from the front end of Aisle Two.

"Honestly, if that's what you're asking."

Abe leaned in close to Darren. "How?"

"That's my business." Abe pushed it back toward him. "Keep it."

Wallace walked to the freezer and rummaged through it.

"I told you before, I don't take charity."

"Let me tell you something. Everybody needs help now and then. Without giving, you don't receive. That's how the world works. You're insulting me by offering me money for gifts."

"Wasn't no gifts. They was handouts. Handouts are charity. I don't accept no charity."

"Gifts are not charity. You ever get a Christmas present?"

"Yeah."

"Did you pay for it?"

"No."

"Well?"

"Not the same."

"Why you so stubborn, boy?" Darren glared at Abe. Mrs. Powell shifted to the front of Aisle One, her back turned to the front counter.

"Tell you what. This money will pay for those groceries and get you started on an account here."

"Only enough there to pay for the groceries I got last time."

"Not as far as I can remember."

Abe counted the crumpled bills and began separating the mound of loose change. Wallace returned with a Blueberry Popsicle, paid for it, and then stepped outside the propped-open front door, where he stood in the lambent sunlight of a second Wednesday in July. Darren remembered Wallace as the man who'd grabbed him. He watched Wallace until he was certain he had no plans of interfering. Abe stacked five dollars' worth of quarters. He put the remaining coins back into the paper bag, telling Darren he would count the rest later.

"As I recall, you received about five dollars' worth of goods. The rest is profit."

"You're wrong, mister."

"Son, if nothing else, I can count."

Darren produced a folded piece of paper out of the back pocket of his plaid shorts and handed it to Abe. Abe unfolded and flattened it on the counter. It was quiet outside. An oscillating electric fan hummed from atop the butcher's display case. Abe wiped sweat from his face with his handkerchief. Darren knelt on one knee and retied the white laces on a new black tennis shoe. When done, he studied it for a moment. Satisfied, he switched knees and repeated the act.

"I don't know the prices of everything on there, but you do," Darren said.

"Yes, I do." Abe paused. Darren wiped his sweaty forehead across the short sleeve of his blue T-shirt.

"I only gave you groceries amounting to five dollars and ninety-three cents. Now, do you want the rest of your money back, or would you prefer I keep it on account?"

"What's that mean?"

"Anytime you need something to eat, you get it here. I deduct its cost from what you have credited to your account."

Darren stared sideways at Abe. He recollected going to the store to buy things for his parents on account. It was something he did not understand at the time.

"Okay," Darren said as he turned to leave.

"Where you going?"

"Home."

Abe wondered where that could be. "To have an account, you must have a name to charge it to."

Abe hoisted his account book out of a drawer next to the cash drawer. He opened the ledger, lifted the red sash out of the way, and then plucked a BIC pen from that same drawer.

"What's your name?"

"Huh?" Darren looked dazed.

"Your name, son. I need it for my records. To keep track of what you spend."

Perry and Dog laughed hysterically at something Tony said as they entered Willie's Market. All three smelled of marijuana. Wallace came in behind them. Perry and Dog frowned at Darren.

"Don't you think it's time you took that Johnson for President poster out your window?" Tony said to Abe. "The man's already in the White House." Perry and Dog found Tony's statement hysterical. Abe's expression caused them to cut their laughter short.

"And we helped keep President Johnson in the White House."

"I didn't do squat. I'm not old enough to vote."

"Yet."

"Meaning what?"

"When you are old enough, hopefully, you won't still be a knucklehead." Perry and Dog burst into laughter. This time, Tony's angry expression caused them to settle down.

"I'll do my part when I'm old enough."

"Not from jail you won't."

"Who says I'm going to jail?"

"That's where they put people they catch doing illegal things. Like smoking dope."

"Man, you're crazy."

"Just in case you are a free man who's registered to vote, I want you to remember that poster in the window. It symbolizes what we can accomplish when we work together to take advantage of our opportunities. That goes for the highest office in the land to the lowest office in your district. Your right to vote is a jewel you should cherish, honor, and protect. More than anything else, it's what defines you as an American."

"Whatever, man." Tony, Perry and Dog smirked at Abe, turned their backs, and walked away. Wallace tossed his popsicle sticks in the tin trashcan to the right of Abe, then went and stood in front of the fan, wiping his forehead clean of a thin film of sweat.

"My name's Virgil," Darren said.

"Virgil what?"

"Virgil Bacon."

"You sure it isn't Reed?"

"If I know anything, it's my own name."

Abe stared at Darren for a moment. Darren stared back.

"Okay, Mr. Bacon. Anytime you need anything, you come here and we'll charge it against your account."

Darren turned to leave.

"You wouldn't happen to need anything now. I mean, it would be good practice. To show you how it works."

Darren eyed Abe until satisfied he was sincere. He looked down at the wealth of candy behind the glass case. Darren asked for a box of Good 'n Plenty and a Hershey bar.

"That'll be ten cents. Now, all I do is write in my ledger the cost, like so." Under a column titled Debit, Abe wrote 0.10. "Deduct it from your credit—which I haven't determined yet. And the candy is yours."

Darren half smiled as he accepted the candy. Tony had meandered toward the back of the store. Perry and Dog loitered near Aisle Three, alternately grumbling to each other. They all had given Mrs. Powell a clumsy greeting. Mrs. Powell shook her head in disgust and walked away. Wallace they ignored.

Before Darren left, Abe reminded him: "Whenever you need anything, this is the place you come to. Got it?" Darren nodded and left. Perry and Dog were leaving right behind him.

"Perry! Dog!" They stopped in the doorway and looked defiantly at Abe. A canary-yellow LTD stopped at the corner in front of the store. Music blared through its rolled-down windows.

"Who Tony chooses to waste his time with is his business. But if either of you knuckleheads lay a finger on that young man," Abe pointed at Darren, "I will kick your sorry asses so bad your shamed predecessors will feel it in the cosmos. Understand?"

Quiet returned with the LTD's departure. Perry and Dog elected to stay inside the store.

A neighborhood boy walked in, wearing damp swimming trunks. He smelled of chlorine. His dark brown skin was ashen.

"You got any Coca Cola?"

"I don't sell that stuff and you shouldn't be buying it."

"I like it," he said with an indignant tone.

"Do you know anything about South Africa?"

"Yeah, it's in southern Africa." The boy smiled. Perry and Dog chuckled.

"African people are nothing more than indigent laborers there; slaves in their own land. Coca Cola does a lot of business with the people who have enslaved them; our ancestors."

"Whatever, man, I'm thirsty. I like Coke. You ain't got none, I'll get it someplace else."

On his way out, Abe overheard the boy say to himself that if he wanted a history lesson, he'd have gone to summer school. Perry and Dog laughed. Ron walked in, said a blanket hello, and then asked for a gallon of Neapolitan ice cream.

"Tony," Abe yelled, holding his palm up to Ron.

"What?"

Wallace stepped up to the front counter.

"Can I help you find something?"

"No."

Abe had found Tony in the convex mirror. "When you're finished doing whatever it is you're supposed to be doing back there, I want to see you up front."

"What for?"

"So I can give your friends a demonstration on what I do to people who steal from me."

"I ain't stealing nothing."

"Then nothing's what I'll find when I turn your butt upside down and inside out."

Tony joined Perry and Dog up front.

"You got no right talking to me like that, Mr. Stone. I ain't no thief."

"Save it for your mother, Tony. I'm just letting you know. She's been covering your sorry behind long enough." Abe walked from behind the counter and squared off with Tony.

"You steal, I squeal, whipping your behind in the process."

Abe paused and looked at each boy, gazing into their reddened eyes. They were edgy. *Tony, if any, would be the one to jump*, Abe thought. *To try to see if he still had that legendary army toughness everyone in East Liberty had heard about.*

"Not one of you should be stealing anything from anybody. You're able-bodied, somewhat bright, young men. Your parents aren't poor. You don't have any excuse doing what you do."

"Like that little bum you let walk out of here with candy?" Perry asked.

"That child's got no one. Each of you has a home and people that love you."

"Right," Dog said. "We outta' here."

"Remember what I said. I'm tired of playing with you fools. Next time, I'm kicking asses and taking names."

Abe tapped Dog on his cheek. Dog leaned toward Abe. Wallace stepped in behind Tony and Perry. Ron removed his watch and placed it on the counter. Dog thought better of attacking Abe. All three left, waiting until they were out of earshot before they boasted about what they would do if that old man ever got in their faces again.

Things settled down. Customers came and went. Ron, Wallace and Mrs. Powell went home, in that order. Abe leafed through *Ebony* magazine, going over a checklist of items in his head that his family would need for the camping trip they were taking with the Hickman family.

Felton Dobbs stopped in the doorway. He wore white shorts, a green skullcap, blue knee socks, a wrinkled purple T-shirt, and brown penny loafers. His arms and legs were ashen. Head shaved bald. For the first time, Abe noticed recognition in his bloodshot eyes as he looked around the store. He was a man fully aware of himself and his surroundings; not fragmented like some figment or specimen of curiosity, as he imagined Felton viewed the world.

He strolled past the counter, down Aisle Three, without as much as a glance in Abe's direction. Abe watched him in the convex mirror as he browsed the top shelf, his forefinger guiding his bulging eyes along a variety of labels.

Felton abruptly made his choices and rushed to the front counter. "Will that be all, Felton?" Abe asked. Felton stared at Abe, his face a ghostly ash; his eyes tired and pained. Felton shoved the can of green beans and box of Fig Newtons across the counter, closer to Abe.

"Will that be all, Felton?"

"Yes." His voice was hoarse. "That will be all, A-bra-ham."

Felton handed Abe a crumpled ten-dollar bill.

"Would you like a bag?" Abe asked.

"Yes...please." After a few seconds of hesitation, he asked: "You are the new owner of Willie's Market? No more Ralph Lingle?"

"No more Ralph Lingle."

Abe noticed tears forming in Felton's eyes.

"Ralph Lingle no more," he mumbled. "Can't help Ralph in the storeroom. Ralph can't help me in the storeroom; can't help me anymore."

The tears were rushing in streams down Felton's cheeks. He kept gently shaking his head. "You Ralph Lingle now; you the only one—only one can help save the truth. A-bra-ham must know. I watch you. Close. Willie's Market know. Ralph Lingle know. Felton know. A-bra-ham must know. Soon truth, yes...yes...yes, soon truth."

Felton rushed by Earl on his way out. Earl said hello. Felton ignored him, crossing the street to stand on the corner, his back to Willie's Market. Earl ambled over near the oscillating fan. Dark rings of perspiration dampened his collar and the underarms of his short-sleeved shirt. He ran his lumpish thumbs along the elastic waistband of his pants, snapping the elastic under his belly where his thumbs met. He wrested a red bandanna from one of his sagging back pockets and mopped his sweaty face, sighed, then complained about the heat.

Abe felt sorry for him. Summer had slowed Earl to a crawl. He got Earl what he wanted and placed it on the counter.

"What's the story on Felton?" Abe asked while bagging Earl's groceries.

"Can't tell you much," Earl answered.

"Arthel said you were in his house."

"Once. That was a long time ago, when he lived over on Shetland. My brother was sick. I came up from York to take care of him. Arthel stayed behind. Back then, only other coloreds lived in this area were the Powells and Dobbs. Clifford was bedridden. Cancer ate him alive. Felton invited me over for dinner. His oldest boy looked after Clifford. I met his wife and the other three children. They were good people; seemed happy."

"Was?"

"Yeah."

"What happened?"

"Don't exactly know. Clifford died, so I wasn't feeling very social. After the funeral, I went back to York. By the time me and Arthel moved up here, Felton was wigged out."

"Any idea what caused it?"

"Somewhat. Ruth could tell you more."

Abe looked out from the storefront. He saw Felton hand Kirby Brown his bag, then run away. Kirby looked after him, holding the bag at arm's length, confused about what to do. Abe walked around the counter and yelled to him through the open door, "It's already paid for, Kirby. Take it home." Kirby closed his mouth and did just that.

"Where does Felton live?" Abe asked Earl.

"Across the Lincoln Bridge someplace, on the Homewood side. Why? You going to pay him a visit?"

Abe thought for a moment. "Maybe."

CHAPTER SIXTEEN

It was the summer of 1963, two years before the Watts riots and before the days of Jesse and Theresa. Humidity was in the eighties. Temperature peaked at a suffocating ninety-six degrees. Abe closed Willie's Market early that Sunday, due to an afternoon drought of customers. Even the vicinal Mrs. Powell had been absent, spending a few cherished days on the Southside in the air-conditioned home of her eldest son and his family.

The day after Independence Day, Winona left to visit her parents in Alabama with a reluctant seven-year-old Dwight in tow. She was not expected to return to Pittsburgh until August 6. They had only been absent from his life for eight days. Home was lonesome and deserted without them. Instead of going home, Abe decided to take a stroll around East Liberty, something he hadn't done for some time.

Neighborhood children played outdoor games, ignoring the oppressive heat. Scantily clothed teenagers lazed on doorsteps and lounged on shaded porches, wiping sweat from their persons with washcloths and dishtowels already damp from perspiration. Every home Abe meandered past on that early Friday evening had open front doors. With summer curtains drawn and screen doors closed, adults sought relief from the heat inside those homes. They sat near electric fans, sipping cold drinks. Their lives drifted out into the street and revolved around toneless conversations, wilted laughter, and soft-spoken televisions and AM radios.

Abe unwittingly paused in front of Carter's Funeral Home to drink in East Liberty's atmosphere, enjoying the serene experience of twentieth century civilization at rest.

He stopped at the corner of Paulson and Carver to wipe perspiration from his face. He looked down Carver. Of all the streets he had passed, it seemed most affected by the weather: ghostly, docile—a block outwardly sparse of any activity. He walked down Carver at a leisurely pace. Sounds of life circled in from neighboring streets. A sleepy medley of staccato noises jostled Abe from his tranquil daze into a disquieted sense of caution.

Theresa Peoples' taut globular hips peeked out from beneath turquoise shorts. Smooth, dark skin shimmered along the back of her long, lithe legs. A scarlet halter top outlined her breasts. Not more than the handful Jessie claimed would be a waste. Jesse had coaxed him into seeing Theresa dance while Winona was away. She proved to be a sultry stripper who strutted through wisps of smoke and bland lighting, mesmerizing a drunken din of horny dreamers with seductive movements that made their manhood pulse in their pants. Abe recognized the view, from behind, of the woman bent over fiddling with the engine of her gasoline-powered lawn mower.

"Can I help?" Abe asked.

"If you could, that would be great," Theresa said, exasperated.

"You shouldn't be cutting grass barefoot, Theresa."

"I always do. I like the feel of the grass under my feet and between my toes."

"It's dangerous. You could lose a toe, or worse yet, a foot."

"Thanks for the lecture, Dad. Now, can you fix the mower or not?"

A quick inspection of her lawn mower revealed a loose spark plug connection. Abe secured the connection, then fired up the lawn mower. Theresa thanked him with an enthusiastic hug. When she released Abe, he backed away. He looked around, pretending nonchalance; attempting to see who might have seen them.

Theresa strained, tugged, and shoved the hulking lawn mower across her small front yard. Abe yelled several times over the noise: "Where's Tony?"

She answered, "I don't know!" Abe looked around. Satisfied no one was watching, he offered to cut her lawn.

"I will allow it under one condition," Theresa said.

"What's that?"

"You agree to have dinner with me."

"What are you making?"

"It'll be a surprise."

Abe pondered the idea for a moment. He had grown weary of eating alone.

"Deal."

Some of Theresa's neighbors happened by, acknowledging Abe with a wave of their hand. First Flea, then Earl Farmer lingered near her green Cyclone fence. Abe used a thinly disguised focus on his labor as a distraction to avoid conversation—a formidable task, considering Theresa's front lawn was not much larger than a modest cemetery plot. It helped Abe's deception that her lawn mower screamed like a VW Beetle in third gear. They became miffed and walked away.

Abe cut, raked, and bagged the grass clippings in less than an hour. He had taken off his shirt to ease the heat. It did not help. Hot and sticky and smelling of fresh-cut grass, he knocked on Theresa's front screen door. Out of protocol, he put on his shirt.

"If you think you're going to sit at my dinner table looking and smelling like that, you've got another think coming." Theresa opened the screen door and pulled Abe inside. She led him to her upstairs bathroom by the backs of his shoulders.

"I can go home and bathe," Abe said. "That won't be a problem."

Handing him a towel, washcloth, and bar of Ivory soap, Theresa ignored his mild protest.

"Lotion's on top of the tank." She pointed at the toilet. "Deodorant's in the medicine cabinet behind the mirror. If you need anything else, just holler." Abe stood, dumbfounded, in the center of the tiny bathroom.

"Leave your clothes outside and I'll wash them for you," Theresa said before she closed the door behind her.

"Use Tony's robe, it's hanging on back of the door." Her voice faded as she walked down the hall. "Dinner will be ready in thirty minutes. Hurry up, or I'll start without you."

Abe stood in place, holding the articles Theresa had handed him, staring at a dingy white terry cloth robe hanging from a hook on the back of the bathroom door. For what seemed eternity, he remained in that spot. An occasional noise from downstairs trickled into his ear. Abe presumed it came from the kitchen. There was a naturalness about being there that made him condemn himself. *Why don't I feel nervous, awkward, guilty, or at the very least, uneasy?* Abe thought. Taking a bath felt normal. Leaving his clothes outside and putting on that robe were acts he longed to complete. No different from home.

Abe emerged wearing Tony's robe. It was snug and reached only to his knees, but covered what needed to be covered. The small heap of clothes he had left outside the bathroom door was gone, along with his shoes. Theresa was humming. Abe heard her as he descended the stairs, wishing he had not surrendered his clothes.

Black bass fried in yellow corn meal, white bread, corn on the cob, sliced white onions, and tomatoes were served up for dinner with chilled red wine in mayonnaise jars on the side. Along with a good meal came soft music and interesting conversation. After a dessert of leftover homemade sweet potato pie, they retired to the living room and plopped down on the couch. They were "Full enough to burst," according to Theresa.

Theresa revealed her past to Abe in desultory and elaborate detail. In summary, she followed her teenage boyfriend from her hometown of West Mifflin to Braddock, where he found work at Westinghouse Air Brake. She met Tony's father in Braddock, a man (Theresa told Abe) he resembled. They married. Tony was born the following year. Three years later, Tony's father and Theresa divorced. On paper, it was due to irreconcilable differences. In life, it was because of his adulterous behavior.

Lacking job skills, Theresa enrolled in a beauty college. For money, she took a job recommended to her by Tina, her best friend at the time. Unlike most strip clubs, Theresa was paid a minimum weekly salary to accompany her lucrative tips. She made enough to support her and Tony and pay for school. Her expectation that a beauty college degree would provide her means for a comfortable living never materialized. She emphasized that she had never prostituted; a fact she took great pride in. She continued stripping because the money was good.

"I bring home more from one Saturday night at the Carlisle than I do in a week at the hair salon." Having seen her dance, Abe believed her.

Theresa was not sweating. Abe asked why. "Baby powder works for me," she said. "Keeps me dry as a bone." She shoved her forearm under Abe's nose. "Smell," she commanded. Abe did so. "Well?"

"Smells good."

"Smells good all over."

"I think it's time for me to leave. Where are my clothes?"

Her kiss stunned him. He assumed she'd had too much wine, and was prepared to dismiss it. Theresa ran her tongue over her lips.

"Yummy," she said. Her eyes lured Abe. He had never before noticed how enticing they were: Umber orbs adrift in pools of marshmallow white.

"Where are my clothes?" he asked. "I'll get them myself."

Theresa said nothing. Her gaze held him fast. Abe had always found Theresa attractive. Seeing her dance had made her desirable. She moved closer to him. One hand massaged the back of his neck. The other slipped inside the rough terry cloth, rubbing his washboard stomach. Abe felt a tingling tear through him. Her breath tickled his cheek. Her eyes were beckoning lights emanating from her center. She moved closer. Her hand slid from his neck to his chest. She kissed him again. The whole act seemed detached, as if it were happening to someone else. Theresa drew her legs up toward herself. She placed Abe's hand on her inner thigh, encouraging him to rub her there by guiding his hand up and down until her assistance was no longer required. He managed to ask Theresa about her son's whereabouts, the neighbors' curiosities, and his wife. She answered each question with a deaf kiss, each more impassioned than the previous.

Abe awoke with a nude, snoring Theresa by his sweaty side. He felt queasy. She smelled of baby powder. Her face was innocent and tranquil. Abe wanted to shove her away from him; push the entire affair out of his mind. Both windows were open, as well as the bedroom door. It still seemed hot enough to steam water. He felt as though he were suffocating. He needed fresh air.

Theresa stirred as he eased out of bed. His clothes were across the room, folded neatly on a stool near her vanity. Abe put on his clothes and tiptoed out of her bedroom. Shame prevented him from looking at her as he dressed.

A glint of light caught his eye from across the dark kitchen when Abe reached for the back doorknob. Tony stood over the sink, drinking a glass of water. He appeared as a dark specter to Abe. They looked at each other for a moment. Neither of them moved. Nothing was said. Abe hung his head and left.

Along shadowy streets lined with silent backyards, Abe hurried until he emerged near his home. That was the only time he had been unfaithful to Winona. Guilt allowed him no sleep that night, although the stagnant heat and oppressive humidity shared blame for his insomnia.

The store telephone had rung ten times that evening. When there was no answer, their home telephone summoned twenty-five times throughout a vacant house.

CHAPTER SEVENTEEN

"That land used to belong to Willie Norton," Winona yelled over the hot currents of air rushing through the rolled-down windows of their Buick LeSabre on the day of Abe's adultery. She tugged at the neckline of her peach sundress, pulling it away from her dampened skin. Dwight was sweating, too, in his shorts and T-shirt, looking small in the Buick's bench seat. Winona glanced down at him. Sunlight beat directly on his face, neck, and chest. His skin had tanned from cinnamon to clove. He squinted at whatever he could see between the sun visor and dashboard. If he had not been such a whiny brat when they'd left, Winona would have remembered to tell him to bring a hat.

"We called him Old Man Norton. He couldn't have been much older than I am now."

"That's nice," Dwight yelled over the rush of air.

"Mama Doe said he passed away a few years ago. Maggie sold the place to a lumber company. Can you see those boards?"

Dwight rose in his seat to try to see the stacks of blond boards near weather-beaten buildings his mother pointed at.

"Un-huh."

"That's the Farr Lumber Company's, now."

"Who's Maggie?"

"Old Man Norton's oldest child."

"Did I meet her?"

"No."

"Oh." Dwight closed his eyes and settled back into his seat. Winona felt sorry for him. *This heat is enough to drive a person crazy*, she thought. *Poor baby, it must be killing him.*

"You want to get in the back seat and lie down? It'll be cooler back there. The sun won't be all up on you."

Dwight looked at Winona with one squinting eye. "I'm all right," he said.

"You sure?"

"Yes, ma'am."

Winona glanced at him. He had both eyes closed. "Let me know if you change your mind." Dwight nodded.

"Funny thing about Old Man Norton's place: he had the biggest barn in Chilton County, fire engine red with white trim. You could see it for miles. Every summer Saturday afternoon, he'd let us kids take it over. We swore it was as big as a football field. It was cooler than being outside. We played hide-and-seek and It-tag and chased each other around until our tongues were dragging."

"That's nice." Dwight had picked up that expression from Winona's mother, without adopting the subtle nuances Mama Doe Perkins incorporated to prevent it from sounding condescending. Winona expected he would drop it shortly after they returned to Pittsburgh. If not, she would have to make him stop saying it until he was old enough to understand what it was he was doing.

Dwight sighed. Winona ignored him. Again, she tugged at her dress.

"Old Man Norton's barn won first prize for being the best-looking barn in Chilton County."

"What was it called?"

"The barn?"

"The prize? What was it called?"

"Can't remember, it was so long ago. They don't do that sort of thing anymore."

Dwight sighed and slumped into his seat. "How much further before we get to Uncle Luke's?"

"Soon, baby, real soon."

Dwight had been excited about this vacation and going to a real farm, meeting relatives he had heard a host of stories about. His litany of questions regarding his unseen family seemed endless to Winona. She answered the ones that she could; at times, not to Dwight's satisfaction.

"What does Grandpa Perkins look like?"

"He's a little taller than me with my eyes, ears and mouth—only his features are bigger because his head is bigger."

Dwight stared at his mother. Winona assumed he was trying to fix her image in his mind, making the features larger.

"Does he look like Dad?"

"No, your Dad's father looks like Dad. My father looks like me."

"What does cousin Darnell look like?"

When they pulled up to her parents' front door, her parents, brothers, and their families were crowded onto the front porch. Winona had to grab Dwight to prevent him from jumping out of the car before it stopped. The way he hugged each of them, one would have thought it was Dwight who had come home after being away for six years. Dwight was so excited, he barely slept at all that first night.

For the first week, Dwight relayed everything he experienced to Winona with uncontrolled exuberance: which members of the family he had met, what he learned about farming and farm animals, and how Grandpa Perkins had taught him to ride a horse, respect the land, and read the wind and sky. As she tucked him in each night, he told Winona what chores he would be responsible for the next day. Before dawn, she could hear him filing out with her father, resurrecting pleasant memories of herself at Dwight's age.

Against her father's wishes, Winona made a special effort to take Dwight to see Sarah and Cleavon Waters. They had moved to a smaller farm over in Dallas County. She introduced them to Dwight as his Great Aunt and Uncle. Cleavon had become a hunchbacked man, appearing exhausted in spirit. He possessed none of the mesmerizing charm or striking good looks that made a renegade young woman drunk with desire. When he looked at Winona, there was a trace of shame in his eyes. Dwight made him equally uneasy. Sarah made them feel at home.

Winona, for the first time, took a good look at Sarah Waters. She was not what some would call a lovely woman. Her mouth was large and crooked, missing more than half her teeth. Uneven eyes, sunken cheeks and a searing scar angled across her nose. She walked with a gimpy right leg that had been broken during Winona's absence and which had never properly healed. But her gentle attentiveness was a wonder to receive. Her voice was grandmotherly in an all-knowing kind of way.

Winona had heard stories that Cleavon beat her. She had witnessed evidence of his verbal abuses when Winona was a child. How could she have possibly believed Cleavon Waters was someone she wanted to spend her life? Winona pitied Sarah Waters. She deserved better than the man she had married.

Dwight's attitude changed during the third week. He had nothing to say about his impending day. He was reluctant to help with chores; he whined about everything but the food and complained he missed his friends, his bed, and his Dad. Winona would see him off by himself. Nothing devised to interest Dwight did more than increase his homesickness. Country life and country people had gone the way of the hula hoop. Dwight was ready to move on.

"Over there is where me and your uncles used to pretend to hunt." Winona pointed toward a small cluster of Southern pines, the same grove fronting the clearing where Niobe had found Winona distraught after her final episode with Cleavon Waters. Dwight stretched to look toward to where his mother pointed. The rising and falling of his eyebrows defined his feelings on the subject.

"That's nice," he said, followed by what he really thought: "When are we going home?"

"Don't ask me that again. You already know the answer."

Dwight sighed and closed his eyes. Coming home had been an enlightening experience for Winona. She had not realized how much she missed the people she grew up knowing; a community she felt at ease in. Much had changed, from faces to landscapes. While she sat on her parents' reupholstered couch answering questions about her life up north at a standing-room-only family gathering, she was overwhelmed by a powerful sense of belonging. Pittsburgh was comfortable; but for Winona, it was good to be home. It would be difficult to leave.

Winona glanced at Dwight, who was staring off in the distance out of the passenger window. She had promised they would visit Luke and Tessie before they left for Pittsburgh. They were in the final week of their month-long stay. If they did not do it now, it might not happen at all.

Winona wondered if she had procrastinated this long because Luke resided in the house she and Abe had lived in during their first two years of marriage. It was there, on their small wooden porch, that a child wrapped in burlap was left outside their front door. It was a foggy morning. Abe almost stepped on the quiet infant smiling up at him.

Abe was furious. He wanted to take the nameless child to Niobe's parents when Abe realized what Niobe had done. Winona talked him down. Winona got him to agree to keep Dwight for a few days. That would give Niobe a chance to realize what she had done and she would probably return for her child. If she did not, then they would turn him over to her parents.

Winona had not seen Niobe or anyone in her family since the child was born. A name was necessary. She decided on Dwight, and told Abe that was the child's name. It never dawned on her to ask people who knew what his birth name was. Years later, she concluded, she had deliberately remained ignorant of that truth. Since Winona named him, that made Dwight all the more her son in her mind and in her heart.

Dwight and Winona became very attached to one another during their wait. He seemed the most contented baby Winona had ever seen. Abe shunned any commitment. When the time came to hand Dwight over to his maternal grandparents, Winona cried but cooperated, as she had promised she would.

Winona was secretly ecstatic when Cleavon Waters, Niobe's father, refused to accept his daughter's illegitimate son. Abe lobbied hard for the Sumpters to take Dwight. Sarah, Niobe's mother, never said much, but Cleavon stood firm. Abe tried reasoning with Dwight's paternal grandparents. Their son, Moses, had denied the child was his. It didn't matter. The Sumpters had already taken in three of their middle son's children born out of wedlock and were incapable of caring for another. Dwight became their child through default. Winona was glad. Abe was angry. Abe finally came around when fate forced the three of them to become a family.

Highway 22 was a quiet stretch of road, serene in its rustic beauty, an artery connecting Dallas, Chilton, and Autauga counties. Their LeSabre rolled along at a steady fifty miles per hour. Sunday afternoon found very few vehicles on the road. The ones they saw were mostly pick-up trucks whose passengers warily eyed the shiny Buick.

Winona remained quiet until they pulled onto Luke's dirt driveway. She warned Dwight to be on his best behavior.

"Don't make me spank you in front of your uncle and everybody." Dwight frowned his understanding.

Moss-hung oaks shaded the car. Dwight took a deep breath. It felt twenty degrees cooler in the shade. Luke Jr. and Christina ran out from seemingly nowhere to greet them. Tessie ushered them inside and made them comfortable with cold glasses of sassafras tea. It was surprisingly cool inside their house. Only the north windows were open, and all the shades were drawn. Luke came in from the barn where he had been replacing spark plugs in his tractor. The grownups talked while Dwight savored his tea, allowing his cousins to entertain him.

Luke filled Winona in on many of the changes they had made to the old house. The front porch where Dwight was abandoned had been remodeled. Luke had added two bedrooms and a sewing room, widened the tool shed, and cleared more of the land for farming. The tree stump Abe used for splitting wood had not been moved and was still being used for that purpose. Tessie showed Winona around. Dwight stayed with his uncle and cousins. When Winona returned with Tessie, Dwight looked bored. His young cousins had become a nuisance that Dwight was in no mood to tolerate. Winona's watchful eye was all that kept him civil.

Dwight had no recollection of ever having lived there. Winona noticed how everything had been walled off and made rectilinear. What was now a living room and separate bedroom were once one and the same. The kitchen had walls and a swinging door. The dining room had walls and sliding wood doors. When she lived there, all of those areas were set into their own spaces inside one room. A wall did not define the confines of a kitchen, but a stove and sink did. Bed and dressers, bedroom; dining table and chairs, dining room. Winona had preferred that layout and was mildly saddened that it was no longer that way.

Dwight groaned at Christina, who was the most adamant about getting Dwight's attention. The four-year-old had said something Dwight apparently found stupid and he told her so. Winona raised one eyebrow. Dwight slouched in his chair and settled down. Tessie made mention of having seen Niobe "awhile back."

"She was here to see her parents," Tessie said. "They moved over to Dallas County, you know?"

"I know," Winona said. "Dwight and I were over there the other day."

Luke and Tessie looked surprised. "Does Papa Walt know 'bout this?" Luke asked.

"Yep, it gave Dwight a chance to meet his great-aunt and uncle." Luke and Tessie looked at each other but said nothing.

"She came all this way to say hi," Tessie said, sensing a need to bring the conversation back on course. "Think she was upset to see me and Luke livin' here, 'stead of you and Abe. She asked a million questions 'bout where everybody was; what you-all was doing."

"Who's Niobe?" Christina asked.

"Nobody you need to worry 'bout," Luke answered. "Now, hush when grown folks talkin'.'"

"You was just a baby," Tessie said, "when Niobe stopped by that day."

"Oh, yeah." Christina's expression reflected her confusion.

"About how long ago was that?" Winona asked.

"Be 'bout four years now," Luke answered. "Ain't seen or heard from her since."

"Anyway, she asked 'bout Dwight," Tessie said. "'Cept she called him somethin' else. Can't 'member now what it was."

"It's not important," Winona said.

"Sure you right," Tessie said. "Anyway, she seemed tickled to death he was doin' all right. Look at 'em, just as big and beautiful as his daddy."

Winona thought about Niobe. Love can be cuddly and soft like a down comforter or it can be as abrasive as sandpaper. Winona had rarely known the rough side. Niobe had known only that. When Winona discovered Niobe was pregnant, she prayed Niobe would be well no matter what happened with the child. Winona knew Niobe was having sex with Moses Sumpter. She had confided that in Winona.

Bad news, that one, Winona had told Niobe: sandpaper all the way. He was only eighteen and had three children in Chilton County alone; was rumored to have two more over in Hale and another in Marengo. Niobe did not seem to care. When Winona asked Niobe if she loved Moses, she told Winona she did. Winona was never convinced. Abe was her down comforter just as Moses had been Niobe's sandpaper.

When they left Luke's house, Winona was glad she had visited. There was a sense of purging as she realized how history had moved on, leaving her with many pleasant memories and a son to enjoy.

Laughter ricocheted in from the living room, filling the kitchen later that night. Winona hung up the telephone in disappointment. She wondered where Abe could be at that time of night. Winona overheard her parents telling two of their friends amusing stories about things Winona did when she was a little girl in the living room. Her parent's friends laughed and shared funny recollections they had regarding their own children.

One story her mother told brought to mind a vivid memory. Winona was five. It was a Saturday afternoon, summer; hot and clear. Papa Walt stepped onto their front porch to check on his "Sweet Potato." He handed Winona a tall, perspiring glass of lemonade. She held it tight with both hands to prevent it from slipping, balancing its bottom on her knees. Papa Walt sat next to her on the wooden steps. He quietly drank his glass of lemonade and stared out over their farm. She imagined her father saw what she saw, smelled the same smells, heard the same sounds, baked (as she did) under a relentless yellow sun, and savored how delicious her mother made lemons, water and sugar taste.

Papa Walt had a sly ingenuity for practical jokes that Winona could only appreciate when she was not one of his victims. Her father convinced her that if she jerked her head around quickly enough, she would be able to see her own ear. First, he demonstrated how it was done. Papa Walt stared straight ahead. He moved his eyes right, then left, toward Winona, keeping his head stock-still. He sharply jerked his head to his left, claiming to have seen his own ear. He told Winona to watch carefully as he demonstrated again. Winona stared in amazement. When Papa Walt was done, he coached Winona on how she could do the same.

Winona listened. She did everything he told her. Kept her head straight, looked toward which ear she wanted to see, and then jerked her head around as fast as she possibly could. She repeatedly attempted to duplicate her father's feat until her mother happened onto the porch and put a stop to it. Winona chuckled to herself about how naive she had been. *Had she learned her lesson?* she thought. *Is absolute trust something anyone should be afforded?*

CHAPTER EIGHTEEN

The morning after Winona and Dwight returned from their trip, Anthony threatened to blackmail Abe while they were alone in Willie's Market. He told Abe if he did not give him free groceries for the remainder of his life, he would squeal to Winona about him and his mom. Tony's blackmail threat only added to Abe's self-torment about the affair. Abe had decided to confess to Winona about his infidelity even before Tony's extortion attempt. When and how had not yet been determined. Tony forced him to move his timetable up to "as soon as possible". How he would break the news was still in question.

Abe told Tony unequivocally that there would be no deal. Tony stormed out, threatening to head straight to Winona. Abe did not attempt to stop him. What good would it have done? Tony was peddling the truth. Besides, he did not believe Tony would play his trump card so early in the game.

All that day, Abe was not himself. His stomach was a pit of knots. Anxiety built up, and his customers noticed. He told them he was not feeling well. He said it was a touch of intestinal flu.

Winona did not confront him when he got home. Tony had not yet done what he had threatened to do. After Dwight was put to bed, Abe told his wife everything. She was furious. He sincerely and repeatedly told Winona how sorry he was, promising her that nothing like that had ever happened before or would happen again. Winona could not so easily forgive him.

Where they came from, divorce was not an option. Abe slept on the couch for a week. Dwight, being a sound sleeper, was never aware of it. By the time he awoke, Abe had cleared away any evidence of him having been there; a benefit of his having to leave early to open the store. What Dwight did notice was the strain between his parents. There was a crisp tension in the air; one, he suspected, blew an ill wind through their once-happy home.

When Winona allowed Abe back into their bedroom, it was to sleep and nothing more. The tension had gradually given way to civility. There was no amnesty in Winona's heart for Abe's transgression. When she looked at the man, a man she had held in such high esteem, she saw a liar and a thief; one who'd stolen her heart, only to abuse it.

Abe needed to do something to regain the trust and affections of the woman he loved. Knowing Winona as he did, it would have to be something drastic; an action worthy of her. Before he closed the store on Saturday evening, he posted a sign on the inside of the front door which informed customers that Willie's Market would be closed from Sunday until one that afternoon.

Dwight and Winona were stunned when Abe decided to attend Sunday church services with them. Winona and Abe walked to church with Dwight between them, recipients of exaggerated smiles and a number of pleasantly surprised expressions.

Abe partially listened to Reverend Baines' fire and brimstone sermon, a predecessor to Embry Wilshire. He was preoccupied, rehearsing his radical action in his own mind.

Reverend Baines concluded his sermon as he always did: "Go in peace and let God watch over you on your journey."

To which the congregation always responded in unison, "Amen."

As everyone stood to leave, Abe spoke. "Forgive me, Reverend, but might I have a word with the congregation?"

Reverend Baines peered out at Abe over his reading glasses. "What about, Brother Abraham?"

"If you don't mind, Reverend, I would prefer to share my..." Abe paused, panning his mind for the right word, "...confession with the entire community."

"We are not Catholics, brother. And if we were, then your confession would be confined to the confession booth."

"I would prefer to confess my sin in God's house, from his pulpit."

This brought a murmur from the congregation. Abe suspected Reverend Baines knew of his sin. The rumor mill had probably ground out various versions of his infidelity. Abe had agonized over his decision; not for himself—he could handle the heat. He deliberated whether it would be best for Winona and Dwight. Gossip in itself has a certain air of deniability attached to it, more like circumstantial evidence in a trail. Once confirmed, the reality of it, like physical evidence, obliterates doubt, leaving the jury to not only issue a verdict, but a punishment, as well.

The reverend eyed Abe for a moment, as if attempting to spirit him out of his decision. "Very well," he said, relinquishing the pulpit and repositioning himself left center stage. The congregation sat.

Abe approached the stage not with feelings of fear or reservation, but with a sense of resolve. He had made up his mind that no matter the outcome, he needed to do this in order to prove to Winona his commitment to her and their family.

Abe walked to the stage. The murmuring became a buzz. Dwight squirmed in his seat, looking around, not knowing what was going on. Winona took his hand and gave him a reassuring smile. It calmed her son. Winona watched Abe, sitting still, not acknowledging the curious stares.

Remembering his Army training, Abe stood at a stance similar to parade rest: shoulders back, chest out, head erect, eyes straight ahead. Reverend Baines raised his hands. The congregation quieted.

"I have sinned in more ways than God may ever forgive in my final days. There is one sin I have recently committed that has been my first. It is the sin of adultery."

There were gasps from the congregation. Someone yelled, "How could you?" The reverend once again raised his hands. His gesture for quiet was respected.

"How could I, indeed? I love Winona with all of my heart and soul. But as some of us know better than others, lust has a way of taking love prisoner long enough to impose its will. During my wife's absence, I allowed that demon to control my actions. Who the other party is in this matter is of no importance. While it only happened once, that was one time too many, for a family man. I apologize before God to my wife and son and ask forgiveness for bringing anguish and disgrace upon them."

Abe saw the closed Bible on the podium. He placed his left hand on the Bible and raised his right.

"I solemnly pledge from this day forward that such a grievous offense will never happen again, so help me God."

Abe felt strangely relieved, as if a giant burden had been lifted from his soul. While Winona greeted her husband with a warm smile and comforting hug upon his return to her, her emotions were mixed. She was angry Abe had made her private humiliation public. She was pleased he loved her enough to make such a grand gesture in order to prove his sincerity. Her absolution was not instantaneous, but it was forthcoming.

Abe attended Sunday services with his family for the next three months without once having to be asked. On the first Sunday of the fourth month, Winona released him from that responsibility. She told Abe in words and actions that she forgave him. His penance had been paid.

CHAPTER NINETEEN

On the last Sunday in August, Willie's Market remained closed in honor of their annual East Liberty Community Barbecue. Cottage Grove at Highland Park was the sight of that year's potluck festivity, for which Abe provided the meat. Almost every customer attended. Those who were without spouses or children—such as Flea, Phillip and Drake—were welcomed members of everyone's extended family. Reverend Wilshire escorted Rebecca Jones. Jesse and Theresa behaved like star-crossed lovers, while Theresa proudly displayed her new emerald engagement ring. Her announcement to retire from stripping met with disappointment from men, skepticism from women, and indifference from children. Darius shared news of an invitation by the Honorable Elijah Mohammed to join him in Chicago for a special Nation of Islam celebration. According to the handwritten letter he showed as proof, Mr. Mohammed wished to thank Darius, on behalf of the faithful, for his exemplary work at Temple 21.

Hickory and charcoal smoke drifted between oval slots of blackened metal grates, embracing steaks, spareribs, chicken, hamburgers and hot dogs. They sizzled, making sounds similar to rain striking concrete. Abe slathered his secret sauce over the meats with a paintbrush. The rain quieted. In his camouflage shorts and white T-shirt, leather sandals, army cap, and dark sunglasses, he was comfortable. Three yards south of the brick barbecue pit was a cluster of wooden picnic tables.

One table was covered with homemade food dishes. Another was blanketed in snacks and homemade desserts. At both ends of those tables were huge tin washtubs filled with ice cubes sprouting refreshments. Two had sodas, two had beer, and the last had wine. Fresh-squeezed lemonade could be found in glass coolers on various tables. Hungry picnickers helped themselves to the offerings. Abe nipped at a sparerib and sipped cold Iron City from a perspiring sorrel bottle while he cooked. The summer neighborhood barbeque of 1966 was well underway.

"Let's go, Bucs! Let's go, Bucs!"

Abe looked down the grassy knoll.

"Now batting number twenty-one, Ree-bert-toe Clee-men-tay!"

A group of neighborhood boys walked across its base.

"Two on, two out, Clemente's two-for-three today with a double back in the fourth to drive in two runs. If he gets ahold of one right here, it's a whole new ball game."

Dwight had his transistor radio volume turned to MAX.

"Right down the pipe, strike one."

Out in a large, flat clearing, teenagers played volleyball. Atop a grassy knoll, northeast of the volleyball game, a lone figure slept beneath the shade of a maple tree.

"Outside, ball one. That makes the count one-and-one. Clemente showed a good eye, laying off that pitch. A crowd of twenty-two thousand chants 'Let's Go Bucs', hoping for a little two-out lightning. Roberto steps out of the batter's box. Knocks a little dirt off his cleats with his bat, sets his feet, eyes the pitcher, and we're underway."

Abe watched the figure for any movement. Only the leaves above him stirred from a breeze.

"There's the windup, and the pitch. Long drive, deep left-center field, going back, *way back, caught on the warning track. Whoa, Nellie*; I didn't think Forbes Field was big enough to hold that one. No runs, two hits, no errors. At the end of eight, it's still the Pirates six and the Dodgers four."

"Reverend Wilshire's good. He beat me worse than I beat you."

"Is that right?" Abe had been staring off into the distance. Wallace slapped him on the back.

"Yes, sir, he throws a mean horseshoe." Abe turned over the meat. "Want me to take over?"

"In a bit." Wallace looked toward Felton. He could not conceive a stranger individual than Felton Dobbs. "How long's he been under that tree?"

"Since we got here."

"Is he dead?"

"Not since I last checked."

"You checked on Felton?"

"Wanted to make sure he was all right. Let him know he's welcomed to our picnic."

"He doesn't live in East Liberty."

"He was one of the first of us who did."

"When we got those thunder showers last week, I saw that fool turning in place outside of Lenton's Pharmacy, looking up at the rain and pointing and laughing like some deranged kid."

"So?"

"The man's loco, goofy, bananas, nuts—"

"I get the picture, Wallace."

"Out of his—"

"What's Wallace upset about now?" Jesse asked. He and Theresa held hands. Since Theresa and Jesse had made their love affair public, they were practically inseparable. Those who disapproved still disapproved, albeit in a civilized fashion. The rest of the community either accepted them or did not care. Wallace and Abe were part of the acceptance crowd.

"I'm not upset," Wallace said.

"Your forehead's wrinkled and your lips are drawn," Theresa said. Abe looked at Wallace.

"Your face does get agitated when you're miffed." Abe subdued a smile.

"I'm not the only one should be upset around here." Wallace jerked his head in the direction of Felton. Theresa and Jesse looked perplexed. Wallace wiped his forehead and jerked his head again. They stared at him as if he were ill.

"Felton," Abe said.

"Oh!" Theresa smiled. "He's a sweet old man."

"*Sweet*, not hardly," Wallace said. "He's dangerous."

"How much trouble can a sleeping man cause?" Jesse asked.

"He'll be awake soon enough."

"Life is marinated with spicy ifs and sweet and sour whys," Theresa said. Abe and Wallace stared in surprise at Theresa. "Felton's just a different flavor of person. He's harmless."

Jesse kissed Theresa, pulled back, and smiled. They heard the squeal of laughter and spirited banter. Each of them looked in the direction of the volleyball game. Adults were competing against teenagers. Tony was amongst his peers. Jesse suggested to Theresa that they join the game.

Theresa agreed. They left Abe paying more attention to barbecuing than anything his friend had to say.

Ruth Powell passed an exasperated Wallace on her way to get a hot dog. Abe saw her coming. She greeted him with a grin. "Earl tells me you've been asking about Felton Dobbs?"

"Yes, ma'am."

"I'll tell you what I know."

"What happened to Felton's family?"

"Vanished."

"You mean, they left?"

"Maybe, nobody saw them leave. And Felton's not talking."

"Police?"

"Searched his house, his car, his property—didn't find a thing. All their clothes were still there. If they left Felton, they didn't take as much as a toothbrush."

"If?"

"I mean, when."

"What did the police do?"

"Took him in, questioned him. Two days later, they let him go. Police seemed convinced his family up and left."

Ruth plucked a steaming hot dog from a roaster full of barbecued meats. She dropped it onto a paper plate Abe handed her, then licked her fingers.

"Were there marital problems?"

"Nothing out of the ordinary. Their kids played with my kids. Taylor and me played Felton and Becky bid whist every Saturday night."

"What do you think?"

"Think?"

"About what happened?"

Mrs. Powell paused for a moment. She glanced toward Felton. "Everybody's got some button sets them off."

Abe nodded. "Do you think he did something to them?"

"No!" Ruth looked around to see who had heard her. Those seated at picnic tables momentarily stared her way. She ate half her hot dog. Abe dropped cooked meat into the roaster; added fresh meat to the grill. He finished eating his barbecue. Ruth moved closer to him. They appeared to be sharing a secret. Abe took a long swallow of beer, and then slathered the fresh meat with his barbecue sauce.

"He's not that kind of man."

"I've seen men do things during the War would shock the devil. Men who'd have given you their last morsel of food got so mean their spit would kill a snake."

"Let me tell you something. I've seen things too, Mr. Stone; long before you were born. Before any Korean War, there were lynchings, burnings, lootings, rapes and starvation. Brutality at the hands of men— and women so mean-spirited they'd just as soon cut your heart out than share a cup of water with you. And I'm telling you, Felton's not that kind of man."

"Maybe."

"What was strange about the whole thing was he was fine for a short while afterwards. A little preoccupied; but in many ways, still the same Felton. He told Taylor and me he was taking this trip to try to regroup. He wouldn't tell us where he was going or how long he'd be. We knew there was more to it than Felton was letting on. He had this pent-up excitement.

"We suspected he and Becky were getting back together and he didn't want to say anything until it was all worked out. We looked after his house; didn't hear from him for six months. I was watering the plants at Felton's place when I heard this whimpering coming from his bedroom. Taylor had come in from weeding Felton's front yard, so we checked it out. Looking bad as a dog after a raccoon fight, hunched over in the corner, Felton was mumbling to himself; stuff we couldn't make heads or tails of. We got him to Mercy Hospital. They cleaned him up then sent him to Mayview. Taylor and me would visit when we could. Most times, he'd be talking normal. Sometimes, without any warning, he'd clam up and stare out in space as if somebody flipped a switch or something. I was surprised when I saw him out walking around. Whatever that man found out there did this to him."

"He knows what happened to his family."

"Yep, I believe so."

***

Working nights made Curtiss a mole during the day. The Community Barbecue offered him a rare opportunity to socialize with friends and neighbors. On that day, he learned of Ron's purchase of a coin-operated Laundromat; Felton's latest episode; Wallace's promotion to foreman;

Ruth's latest grandchild; and Virginia's severed romance with Neville. There were games for young and old and, in between, along with sordid gossip, great food, pleasant surprises, and discreet rendezvouses.

Roberta was absent. Anyone who had not known of Roberta's drinking and infidelity learned about it at the barbecue. Because of this awareness, Curtiss, Marvin and Kevin were, at times, treated as homeless orphans. Abe told Curtiss what he knew about Roberta's misdeeds. Curtiss had foreknowledge of some of what was said to be fact. He'd suspected the rest.

The highlight for Curtiss came when Virginia joined him on a blanket beneath the shady tree Felton had abandoned. She had given him a paper plate full of food. They talked. Virginia touched him, at times— particularly when she laughed at something funny he'd said, or complimented him on some part of his person. Curtiss had given it little thought.

Curtiss smelled no liquor on her breath. Had Virginia been drinking alcohol, he might have been able to explain away her attentive behavior. They carried on in such a playful manner; other picnickers teasingly warned them to behave themselves. Virginia would only reply, "Misbehaving is much more fun."

Virginia hugged Curtiss before they parted. Curtiss welcomed her soft breasts pressed against his chest. He held Virginia longer than he intended; longer than was socially acceptable among friends. Virginia didn't seem to mind. Curtiss felt embarrassed, lecherous, and desperate for affection. Curtiss watched Virginia walk away, her hips swaying left then right. Her waist, back, neck, head and shoulders were a straight, firm line pointing toward the rich blue sky.

"Long before Curtiss got involved with Roberta," Arthel said, "he and Virginia were a couple."

"Everybody just knew they were destined for the altar," Eva said.

"What happened?" Winona asked.

"Roberta's what happened. She came along with her puny band and big ideas and stole that man right away from that poor girl. Darn near destroyed her."

"Shouldn't have messed with Roberta in the first place," Arthel said. "Woman ruined two good men before Curtiss came along."

"Roberta's quicksand, all right," Lisa added.

"Curtiss know?" Debbie asked.

"Not a thing." Arthel answered.

"Know what?" Winona asked.

"About the two men Roberta ruined. Winona, you got to keep up, honey."

"Over her singing career?" Winona asked.

"If you ask me, that whole Butterbean thing wasn't nothing but a scam to get money," Lisa said.

"I've heard Roberta sing. She sounded pretty good to me," Winona said.

"Really? Then why hasn't she tried out for the church choir?"

"Has anybody asked her?" Winona asked. Eva, Arthel, Debbie, and Lisa stared at each other.

"Every year we have tryouts," Debbie said. "Everybody's welcomed."

"All the time making Curtiss feel guilty 'bout her throwing away something," Lisa said. "Poor thing."

"She didn't give up no career," Eva said. "It gave up on her. She wasn't that good a singer no how."

"Payback time," Arthel said.

"Un-huh, this time she's taking the fall."

"What did she want with Curtiss?" Winona asked.

"Come again?" Arthel said.

"I mean, those other men had money, didn't they?" Winona asked. Everyone except Winona nodded. "Unless I miss my guess, Curtiss ain't rich."

"Roberta wanted him because he belonged to Virginia," Arthel said. "She never liked Virginia."

"The way Virginia behaves, I'm not too crazy about her myself," Lisa said.

"She likes to flirt," Arthel said. "Don't mean nothing by it."

"Roberta was jealous of Virginia," Lisa said. "Always talking 'bout how stuck-up she thought Virginia was and how she'd like to bring her down a peg or two."

"She willfully stole another woman's man," Eva said.

Winona thought of her and Cleavon Waters by Jackson Pond. "It takes two."

"Look at 'em, honey," Arthel said. They stared at Curtiss and Virginia. "If that ain't love, I don't know what is."

"I suppose," Winona said.

"Roberta caught that man like a spider in her web," Lisa said.

"Before he knew what hit him," Eva added.

"Only reason she had those boys was so Curtiss wouldn't leave her," Lisa said.

"And she knew it," Eva said.

"I had no idea," Debbie said. Arthel gave a knowing nod. "If it hadn't been for Sam Edwards, no telling what would've come of Virginia. That sweet man mended that poor child's broken heart."

"Virginia was a suicide watch for sure," Eva said.

"Un-huh," Arthel added.

"Whatever happened to Sammy?" Eva asked.

"Moved to Wisconsin," Arthel said. "Wanted to be a dairy farmer."

"You're kidding?" Arthel slowly shook her head, emphasizing her seriousness to Eva.

"Where in the world could a city man get an idea like that?" Debbie asked.

"Don't start me to lying," Arthel said. "He must've had an awful powerful craving for milk and cheese."

"Here comes Virginia. Shush up about that," Lisa said.

"It ain't like she don't know what happened," Eva said. Lisa, Winona, Debbie, and Arthel eyed Eva.

"All right, I won't say a word."

Virginia joined the women gathered near a large cooler chest. She was informally received into their lot. Curtiss wondered what they talked about that made them so vibrant.

"Hey, Virginia, you looking extra special today," Eva said.

"Thank you." Virginia took the compliment in stride.

"Saw you over there spending a little time with Curtiss."

"Something going on we should know about?" Arthel asked. Winona noticed that Virginia blushed. It surprised her how a woman as brash as Virginia had become a bashful girl before her eyes.

"Nothing I can think of," Virginia said. Winona felt guilty. She disliked Roberta, but she and Curtiss were married and family. Something inside made her want to put a stop to what was going on.

"Hope Curtiss goin' be all right," Eva said.

"I'll make certain of that," Virginia said.

"I know you will," Arthel said. Eva, Debbie, Arthel, and Lisa laughed. Virginia looked back at Curtiss and winked. Curtiss smiled. Debbie giggled at something Virginia said. Aside from Winona and Virginia, the remaining women could not contain their amusement. They smiled in Curtiss's direction. Arthel raised an eyebrow in a mock seriousness that made Curtiss's smile broaden. Feeling silly, he turned away.

Marvin's eyes met his. Curtiss flashed backed to a conversation they'd had before they left home for the picnic.

"Why can't we wait for Mom?" Marvin asked.

"We're already late," Kevin said.

"We can give her another hour," Marvin said. "If she's not here by then, then we can go."

"Marvin," Curtiss said. "I don't think your mother would want to go even if she were here. This is not the sort of thing she enjoys anymore."

"Why not?" Marvin asked.

"I wish I knew," Curtiss said.

"We can at least wait and ask her," Marvin said.

"If she wanted to go, she would be here," Kevin said. "Obviously, it's not important to her. *We're* not important to her."

"Look," Curtiss said to Kevin. "I'll leave your mother a note to remind her where we are in case she's forgotten. That way she can still make it to the picnic if she gets home in time."

"I guess," Marvin said, sulking. "Where is she?"

Kevin and Curtiss looked at each other. They both had a good idea where Roberta was—or at least, who she was with.

"Your mom didn't say where she would be, and I forgot to ask," Curtiss said.

Curtiss became ashamed of flirting with Virginia and how he felt about her, as well. His shoulders slumped forward. His face went limp. Virginia called to Curtiss. She blew him a kiss. He attempted a smile that fell short of a grimace. Virginia and most of the women moved off toward a shaded picnic table. Winona left to check on Abe. When Curtiss looked to where his youngest son had been standing, Marvin was gone.

During the drive home, the car of three could be heard, loudly singing whatever song played on the radio. Curtiss assigned each of his boys a part that they shouted to the best of their limited abilities.

Their three-part discord was mutilating "Foolish Little Girl" by The Shirelles when they parked in front of their house. They concluded a raucous second verse before Curtiss switched off the car.

A tumult of music accosted them when they entered their home. Curtiss rushed to the stereo. He lifted the needle from a scratchy Bessie Smith record. Roberta's drunken wailing tumbled down from upstairs. Marvin and Kevin stood in the entranceway, staring at their father. Marvin took steps toward the stairs. Curtiss raised his hand. Marvin stopped. Curtiss ushered them through the kitchen and out into the back yard, where he ordered them to wait until he came for them.

Curtiss pondered the future of their marriage during his ascent of the stairs. Could he allow Roberta to continue to ruin their lives in the way she claimed he had ruined hers? If she was willing to continue her descent into debauchery and alcohol, then what future did they have?

A dream came to mind—one which Curtiss had had three days ago. He was standing on the rooftop of the U.S. Steel Building, gazing out over the city. Dark clouds rushed by him at a dizzying rate. From behind came the sound of a familiar voice. Curtiss turned as if standing on a revolving pedestal. Dressed in a long, satiny nightgown and white kid gloves was Roberta, grinning, her eyes agleam in the burgeoning light. She reached out her arms to him. He stood firm.

Roberta was singing as she ran toward Curtiss. She seemed overjoyed about something he could not discern. Curtiss was sad. The closer Roberta got, the deeper sadness burrowed into his soul. Roberta stood before him, singing as loud as she could into his face. Curtiss backed away from her, stepping out into space. Curtiss looked up to see Roberta leaning over the edge of the roof, singing vigorously down to him. He watched her until she vanished from sight. When he awakened, Curtiss retained that sensation of free falling around Roberta, which had not stopped since.

Roberta slurred the words to "Weeping Willow Blues." Curtiss stepped into their sweltering bedroom to find her slumped over at the foot of the queen-size bed, her head fallen toward her drooping breasts. Her body drenched in sweat. An empty bottle of Jack Daniel's Green Label lay on its side at the head of their bed like an abandoned, gigantic jewel. Roberta did not notice Curtiss.

"Can you believe that shit?" she said to herself. "Fuckin' bastard goin' give me the boot. I fix his ass."

Roberta attempted to rise, but collapsed from her own weight. Curtiss eased the door closed. He waited on the other side. *The children can't see their mother like this*, he thought. Her tirades snapped like firecrackers and died as quickly. Curtiss knew her affair with Melon would run its course. He had hoped they would grow closer, from its shame. Curtiss believed that in some distorted way, Roberta would come out of it needing him more than ever.

He opened the door and sat beside her on the floor, clutching her in his arms. Her breath reeked and she smelled of recent sex. Weakly, Roberta struggled to break free. Her moods swung from ironic laughter to hysterical tears.

"Do you know what he said to me?" Roberta asked Curtiss, slurring her words so badly he barely made out what she asked.

"What did he say?"

"Do you know what he said *to me*?"

"What?"

"He said my voice ain't what it used to be."

"You have a beautiful voice."

"I know I have a beautiful voice. You don't have to tell me I have a beautiful voice. Tell that *fool* I have a beautiful voice, because somebody needs to tell him *something*."

Curtiss could no longer understand Roberta. Her slurred speech had become gibberish. Curtiss decided to listen but remain quiet.

"He told me we were going to get the band back together. He promised me it was going to happen, Curtiss. But it ain't going to happen. Melon said it wasn't just him. The band thought it was a bad idea. The whole band—how is that possible? If it was a bad idea, why'd they bother making such a fuss in the first place?"

Curtiss said nothing.

"They got my hopes all up in the sky, then dropped them like a rock from the clouds. That ain't fair, Curtiss. That just ain't fair."

Curtiss said nothing.

Between the laughter and tears, Roberta repeated her lament of dashed dreams. Even in her drunken state, she managed to leave out the part about her affair with Melon coming to a close.

Curtiss had made out little of what Roberta said. How she behaved told him all he needed to know. He would carry her to the car when she passed out. If he claimed she had collapsed while drinking, Mercy Hospital would admit her overnight for observation. That would give him time to think. The boys would be safe alone, for a while. He would leave a note with Abe to explain his whereabouts and ask that he check in on his sons if he had not called by eight o'clock that evening. Curtiss had a reoccurring thought while he waited for Roberta to tunnel into sleep: had he done this to her?

CHAPTER TWENTY

Abe was home on thirty days' leave from the Army after completing basic training. Each day, his brother Clay dropped him off, and Abe would march across a meadow east of Winona's house. Niobe could hear his approach from the tall grass: austere footsteps, uniform and military in cadence. Her nostrils flared, inhaling fragrances of rich earth, fresh green grass, and the clean cotton spread like a blanket under her naked backside.

This morning, Abe was coming for her. Niobe knew it. Abe wanted her as much as Niobe wanted him. Eyes cannot lie, and her eyes had penetrated deep into his. Ardor spread on lust, creating a sandwich of wonder which Niobe had discovered by eavesdropping on whispering women basking between its succulent layers; elder women of experience— women who drank deep from brimming gourds and swooned from their prurient nectar.

Never had she known fires that bright; that tumultuous. Tremors were as close as any of her liaisons had come. Teenage boys had no such knowledge. They were children, flailing about in uncharted seas. Older men were the answer: men who had sailed oceans of ecstasy and navigated tempestuous waters, who'd caught that sexual dragon by the throat and slain it time after time. They were the ones who could provide her with wings to soar to heaven and be there to catch her when she fell.

Rain was certain. Niobe could smell its delicate musk; could feel its fragile touch on her hair, her face, and her nude body. Abe nearly stepped on her. Niobe said nothing. His eyes moved over her body with considerable care. Her eyes watched only his eyes. Niobe saw longing. Her legs drifted apart. Niobe saw the yearning. When Abe looked at her face, Niobe smiled a soft smile—an easy smile; a visage of comfort. This was her sensual invitation to experience sunrise from inside her golden passage.

Abe leaned forward, but his feet remained anchored in the earth. Niobe reached for him. One foot moved back (his right foot). After his eyes passed once more over her body, Abe left, his cadence the same in leaving as in coming.

Niobe lay there awhile, her arms reaching toward heaven, wondering why he'd refused her pristine summons and hoping he would return with gourds for each of them.

***

Niobe Painter sat erect on the high-backed seat of a passenger train bound for Pittsburgh, appearing dignified in her pink shoes, gloves, skirt, jacket, and pillbox hat. A fresh red carnation pinned to her lapel subtlety contrasted the stark whiteness of her silk blouse. Over the years, Niobe had become a plump woman of motherly ways and sensual charm. Her face was fuller and rich with kindness. Marcel waves outlined her reddish brown skin. One's initial observation would conclude a contented person sat in her place. Only her eyes, black pearls staring blankly at the Pennsylvania countryside, revealed her apprehension.

She was fifteen when she gave birth to her first son. Her parents had not approved of her relationship with the apparent father, a wanton and restive dark brown man of twenty, who bore an alluring, disarming smile on his handsome face. He positioned his stocky body close to women when he spoke to them in his silky bass voice and touched them in a way that encouraged more; drank in their faces with his bedroom eyes. Her mother claimed he could charm the devil's wife. "Bad seed of a bad seed" was how her father had dismissed him.

Moses Sumpter fled when local authorities sought to arrest him on assault and battery charges. Niobe followed him, abandoning her son with the only person she trusted would care for the child now known as Dwight.

Niobe found Moses in Birmingham in a Negro boarding house in the dirt-poor Colored section of town. Moses took what little money Niobe had and gambled it away. Moses called himself a professional gambler. Sadie Lee Futch, proprietor of the local gambling house, called him a pitiful loser.

To pay his backlog of IOUs and finance his bankroll, Moses coerced Niobe into selling herself, convincing her it was a temporary circumstance. They would marry once he made his fabled big strike. Then Moses would treat Niobe as the queen he told her she was.

Somehow, his fortune remained one card or roll of the dice away. Niobe took to drink to numb her shame. The more she prostituted, the more she drank, until her life became an incessant drunken stupor of nameless, faceless patrons.

Moses Sumpter had his throat slashed in a back alley knife fight over twenty-three dollars of craps money. Niobe discovered untapped strength from his murder. She escaped north, landing—exhausted and hungry—in a quiet little town named Cullman. There, a local pastor and his wife took her in. They dried her out and helped her clean up her life. To this day, Niobe credited that pastor and his wife (along with God) for her salvation, although not in that order.

Small town existence could not satisfy Niobe. She craved more people, activity, and choices. The pastor's wife sensed the restlessness in her and told Niobe of a cousin who was also a pastor, who lived in East St. Louis. He was in need of a secretary. Niobe learned the necessary skills under the tutelage of the pastor's oldest daughter. She applied for the position and got it.

In St. Louis, Niobe met Calvert Painter, a gaunt, tan colored man with an echoing laugh, bright brown eyes and two front teeth missing from his dimpled smile. He was a carpenter and bricklayer by trade, high school educated, single, and in search of a wife.

Calvert fell in love with Niobe when he first saw her at New World Baptist Church. Niobe found Calvert mildly interesting. It took two years of persistent courting on Calvert's part before Niobe answered yes to his numerous marriage proposals. Three children and an eight-bedroom house later, Niobe returned to Alabama with her new family.

It was then that Niobe learned of Dwight, a boy as handsome as she was beautiful. From what she gathered, Dwight Stone was unaware that Winona and Abe were not his natural parents. Her parents saw no reason to tell Dwight otherwise. He was a Gift Child to the Stones, as far as they were concerned. Outwardly, Niobe agreed.

Niobe felt a nagging void, watching her three children grow. Thoughts of Dwight troubled her night and day. Niobe's parents had given her Winona's address and telephone number. Niobe wrote Dwight several times, but she never received a response. Her suspicions were that Dwight had never received the letters. If Winona and Abe loved Dwight as much as she loved her other children, then they probably intercepted them. That's what she would have done if she were in their position: protected a child she loved from any impending threat.

A telephone call was out of the question. In her mind, words on paper could be misinterpreted in many ways. There was safety in that. To hear Dwight's voice and not be able to see or touch him would be unbearable.

Calvert urged her to make the sojourn to Pittsburgh. When she finally gave in, Calvert wanted to come along. Niobe convinced him it was something she needed to reconcile for herself. Calvert reluctantly agreed, making all of her travel arrangements. He wanted to notify Winona she was coming. Niobe told Calvert she would rather surprise them. What concerned her was that Winona might not want to see her at all, judging by what her parents told her about the pride she took in claiming Dwight as her own.

The train entered a tunnel. Dense dark walls enveloped the car's light. Niobe stared into the darkness, at first. The window became a mirror, reflecting interior images she had neglected. A middle-aged woman in blue read her Bible while a middle-aged man slept in the seat next to her, his head resting on her shoulder. Matching wedding bands told their story. Seated behind them were twin girls who were divulging secrets to each other that they wanted no one else to hear. In the seat in front of her was a glum-looking man, his face drawn, his weary eyes staring ahead. Niobe wondered what grief he harbored. Could it be worse than her own?

"Can I get you anything, Miss?" asked an obsequiously smiling man with skin as smooth and glossy as anthracite. *Where did he come from?* Niobe thought. She stared at the porter as if puzzled by the question. She thought about answering: *my youth, my dreams, my son.*

"No thank you," she said. They emerged from darkness into sunlight. He walked away with a slight nod of his head.

CHAPTER TWENTY-ONE

Abe opened Willie's Market at the usual time that bright Tuesday morning, scooping up mail scattered at his feet inside the store. A manila envelope immediately caught his attention. "To the owner of Willie's Market" was written in large, irregular print with green, yellow, orange, and purple crayons. There was no forwarding or return address. No postage, either. He dropped it on the counter along with bills and junk mail and went about preparing the store for the day.

Felton stopped in front of Willie's Market, smiling and talking to himself. He stared at Abe through the window. His face turned grim. He placed a forefinger to his puckered lips as if asking for silence. He rubbed his fists across his eyes, bowed his head, and walked away, taking cautious baby steps.

It took Abe a full minute to rip open the envelope that had been heavily secured with packing tape. Stick figure crayon drawings were done on various colors of construction paper. The words "PAIN, LIGht, Dark, NIGHTmares, HuRT, Can't BREAThe, WON'T STOP, Rain, snow, COOL, COLD, GOOD, FIRE OuT, HuRT GO AWAY, WHY, GoD, whY" were scribbled in blue ink on the drawings.

Each drawing had a stick figure strapped to what appeared to be an operating table. Crooked lines struck the table figure in the head and groin. One figure showed other stick figures standing around, looking at the stick figure on the table, checking dials on a wall and doing something to its straps. The egg-shaped head of the stick figure on the table had large tears dripping from his dotted eyes. There were zigzagged lines one could call a mouth. It was an expression of excruciating pain.

Customers came in. Abe tossed the material into a drawer and waited on them. Once he knew a lull in business was forthcoming, Abe retrieved the manila envelope. He leafed through the drawings, disturbed at the contorted images of suffering they clearly exhibited. The last part of the strange envelope's content that Abe saw was a letter addressed to Felton Dobbs at his old East Liberty Residence. The envelope was weathered, but Abe could make out a Richmond, Virginia postmark. It had no return address.

Abe looked around, as if expecting to see Felton watching him. He checked about the store, then outside, taking the letter with him. He saw a few people on their way to work. They waved. He waved back. In the store, Abe read the letter:

Felton:

No apology can erase the memory of catching you and Ralph in that storage room. I don't believe you wouldn't do it again. Another woman would have been painful, but at least I could have some frame of understanding. *Another man*—how could you do something so foul and repulsive? It goes against nature. What did he do for you I couldn't? I loved you. At least, I loved the man I thought you were. Who—or what— you are, I don't know. In any case, I refuse to let our children—especially our sons—be raised by a pervert. Drugging you and leaving was the least destructive thing I could think of. Don't try to see or talk to us or I will have you arrested. Being a faggot is against the law in Pennsylvania. You disgust me, Felton. May God forgive you, because I certainly cannot.

Goodbye, Becky

Ruth Powell walked in through the propped open door. Startled, Abe gathered up the drawings—along with the letter—and tossed them into the drawer.

"Good morning, Abe."

"Good morning, Mrs. Powell." Abe checked his watch. Ruth was early. She walked back to the end of aisle three. Abe watched her. Ruth had not reacted as if she saw what he did, but he was convinced she had. It was of no consequence now. There were things he needed to know about Felton, and Ruth Powell was one of the few people who could tell him. He had to be patient so not to draw suspicion to his earlier actions. Theresa came into the store, shopped, and held a few moments of polite conversation with the widow Powell, then Abe, and left. So did Arthel and Curtiss. Ruth perused Aisle Three, then Aisle One. Abe was about to approach her when she brought a package of Fig Newtons to Abe for a price quote.

"Twenty-nine cents."

"Hmm, I'll leave them here for now, 'til I get a chance to think about it."

"Ruth." Mrs. Powell stared at Abe, waiting for him to continue. "Did Felton and Ralph Lingle have some sort of arrangement?"

"What'd you mean?"

"Did Felton sometimes help Ralph out—around here?"

"Oh! Yes. Felton used to help Ralph with his storeroom inventory, once a month. They did it very early, usually on the last Saturday of the month."

"Why didn't Ralph get his boys to help him—or his wife?"

"Ralph's wife barely had enough energy to help out with customers at the store between housework and cooking. And them boys was as lazy as pouring molasses out of a cold pitcher, and spoiled as rotten eggs. Ralph needed someone who was reliable and hardworking helping back there. If anything, that was Felton. What made you ask that?"

"No particular reason."

"How'd you find out about it, anyway?"

"Ralph must have mentioned it to me."

"He did?"

"Must have."

Ruth gave Abe a sideways glance. Abe realized that Ruth saw more than what he first believed. Whatever was at the heart of Felton's collapse, Ruth would not be the one to tell it. Maybe it was time to pay Felton that visit Abe had thought about for so long.

Jesse walked in. Ruth said good morning, and then took to perusing Aisle One. Abe could feel her watching him as he washed his hands to cut Jesse a pound of bologna and half a pound of American cheese. It was quiet in the store. No one spoke. Ruth watched Abe. Jesse watched Ruth, and Abe watched the meat cutter. None of them saw Felton staring at them from across the street.

CHAPTER TWENTY-TWO

"Think the Pirates going make the play-offs?" Kevin Bankhead asked Dwight.

"Yeah," Dwight answered.

"Who's your favorite Pirate?"

"Roberto Clemente."

"He's good, but I like Willie Stargell better."

"I like Matty Alou," Marvin Bankhead interjected. "Him and that Baltimore Chop."

"Nobody asked you, Mama's Boy," Kevin said.

"Forget you, Peanut Head," Marvin responded.

Kevin tried to reach across Dwight to grab Marvin. The bed groaned from the sudden shift in weight. Dwight pushed Kevin's arms away.

"Stop it," Dwight said.

"Tell him to stop it," Marvin said. "He's the one always startin'."

"Shut up," Kevin said.

"Both of you shut up." Dwight sat up. He looked from side to side at Kevin, then Marvin.

"He wouldn't talk like that if Mom was here," Marvin said; then sat up himself.

"Well, she ain't, Mama's Boy—ain't nobody 'round to stop me from kicking your chicken butt."

"Dad will."

"Dad ain't here."

"As long as I'm here, won't be no butt kicking by either one of you in this house."

"Who you talking to?" Kevin threw back the light summer blanket and got out of bed. He walked to the center of the room. His blue pajamas hung on him as if they were three sizes too large. He posed in his best boxing stance, his fist balled tight. Marvin prodded Dwight to accept his challenge.

"I'll take you both on," Kevin said, staring menacingly at them.

Marvin fell back on the bed and pulled the blanket over his head. Dwight accepted the challenge.

Dwight's red pajamas hung on him in the same manner as Kevin's. Marvin emerged from beneath the blanket and made himself comfortable. Kevin and Dwight circled each other like wrestlers in a ring. They tussled. Marvin rooted for Dwight, his voice rising as the action heated up. No punches were thrown. Dwight had escaped a full nelson by Kevin and had him in a headlock on the floor when Abe separated them.

"What are you boys up to?"

"Wrestling," Dwight said.

"Yeah, and you're in time to see me turn the tables," Kevin said.

"In your dreams," Dwight said as he and Kevin prepared to square off again.

"Stop wrestling and shake hands."

"Shake hands?" Kevin said.

"For what?" Dwight said.

"Because I said so, and you're family. And family doesn't treat each other this way."

"Since when?" Dwight said.

"Since right now," Abe said.

"We were only playing, Dad."

"It didn't look like it to me."

"We were," Kevin protested.

"Play time's over. I want you two to shake hands and apologize to each other."

Dwight and Kevin shook hands in complete confusion as to why.

"I'm sorry," Kevin said his words as empty of sincerity as space.

"Me too," Dwight said, sounding the same.

"Good," Abe said. "Now get back in bed."

Abe escorted Dwight and Kevin back to bed and waited for them to settle in.

"I want peace and quiet in here for the rest of the night. That means no roughhousing."

Dwight and Kevin nodded in agreement.

"If it happens again, I'm coming back in here to whip some tail."

"Yes, sir," Dwight and Kevin said in a scattered response.

"That goes for you too, Marvin." Marvin continued pretending as if he were asleep.

"All right, don't test me."

Shortly after Abe settled into his own bed next to Winona, the boys started talking again.

"I didn't mean to get you in trouble," Kevin said.

"No problem," Dwight answered.

"I'm sorry too, Dwight."

"Shut up, Marvin," Kevin said.

"Both of you please stop arguing. You'd think with your mother being sick…" Dwight stopped talking. He did not know how to finish his sentence. While he did not like his cousin Roberta, he loved her. He loved Marvin and Kevin, too. He'd never realized how much until tonight. What he wanted least was to see them sad.

All the boys lay still, staring at the ceiling, their hands tucked behind their heads. A long silence would lead one to believe that they had fallen asleep. Kevin's voice dispelled that perception.

"Mom's been drinking a lot lately."

"Yeah," Marvin said.

"She was always talking about her old band."

"Her and that dude—what's his name?"

"Melon," Kevin said.

"Yeah, talking about how he say she can still sing and stuff," Marvin said.

"Your mother can sing," Dwight said.

"Yeah," Marvin said.

"She is good," Kevin said. "But I don't like that dude, Melon. When I get big enough, I'm ah kick his butt."

"Me too," Marvin said.

"Hope Mom won't be drinking anymore when she comes home."

"Yeah."

"She'll be all right," Dwight said.

"She blames your folks for why she's not a star," Kevin said.

"I know," Dwight said. "You believe that?"

"No," Marvin answered.

"Dad says it's not true. I don't believe it, but it's hard watching Mom go through this."

"Mom gets mean when she gets drunk," Marvin said.

"Sure does," Kevin replied. "Says some nasty things—hits, too, sometimes."

"Yeah."

"What'd you mean *yeah*, Marvin? She never hit you. I'm the one she beats up on when she's like that, so shut up."

Marvin turned over on his side, his back to Dwight and Kevin. Dwight reflected on a time Kevin had come outside to play with a bruised cheek— one he hadn't had the night before. No sooner had Kevin walked inside his house than he'd heard Cousin Roberta yelling at him. Dwight cringed when he heard the sharp, crippling sound of flesh striking flesh. The next day, Kevin explained his wound as an accident. He'd tripped and hit his face on the arm of a living room chair. No one believed him, but no one disputed his explanation. It made Dwight suspicious. How many times had his seemingly accident-prone cousin been a victim of his own mother's misplaced rage?

Dwight jumped out of bed. Kevin and Marvin stared at him as if he were crazy. From his underwear drawer he fished out his tape recorder, along with its earphone. He brought them over to his awestruck cousins, who sat up beside him at the head of the bed.

"That's cool," Kevin said. "When you'd get that?"

"Last Christmas, I'm not allowed to take it out of the house. I buy blank tapes with my allowance money."

"That's why I ain't seen you buying any candy lately," Kevin said.

"Yep."

Dwight rewound the tape to its beginning. After he plugged in the earphone, he handed it to Kevin, who inserted it into his right ear. Dwight turned it on and carefully aligned the tape recorders dial to PLAY.

"Listen," Dwight said.

"I want to hear," Marvin said.

"You'll get your turn," replied Dwight.

"I don't hear anything," Kevin said.

"Wait a minute."

Kevin's face lit up with a smile. "The Supremes," he said.

"I taped it off the radio. It didn't come out all that good."

Kevin bobbed his head in time to the music. Dwight let him listen to it until that song ended, then gave Marvin a chance. While Marvin listened to a song by B. B. King, Dwight explained to Kevin how it worked.

Dwight snatched the recorder from Marvin when he heard the front doorbell. Kevin and Marvin scurried under the blanket while Dwight scrambled to put away his tape recorder. As his father's footsteps drew nearer, Dwight squirmed himself between his cousins, who were already feigning sleep.

Abe passed Dwight's bedroom and descended the stairs. The doorbell rang again on his way down. Two sets of muffled voices could be faintly heard. One was his father's. The other, lighter in tone, the boys did not recognize. The front door closed. Both voices moved to the living room. A softer set of footsteps followed the path of their predecessor, bypassing the front door for the living room. There was quiet. Dwight and his cousins remained still. They were sound asleep within moments.

CHAPTER TWENTY-THREE

Abe was unprepared for whom he saw when he opened the front door. He expected to see Curtiss, with an update about Roberta. Standing in his yellow porch light was a mystery woman in pink. When she stepped forward, he saw her face.

"Hello, Abe."

Abe was dumbfounded. "Niobe?"

Niobe nodded. "I'm sorry it's so late. I just couldn't wait any longer."

"Wait any longer for what?"

"May I come in?"

Abe stepped to the side. Niobe walked in. Abe closed the door behind her. He led Niobe into the living room. She sat in the center of the couch. Abe sat across from her in his reading chair.

"Niobe, why are you here?"

Niobe took a deep breath. "I'm here to see—"

Winona entered before Niobe could finish. Niobe rose, smiling and putting her arms out for a hug. Winona glared at her. Embarrassed and shocked, Niobe sat, folding her gloved hands in her lap. The outline of a ring could be seen through the thin gloves. Winona noticed.

"I see you're married," Winona said.

Niobe removed her glove to proudly display a gold wedding band.

"My husband's name is Calvert. We've got three kids: two girls, one boy." Niobe dropped her hand back into her lap and looked down at her feet, ashamed she had forgotten Dwight. Winona stood next to Abe. Without looking at each other, Abe offered his hand and Winona grasped it.

"We thought you were dead," Winona lied. Niobe looked at Winona. Her eyes narrowed.

"You say that like you're disappointed."

"We're just surprised to see you after all these years," Abe said.

"I wrote letters. Nobody answered."

"We didn't receive any letters," Abe said. "Are you sure you sent them to the right address?"

"Now I am."

Winona let go of Abe's hand. She sat on the couch next to Niobe.

"How'd you find us?" Winona spoke with a tight jaw.

"I'm not here to start any trouble," Niobe said. Niobe angled her body to face Winona. Her stare softened. Winona was still one of the most elegant and regal women she had ever known. That was how Niobe had described Winona to Calvert. A woman whom, once you've met, you would never forget. "You gave my parents your address, remember? They gave that information to me."

"I gave them our telephone number as well. Why didn't you call?"

"I couldn't. It would seem…inconsiderate." Niobe looked to Abe for help. "I know it's late, but it was like I told Abe. I couldn't wait any longer."

"You've waited this long," Winona said. "Seems to me a few more hours wouldn't make much difference."

Niobe looked back at Winona. Anger rippled Winona's tightened jaws.

"I didn't come here to argue."

"Why are you here?" Winona asked.

"To see my son."

"Your son," Winona let out a derisive laugh. "You gave up that right ten years ago, when you left him on our doorstep."

Niobe felt a rush of hot anger followed by icy shame. She wanted to slap Winona and then beg her forgiveness. Her hands wrung her left glove. She looked again at Abe. His eyes showed embarrassment for Niobe, but he exhibited no signs of intervening on her behalf.

"I know what I did, and I'm sorry. That was a different person. I only want to see my boy. I need to see him."

Niobe's bottom lip quivered. Her eyes welled with tears that she wiped away before they spilled over onto her cheeks.

"It's a bit late for that," Winona said.

Niobe continued to wring the glove between her hands, her head bowed forward.

"What Winona means, Niobe, is that Dwight's asleep," Abe said. Winona glared at Abe. He ignored her by keeping his eyes on Niobe. Niobe looked up at him.

"Of course," she said.

"Why don't you come for dinner tomorrow? That'll give you a chance to see Dwight."

Niobe wiped her eyes with her glove and donned a nervous smile. Winona continued to glare at Abe. Her breathing quickened.

"Do you know the Bankheads?"

"No."

"They're our cousins. They'll be at dinner as well."

"How'd you get here?" Winona tersely asked.

Niobe answered without looking at Winona. "By jitney."

"From St. Louis?" Niobe looked at Winona. She wondered how Winona knew she came from St. Louis without her having said. Abe thought the same.

"I took the train from St. Louis and a jitney from the rail station."

"Where are you staying?" Abe asked.

"The Ellis Hotel, Room 319."

"I'll have Curtiss pick you up tomorrow at five," Abe said. "He's one of our cousins."

"Thank you."

Winona raised an eyebrow as she looked back and forth between the two. Neither would acknowledge her stare. All three stood. Winona and Abe walked Niobe to the door. Abe put his arm around Winona. Winona crossed her arms over her chest.

"If I can use your phone, I'll call a jitney. The driver gave me the jitney number out here."

"Out here is East Liberty," Winona said.

"No need," Abe said. "I'll take you."

Abe left to get dressed. Winona watched him leave, then her eyes bored down on Niobe.

"It's good to see you again, Winona."

Winona said nothing, but continued to stare. Niobe leaned forward as if to hug her. Winona's eyes narrowed. Her back stiffened. Niobe straightened; gained composure. Her shoulders drew back.

"We can fight all day. But I ain't leaving until I see my son."

"No matter what you may think, Dwight will never be your son."

Winona and Niobe defiantly stared at one another.

"What are you going to say when you see him?" Winona asked. Niobe paused for thought. Her eyes did not waver. "I don't know."

Niobe decided, as she put it, to wait on the porch on such a beautiful night. Winona sarcastically agreed with her idea.

"He's my baby," Niobe said from the porch. Winona slammed the door in her face.

Winona bolted the door and ran upstairs. Abe was tucking a tan silk T-shirt inside his khaki shorts. He did not look at Winona when she burst into their bedroom. Only his bedside lamp was on.

"What do you think you're doing?" Her fists were pressed into her hips; her left foot tapped out a threatening rhythm.

"I'm getting dressed." Abe searched for his leather sandals, careful to steer clear of Winona. Their bedroom was hot. The open windows did nothing to relieve the stuffiness. Abe was almost grateful to take Niobe home. It would give him a chance to feel out her motives for being there. Also, by the time he got back, their bedroom would have cooled enough to get a few hours of sleep—if Winona let him.

"You know exactly what I'm talking about," Winona said.

Abe found his sandals. When he sat on the bed to put them on, Winona plopped down beside him. He looked over at her. She seemed more pained than angry. After he put on his sandals, Abe hugged her. Winona fought off an impulse to shove him away.

"Winona, honey, listen. No matter what we do for Dwight—no matter how much we love him - he will forever be Niobe's child."

Winona pushed her face into Abe's chest. Her voice was muffled. Abe told her he could not hear what she had said. She turned her head to one side. Her arms encircled Abe's waist.

"It takes more than having a baby to be a mother."

"I agree. But we can't deny her the right to see him."

"Abe," Winona stopped. Abe felt her body tremor. "What if she tries to take Dwight away from us?"

"She won't."

"You don't know that. What if she's here to take him with her?"

"We'll stop her."

"How?"

Winona looked up at Abe. He brushed back her tears with one hand. "By whatever means necessary."

Winona's head fell upon Abe's chest. He held her until the shuddering stopped. When her body calmed, he left to take Niobe home.

Winona went to her closet. In the farthest left corner was a stack of beige shoeboxes. She slid out the one at the bottom. Winona sat on her side of the bed, resting the shoebox in her lap. She remained mesmerized by an invisible terror, staring out into empty space for a few minutes. Her lips quivered when she looked down at the shoebox. She lifted its lid. Four unopened letters were strewn inside. All addressed to Dwight.

CHAPTER TWENTY-FOUR

The doorbell rang at six minutes past five. Abe answered it. Curtiss and Niobe greeted Abe with broad smiles. Niobe shared a joke about a priest, a rabbi and a Baptist minister as Abe escorted them into the living room. Abe relieved them of Niobe's brightly wrapped packages after she finished her joke. Abe had heard it before. He laughed anyway. Niobe and Curtiss made themselves comfortable on the couch while Abe stacked her packages in the hall closet.

"Where're the boys?" Niobe asked when Abe returned. By that, Abe knew Niobe was really asking where Dwight was.

"Upstairs, in Dwight's room," Abe answered. "They'll be down soon."

Curtiss seemed upbeat. He had telephoned Abe earlier with news of Roberta's voluntary admission to Mercy Hospital's Detox Ward. That, in and of itself, had given Curtiss hope. Indications he had, from listening to Roberta, convinced Curtiss that she intended to slay her alcoholism and begin rebuilding their lives together. A major breakthrough for the Stones was that Roberta had sent along her appreciation for what they were doing for her family during her "Down Time," as she phrased it. Abe offered them a drink while they waited for dinner to begin. Both declined.

"Who are those packages for?" Abe asked Niobe.

"You'll see after dinner," Niobe said, smiling. Niobe was a different person from the previous night. Infectious energy resonated from her. Curtiss had caught it. Abe felt it, too. When the boys ambled down the stairs, asking about dinner, they immediately became swept up in the person introduced to them as 'Aunt Niobe'.

Dinner was magnificent. Dwight sat next to Niobe. Curtiss, Niobe and Abe had high praise for everything, from the table setting to the lemon iced tea. Kevin, Dwight and Marvin chimed in their accolades to prevent being left out. *The way they're heaping it on, you'd think I was dying from something,* Winona thought. Niobe claimed that if she closed her eyes, she'd swear she was back in Alabama eating her mother's fine cooking. Winona resisted the urge to tell Niobe that back in Alabama was where she wished Niobe were. Instead, Winona accepted all compliments with a modest smile.

Winona could not ignore the threat Niobe posed. Each time Niobe placed a gentle hand under Dwight's chin, or was first to answer one of his questions, Winona barely resisted the impulse to strangle her.

"What's it like in St. Louis?" Dwight asked.

"Not much different than here," Niobe answered.

"How old are your kids?"

"Jacob's six. Marion's four. And Paulette's two. I've got pictures back at the hotel. I'll bring them next time I come."

"Why didn't you bring 'em?"

"Who?"

"Your family?"

"Next time."

"What're your kids like?"

"Much the same as you three." She looked around the table at each of the boys. "Except, two being girls, of course." The children nodded their grinning faces in agreement.

"Why don't you stay with us?" Dwight asked.

The question caused Winona to drop her fork in her plate. Abe stiffened. Winona reared back. Niobe became nervous for the second time that evening; the first being when Winona refused her hug. Niobe told Dwight she didn't want to be a bother. Dwight would not concede.

"It's no bother. That's what the guest room's for; huh, Dad?"

"With your cousins here, it might make things a little crowded," Abe said.

"True," Niobe added. "I'm very comfortable at the Ellis."

"I forgot to tell you." Curtiss finished chewing a mouth full of roasted chicken, inadvertently pointing his fork at Abe. "Virginia's going to be staying with us for a while until Roberta gets on her feet."

Winona and Abe looked at one another. They both scrutinized Curtiss. Marvin appeared confused. Kevin seemed pleased.

"What brought this on?" Winona asked.

"She's getting her house painted. I suggested she stay with me—us—instead of some hotel." Curtiss took a gulp of his iced tea and then wiped his mouth with his napkin. Every adult had stopped eating and stared at Curtiss in disbelief. Niobe was more curious about the whole situation than anything else. The children kept eating.

"The main thing is that someone will be there in case something happens while I'm at work."

"I don't need a babysitter," Marvin said. Kevin and Dwight kept eating. Curtiss looked at Marvin with a raised eyebrow. Marvin acknowledged his father's meaning by stuffing a forkful of mashed potatoes into his mouth.

"The boys are welcomed here for as long as you need us," Winona said. *They're family*, she almost added; but she did not want to refuel the Niobe issue.

"I know, I know. There's just no place like home. Know what I mean, Niobe?"

Niobe answered "Yes," then changed the subject. "Abe, aren't you usually at the store 'bout now?"

Abe wondered to himself how she knew about the store.

"We're closed on the Monday after our Community Barbecue. It's tradition: everyone knows about it. I was down there most of today, doing inventory. The boys helped." Dwight nodded his head in confirmation.

"Community Barbecue; what's that all about?"

Dwight and Kevin alternately explained to Niobe about the East Liberty Community Barbecue. Marvin added his knowledge, when allowed. Niobe complimented them on their speaking voices and exceptional vocabularies. Abe and Curtiss beamed with pride. Winona turned a wary eye toward Niobe.

"What's the name of your store?"

"Willie's Market," Abe answered. Winona thought to herself, *she probably already knows.*

"Why'd you name it that and not something like Stone's Market?"

"The name had a solid reputation throughout the community, so we decided to keep it. People had come to expect quality goods and quality service from 'Willie's Market'. If we—Winona and me—could convince people to look past the new faces and give us a chance, we were certain we could maintain the same level of excellence."

"Can I kick the tires and take it for a spin?" Niobe chided. Everyone but Winona laughed.

"I do sound like a used car salesman."

"Just a little," Niobe said.

"Well, it worked, didn't it?" Winona snapped like a fresh green bean being readied for the pot. The room went silent. Conversation was done, and so was dinner.

The children wanted to rush outside to play. Niobe asked that they wait in the living room for a few minutes. She had surprises for everyone. With firm nods from their fathers, the fidgety boys did as she asked.

Curtiss, Winona, Abe, and Niobe cleared the dining room table. Niobe slipped away while the other three tended to kitchen detail. They joined Niobe and the children when they finished. All agreed that dessert could wait.

Niobe had given the boys their presents. Marvin ran to his Dad to show him the G.I. Joe he had gotten. Less exuberantly, Kevin showed everyone his crime fighting kit, complete with tin police badge, plastic handcuffs, plastic nightstick, and plastic thirty-eight pistol.

"You're under arrest," Kevin told Winona, pointing his pistol at her, warning her not to move. Winona allowed him to lead her by her wrist to maximum security (her reading chair near the couch). Kevin came back for his father, who was playing with Marvin and his G.I. Joe. Curtiss refused to go peacefully. They playfully tussled. Curtiss surrendered when he declared Kevin had the drop on him. His crime? Resisting arrest. Charges against Winona had never been stated. Curtiss was placed in minimum security on the couch next to Niobe. Dwight sat on the other side. Niobe had her arm around his shoulders as he coddled his presents. Everyone could see they were albums, just as they could see Dwight reading from the back cover of The Bird and The Bush to Niobe. She reveled in every word, aiding him when he stumbled and correcting his phonetic blunders. Jealousy flashed through Winona. Abe noticed. Curtiss noticed. Her face tightened. Winona squinted at the sight.

"What you got there, Dwight?" Curtiss asked.

"Silence, prisoner! No talking allowed," Kevin said. Curtiss pulled Kevin to him by his belt. He rubbed his stubble beard across the back of his son's smooth neck. Marvin jumped in. Both laughed and squealed from the throes of levity. The two were no match for Curtiss. He pinned them on their backs; Marvin under his weaker left hand, Kevin under his right.

"Dwight, Cousin Curtiss asked what you've got." Dwight looked up when Winona asked her question, as if he were startled anyone else was in the room.

"Louis Armstrong," he answered. He fanned them out with Niobe's help. "Look, ten of 'em."

"Great," Abe said. Winona adjusted herself in her chair. Her eyes relaxed. Curtiss released his children. They scurried to their feet, ready for more. Curtiss put both hands up, palms out. They hugged him instead.

"All right, you boys go outside and play," Curtiss told his sons.

"You coming?" Kevin asked Dwight.

"I'll be there in a minute."

Kevin, with his police gear, and Marvin, with G.I. Joe, headed for the front door.

"Hey!" Both boys stopped. Kevin had his hand on the doorknob. They stared at their father. "Did you say thank you?" They said, "Thank you" in unison before rushing out of the house.

Dwight finished his reading. Niobe applauded, which coaxed the same from everyone else. Niobe hugged Dwight, kissed his forehead, and squeezed his cheeks. When Winona did those things to him, he squirmed; was uncomfortable. He only wanted to get it over with. Niobe's affections were accepted with a joyous grin.

Curtiss noticed something for the first time upon seeing Niobe and Dwight together: a resemblance they shared which was not evident in either Abe or Winona. Their eyes and nose had identical shapes—his still maturing and hers feminine; but clearly strong in similarity. The shape of his head and breadth of his cheeks were Niobe's, without question. Dwight's smile was solely his—or perhaps that of his natural father.

Neighborhood people had gossiped amongst themselves about how no physical likeness existed between Dwight and his parents. Adoption was a silent assumption. No one ever brought up the subject with Abe or Winona. Most believed it was none of anyone's business.

Roberta almost let something slip, once. She was drunk, and was being tolerated at a social gathering at the Bankheads. Roberta stood near Abe when she shouted, "That boy ain't none of—" Curtiss yelled at her to shut up before she could finish. Her chin dropped to her bosom. For ten minutes, Roberta was presumed to be asleep on her feet before her head popped up. Roberta left the party, staggering upstairs to bed. Curtiss never brought up that incident. No one else did, either. They'd said Dwight was their son. That had always been good enough for him. Now, he wasn't sure.

Dwight went on to tell everyone he already had five of his gifts—ten Louis Armstrong albums. That was okay, he explained. "Two Louis Armstrongs are twice as nice."

Curtiss ooed and ahed when Dwight showed him the albums. Abe made an unconvincing attempt to appear impressed.

"They're nice, honey," Winona said. Winona would not touch them. She held Dwight to her with one arm around his thin waist, nodding her head in approval as he elaborated a bit on each album.

Niobe's eyes gleamed. She watched Dwight put away his records with the other albums on the storage side of the console stereo. He let everyone know he would sort them out later. They agreed it was a good idea. Dwight again stressed that he could not understand why Aunt Niobe could not stay with them.

"Enough, Dwight," Abe said.

"I told you. I'm fine where I'm at," Niobe said.

"You're family," Dwight said.

"Dwight," Abe said, his voice sharp and final. Winona thought: *Abe may not be Dwight's natural father, but Dwight sure has inherited his stubbornness.*

Dwight fell silent. Winona saw the smile vanish from Niobe's face. Curtiss noticed, too. Before Abe could see her reaction, Niobe's smile had reappeared. Dwight ran over to Niobe. He hugged her around the neck, from behind. Dwight thanked her and kissed her on her cheek. Niobe patted his arms.

"Go play," Niobe told Dwight.

"How'd you know I liked Louis Armstrong?" Dwight asked.

"Your mother told me."

Winona forced a smile that fooled no one. Dwight went outside to play. Winona rose after Dwight left. She asked if anyone wanted dessert.

"Sit, there's more," Niobe said. "I've got presents for everyone." Niobe rose. "I'll get 'em; just sit."

Vaguely masking her disdain, Winona did not move. Abe watched his wife. He wondered how Niobe could stand it; how she remained at ease. Was it from seeing Dwight? No, she had arrived spirited, exhibiting the same zeal she'd had as the young girl he knew back in Alabama who had attempted to seduce him in a grassy meadow.

Niobe excitedly handed out the nameless packages. Curtiss's gift was an indigo silk shirt; Abe's, a black felt derby. Winona stood before the chair that once was her prison. The present sat at her feet.

"What's the occasion?" Winona asked.

"It's my way of saying thanks for making me feel like family."

"As far as I'm concerned, you are family," Curtiss said.

"Would anyone care for some blueberry pie?" Winona asked.

"Ain't you going to open your present?" Curtiss asked. His eyes shifted toward Niobe for an instant. Winona stared at him.

"I would," Abe said, in response to Winona's question about dessert. Curtiss sighed, then said, "Me, too." Winona glared at Niobe. Niobe was not smiling. Niobe made momentary eye contact with Winona.

"None for me, thanks," Niobe said. Winona walked toward the kitchen.

"Need any help?" Abe asked.

"No," Winona answered without stopping. "I'll handle this myself."

In the kitchen, the voices were murmurs emanating from the living room. The kitchen windows were opened and screened. The back door was open; the screen door unlatched, but closed. The boys' voices danced throughout the kitchen; Marvin rat-a-tat-tatting his toy soldier at everything while Kevin arrested any child who would allow him. Dwight laughing about something she could neither see nor hear.

Winona lifted one of two blueberry pies from a cookie sheet atop the stove. Through the potholders, she felt its dense warmth. Winona placed the pie on top of a spread dishtowel on the kitchen table. From her butcher's block, she extracted her eight-inch carving knife. It sliced through the pie with ease. The murmurs moved closer, becoming discriminating voices. Winona heard the front door open. Curtiss, then Niobe, expressed their gratitude for a lovely dinner. They asked Abe to give Winona their thanks. Winona heard the door close. Abe walked into the kitchen. Winona repeatedly ran the knife along the same fine cut, her grip tight on the knife's handle. The blade scratched the bottom of the metal pie pan.

"Honey." Abe startled Winona.

"I'll have this dished up in a minute. You want to get some saucers out of the cupboard?" Winona turned the pie to make a perpendicular cut.

"They're gone."

"What?" Winona stopped, knife trembling above the pie. Abe took the knife from her. He led Winona by her hand into the living room as Dwight laughed at Kevin, who tried to catch him. Abe sat Winona on the couch then sat beside her. Abe held her hand between his. Winona looked disoriented.

"You're wrong, sweetheart. I know what you're thinking. I thought it, too."

Winona searched Abe's face for assurance that what he said was true.

"Niobe's not here for any other reason but to see Dwight. She's seen him. Before you know it, she'll be gone. We can get back to normal around here, and Dwight will be all yours again."

Winona's breathing became deeper; quicker. She squeezed Abe's hand.

"You don't know, Abe. I see it in her eyes. Niobe wants him. She wants to take our baby. I know it as sure as we're sitting here."

"You're wrong, sweetheart."

Winona rocked forward and back. Her eyes looked off in the distance. No matter what Abe said, Winona saw only one thing: Niobe leading Dwight away by the hand. Him smiling, Louis Armstrong records under his free arm. Her little man gone.

"She's got three of her own. Why she want to take Dwight?" Winona asked. Abe realized he was not getting through. He took Winona by her shoulders and led her to their bedroom. He undressed her; guided her into a nightgown, put her to bed, and left her lying on her back, gazing at the ceiling, arms limp by her side.

"Dear Lord, why she got to take my baby? She got three of her own. Why she got to have mine?"

Abe left the door open. He returned to the kitchen to clean up. It was a dry eighty-seven degrees in Pittsburgh. *Not many more summer days left*, Abe thought. School was about to start, with autumn on its heels. He stepped out onto the porch. Kids were running about playing, oblivious to grown-up problems—a sweet naiveté Abe relished. What would he do if Niobe decided to take Dwight? He would telephone his attorney before going to bed. Phillip would know how to handle this matter.

"Dwight!" Abe yelled. Dwight, Marvin, and Kevin stopped what they were doing. They waited with open mouths. "Fifteen more minutes, then it's time for you three to come in and take your baths."

"Do we have to?" Dwight asked.

"Yes, fifteen minutes." Abe started to say, "Don't make me come looking for you;" but somehow those words dropped in his stomach like granite marbles.

Abe went back inside. On the floor, where Winona had left it, he noticed her unopened present. Abe locked it away in his basement tool shed.

Upstairs, Abe found Winona standing near the open west window. He walked up behind her and surrounded her in his arms. She leaned back into him; two persons into one. It was that way when they made love. Her smile was slight. They watched the children at play. Kevin had handcuffed Marvin. Kevin was having trouble unlocking the handcuffs. Dwight took charge. Marvin was freed. Parents could be heard all over the neighborhood, beckoning their children home. Dusk had fallen. The boys walked toward the house. They noticed Abe and Winona in the window and did a silly dance for them. It made Winona laugh. Dwight started it. Kevin and Marvin joined in after they noticed Abe and Winona's favorable reaction.

They heard the front door open and close. Abe nuzzled the back of Winona's moist neck. He smelled Dixie Peach and strawberries. He embraced her tighter. Winona reached a hand back to touch his face. The boys stomped up the stairs, roaring and growling like wild animals. Abe rested his chin on Winona's shoulder. They watched a crest of daylight fade beneath an advancing night sky.

"We won't lose him, Winona."

"I know," she said, as if she had experienced a sacred revelation.

"No matter what happens."

She sighed. "Dwight will always be our son."

CHAPTER TWENTY-FIVE

Phillip Davenport had orchestrated the legal transaction transferring ownership of Willie's Market from Ralph Lingle to Abraham and Winona Stone. Abe and Winona were impressed by his thoroughness and efficiency. They had been searching for an attorney who could handle both their business and personal legal affairs. Phillip fit the bill.

En route to pick up fresh produce from the Strip District, Abe stopped by his attorney's office, which was located in a three-story red brick building in the heart of the East Liberty Shopping Center.

Eva Hearn looked surprised when she saw Abe walk in. Eva asked about Winona. Dwight? Abe answered each query with one word, "Fine." While her expression relaxed, Abe could feel her eyes probing his person for evidence revealing the nature of his visit. Eva took a minute to leaf through a leather-bound appointment book on her desk.

"I don't see your name in my book, Abe. Do you have an appointment?"

"I spoke to Phillip last night. He said he'd squeeze me in right after lunch."

"Regarding?"

"He'll know."

Eva stared at Abe for a long moment. There was a vacancy in her eyes that suggested to Abe that she was looking at a stranger. Eva had heard about Niobe through the East Liberty grapevine. She had also heard that Niobe strongly resembled Dwight. That left her to draw her own conclusion.

"I'll let Mr. Davenport know that you're here. Would you like to have a seat?"

"I'll stand, thanks."

Eva knocked on a dark wooden door a few yards behind her desk. Abe did not hear a response. Eva did. She opened the door and disappeared inside. Rumor had it that Eva and Phillip were having an affair. Abe had never seen any signs of romance between them. No intimate touches, yearning glances, clandestine whispers, or prolonged hugs. Eva was married; Phillip a bachelor. For eight years, Eva had been his receptionist—as long as Phillip had practiced law. Abe had known of five of Phillip's liaisons at that time. Eva let everyone know that none of those women were good enough for her boss.

"You can go in now, Mr. Stone." Eva stood to the side, holding the door open for Abe.

"Thanks—and it's still Abe, Eva," Abe said, walking past Eva into Phillip's office. Eva eased the door closed behind him.

"Good to see you, Abe." Phillip walked briskly from behind his desk with his hand extended, displaying his engaging smile. He wore a gray herringbone suit, white shirt, and dark tie. Phillip's black hair was brushed back into soft waves; fingernails manicured; teeth perfect and white. *Spit and polish*, Abe thought. His nutmeg skin, hazel eyes, and deep dimples made women swoon. Husbands watched their wives around Phillip Davenport. Alex Hearn was known to drop by the office unannounced, bearing gifts or news that could not wait until Eva got home. Abe had noticed an occasional glint in Winona's eyes in the presence of Phillip. He could see Eva being attracted to Phillip, although he disbelieved the rumor.

Phillip offered Abe a seat. His chairs were plain and dignified, just like his office. Phillip sat in the chair behind his desk and scooted forward. Abe sat across from him. It was the first time Abe could remember seeing Phillip without a smile.

"You're here about Dwight?"

"Yes."

"To be honest, Abe: without legal adoption papers, we don't have much to work with. If the biological mother decides she wants her son, she has every right to take him."

Had Abe been standing, he would have collapsed. Phillip continued.

"However, there are some possibilities worth pursuing. I want you and Winona to file for legal adoption. Do you have a copy of Dwight's birth certificate?"

"Yes. It's in our names."

"How did you manage that?"

"He was registered by the midwife who delivered him. When she heard he'd been abandoned, she signed our names as Dwight's parents."

"Has Niobe said anything about taking Dwight?"

"Not yet."

"What about the father?"

"No idea where he's at."

"That's a plus. For now—understand, I'm not officially advising you to do this—lose Dwight's current birth certificate. Have a new one issued, naming his biological parents. If there are any copies of it floating around, have those parties replace them with the revised copies. When all of that's squared away, file for adoption."

"What about the father? I don't know who he is."

"Put down 'unknown'. It happens all the time."

"Does Dwight have to know any of this?"

"Not yet, but there's no avoiding him discovering the truth if it goes to court."

Abe bowed his head. He had expected Phillip to reassure him that his son would not be taken away. Phillip smiled.

"Don't worry, Abe. We'll find some way to work this out."

Abe looked up. "How?"

"Without getting too specific, neglect and abandonment will be our strong suit. We've got a strong case against her with what we have—even if the father should show up."

"A minute ago, you said Niobe had every right to take him."

"I was preparing you for the worst. Is she married?"

"Yes."

"Children?"

"Yes."

"That may work in our favor. The court might feel leniency toward her, if she were childless. Dwight is your only child, which helps. One other thing." Phillip paused. "Ultimately, the decision may come down to Dwight."

"Mr. Davenport." Eva's voice came through the intercom.

"Yes."

"Mr. Keenau is here for his consultation."

"I'll be right with him."

193

Abe stood. Phillip escorted him to the office door.

"You know I think of Dwight as a favorite nephew," Phillip whispered. "If anything can be done to prevent you and Winona from losing your son, I'll do it."

They shook hands. Abe smiled faintly. Phillip opened the door. He patted Abe on the back as Abe left.

CHAPTER TWENTY-SIX

"Hello?" Winona answered the telephone on the fourth ring. It was mid-morning. No one else was home.

"Winona?" It was Niobe. Winona recognized her voice.

"Yes."

"I just wanted to say thank you for dinner yesterday."

There was silence.

"Is Abe there?"

"No."

"Can I say hi to Dwight?"

"Dwight's out playing with his friends."

"I was wondering: would it be too much trouble for me to stop by today? I've got those pictures I promised to show Dwight."

"I'll have to get back to you. What's your number?"

Niobe gave her the telephone number of the Ellis Hotel, along with her room number.

"I'll call you later to let you know."

"Winona," Niobe hollered into the telephone as Winona was about to hang up.

"What is it?"

"There's something you ought to know."

"That is?"

"I know all about Dwight."

"What's that supposed to mean?"

"The Stones never adopted a child—legally, that is. You and Abe never filed papers on Dwight. I checked, last time I was in Alabama. I checked here, too."

"You know we don't adopt where we come from. There's no need. If you take a child in and care for him, he's yours."

"I know, but it still ain't legal. Dwight is still my son by God and law. Don't make me exercise that right."

Winona clutched the receiver to her chest. Her breathing quickened. Her mind raced over what to say.

"Winona?" No answer.

"Winona?"

Niobe's voice vibrated directly into her heart. Winona composed herself before she spoke.

"If you think you can blackmail us into seeing Dwight, you got another think coming. Bring your pictures. Be here by seven-thirty."

"Thank you."

"For what?"

"I'm sorry I had to do that. I promise it won't happen again."

"Whatever it takes to keep Dwight, I will do it. You will not take my son from me. Do I make myself clear?"

"What are you saying?

"*Whatever…it…takes.*"

"Winona?"

Winona's eyes fluttered. It took her a moment to realize where she was.

"Are you all right, dear?"

Mrs. Powell stood before her at the front counter, a large jar of dill pickles in her hands. Her face was drawn with concern. She studied Winona much as a doctor examining a patient.

"Yes, ma'am. I'm fine." Winona took a deep breath. She glanced through the open door. The day had gone in and out of cloud cover. She wondered if Dwight were still at Mellon Park.

"Can I help you with something?"

"Are you sure you're all right?"

"Yes, ma'am."

Mrs. Powell did not believe her. She let her know by her expression.

"How much are these pickles, dear? I don't see a price on them."

Winona took the jar from her and examined it. She could not find a price, either.

"Sixty-eight cents," Winona said.

"Hmm, maybe I'll look around for something a little less expensive." She smiled. Winona attempted a smile which faltered midway. Mrs. Powell turned to return the pickles. As if struck by a sudden thought, Mrs. Powell stopped, turned, and asked Winona when she would get an opportunity to meet her cousin from St. Louis. "Soon," Winona told her. Mrs. Powell returned the pickles to Aisle Three, where she browsed the shelves. Winona grabbed a *Jet Magazine*. Her concentration waned. Niobe continued to invade Winona's thoughts.

Customers came and went. When they attempted to strike up a conversation with Winona, she was disoriented and distracted. No one was successful at brightening her mood. They left, concerned. Mrs. Powell had canned peaches, a box of Vanilla Wafers, and three bananas charged to her account before she went home.

"Are you the owner of this store?"

Winona looked up from a page she had been staring at for five minutes. A uniformed police officer stood before her. He removed his hat and held it in front of his sternum with both hands. A young man with dark brown hair, brown eyes, freckled skin, and a nose that hooked down toward his mouth, his speech was clear and concise. He stepped towards Winona, as close as the counter would allow.

"In part. My husband owns it, too."

"Is he around?"

"No. He had to pick up some produce we ordered."

"Your name is?"

"What's this all about?"

"I believe we have your son in custody."

Winona gasped. "For what?"

"Shoplifting."

"*Dwight?*"

"No, ma'am. He said his name was Virgil Bacon. He also said your husband was his father. Know anything about it?"

"The only family we've got in the area are the Bankheads—and an old acquaintance visiting from out of town."

"Your name, Miss?"

"Winona Stone."

"I assume Stone is your married name?"

"Yes."

"Your husband's first name?"

"Abraham—why would the boy lie?"

"He's scared. This is the third time he's been caught shoplifting. But this time, it's a little more serious. He assaulted a security guard with a straight razor. We know his mother was murdered. His father is missing. We're trying to locate an aunt and a sister. We've had no success so far."

"Wish I could help."

The officer laid his hat on the counter and then pulled a small pad and pencil from his shirt pocket.

"If your husband remembers anything about a boy who might have been in here—scraggly looking, about four-foot-five, dark eyes, brown-skinned, weighs between 70-80 pounds—have him give me a call. I'm Officer Carl McClusky. The boy's real name is Darren Reed."

"Marcia Reed's boy?"

"I believe that was his mother's name. Did you know her?"

"Only for a short spell. That poor baby."

The officer handed Winona a piece of paper with his name and precinct telephone number scribbled on it. Winona took the paper from him.

"What will happen to him?"

"Juvenile hall, then foster home; in that order."

The officer put his hat on and left. Winona put the piece of paper in her purse. Mrs. Powell returned shortly after the officer had left. She positioned herself in the middle of Aisle Two. Picking a can of sardines off the shelf, she called Winona over to ask their price. Winona quoted it to her.

"What'd that officer want?" The question didn't surprise Winona.

"He was asking about a child who claimed to be Abe's son."

"His son!" Winona touched Ruth Powell on the shoulder.

"There was nothing to it."

"I wonder if that was that boy Abe caught stealing in here one time."

"I'm sure it was. I'm just thankful it wasn't Dwight."

"Amen."

Abe returned with their produce. Winona and Abe unloaded their van. She told Abe what Niobe had said about Dwight not being legally adopted. He explained to her what Phillip had said on the same subject.

His wife's reaction surprised Abe. He expected frustration, anger, denial—a woman bereft and confused. When Winona searched his eyes for something he could not pinpoint, Abe saw a twinkle of hope, much like you would find in the eyes of a child on Christmas Eve. Winona kissed her husband, smiled, and then left. Abe fought the impulse to follow her. Mrs. Powell watched the tail end of the scene unfold. The major portion of their conversation had taken place in the storage room.

Winona took the long route home. Her steps were light and free. Each person she saw was greeted with a pleasant smile and a hearty good afternoon. Most were asked about family, themselves, their lives. When Winona arrived home, nothing had changed. She walked around the house, noticing things she had not noticed in years. In all of this, Winona had forgotten the most important person involved in this selection. It came from the last piece of information Abe told her that Phillip had said.

Ultimately, if Dwight wanted to stay with them, there would be little that Niobe could do. If Niobe dared tell Dwight, he would be the one to decide on who was his mother. That knowledge would be her triumph and Niobe's downfall. It would turn what their attorney termed as "possibilities worth pursuing" into a favorable outcome. The time had come to fight for her son. Winona had forgotten to mention the police officer to Abe.

CHAPTER TWENTY-SEVEN

Niobe sat in silence on the disheveled single bed. She had dressed late that morning in preparation for a casual walk to combat her mounting sense of claustrophobia, long after she found the courage to call Winona to ask to see her son. On the opposite side of the single room, both windows were fully open. She stared, mesmerized, at a red brick office building across Centre Avenue. Sounds of urban life spilled into her hotel room. In her mind, she dissected and identified its music and meditated on those notes that were soothingly familiar.

Children's voices affected her the most—young children at play: laughing, arguing, yelling and squealing in that unbridled manner only children are capable of achieving. It was a warm day, reminiscent of the one on which she had decided to give up her son. No one was suspicious. Niobe would often take her son with her and vanish for days, returning home only for a change of clothes and clean diapers for her baby.

Her mother was always glad to see them. Her brother, John, displayed his affection in their father's absence. Cleavon Waters always seemed disappointed when Niobe returned; as if he was chagrined they were not dead. Niobe never told them where she went or what she was doing. Sarah Waters gave her daughter whatever she needed, against her father's wishes. Sarah Waters received cuts and bruises for her disobedience—injuries she attempted to conceal or excuse as accidents.

On the edge of Old Man Norton's property, Niobe had found a place he had begun building some time ago, when he thought a disagreeable uncle would be coming to live with them. Maggie Norton discovered them on a day when she heard Niobe's baby crying. Maggie began bringing Niobe food, water, and milk for the baby, twice a day. Niobe suspected word was sent to her mother to let her know Niobe and her child were safe. Sometimes Moses would stay with her. It was then that she felt as though they were a family. He played with his son. Made love to her. Was attentive and treated Niobe with the type of dignity she had always wanted from the men she loved, but rarely got.

By that day, Niobe had not heard from Moses in weeks. Friends of Moses informed her that the Sheriff had been looking for Moses with a warrant for his arrest for assaulting two white men in Monroe County. To hear Moses tell it, he had defended himself from two liquored-up sore losers he had beaten fair and square at blackjack. Moses said that, in any event, he had to get away. He didn't tell anyone where he was going. Niobe was determined to find him.

All night, Niobe waited in the clearing where she and Winona had spent so much time together. She talked to her baby, played with him, and kept him dry and close and warm. Niobe had not expected to love her child. He was—by her own account—a means to a spiteful end. But she could not take him with her. She could not trust her mother to care for him because her father ruled the house, and he hated her child as much as he hated Moses Sumpter. Winona was the only one. Niobe knew Abe would be reluctant, but her big sister would find a way to make it work.

Her movements were unconscious when she laid her son, dressed in his best summer outfit and wrapped in burlap, upon the Stone's dewy porch. Tears dripped from her chin. Niobe kissed him and whispered into his ear for him to mind his new folks. "You belong to them now," Niobe told him.

He threatened to cry. Niobe rubbed his belly, put her lips close to his ear, and hummed The Itsy-Bitsy Spider until he gurgled and smiled. She caught wind of his sweet and sour odor; nuzzled her nose into the side of his neck. Before Niobe could change her mind, she kissed her child one last time, closed her tear-filled eyes, and ran. A girl left that infant behind; one whose heart was so consumed with love for Moses Sumpter that she did not have enough room left in it for her only son.

Niobe stretched out on the bed. Her body felt like what her mother would describe as "too much hay and not enough wagon". For a moment, she stared at the ceiling before turning her head to gaze at the red bricks. Married with children, Niobe asked herself if she had changed. She felt that she had. Believed she had. Then, why did she have to fight the impulse to run away whenever she saw Dwight?

CHAPTER TWENTY-EIGHT

Abe checked the directions Ruth Powell had given him. "On the Homewood side of the Lincoln Avenue Bridge, to your right, you'll see a blue and white, two-story house. That's where he lives. You can't miss it!" Abe refolded the piece of brown butcher's paper and returned it to his pants pocket. He was stunned by what he saw. A pristine concrete walk—flanked by scrupulously groomed boxwood hedges—led to a set of cobalt blue plank steps that shined as if they had just been painted. As Abe got closer, it seemed to him as if the entire house had been freshly painted in cobalt blue and trimmed in eggshell white. Beneath the porch, a white latticework protected the crawlspace from intruders. Planted in a dirt strip in front of the crawlspace were tulips, begonias and daffodils. When Abe stood on the porch, he looked around to see two small lawns groomed to perfection, an oak sapling growing in the center of the one to his left.

Abe turned to face the house. He noticed glistening picture windows on both sides of an ornate screen door. He pressed a shiny black button protruding out of a polished brass plate. It played a music box version of Auld Lang Syne. Abe waited, looking around in amazement, not knowing what to expect. He noticed there were no light fixtures. That struck him as odd. Abe wondered how Felton saw outside at night. Then he thought to himself: *would it matter?*

Wind chimes tingled from a breeze. Abe rang the doorbell again. He thought he heard what sounded like voices coming from inside. Abe went to one of the windows. The drapes were open. He peered inside. The dominant furnishing theme was Victorian, from the white marble top table to the long mahogany case clock to the crystal chandelier. Everything was neat and spotless and orderly, as if it were part of a sterile Victorian museum exhibit. *Maybe Ruth is playing some kind of warped practical joke,* Abe thought. *This can't be where Felton Dobbs lives. From Earl, I'd expect this sort of thing—but Ruth! Her sense of humor generally doesn't lean in this direction.*

There was something else Abe found odd about what he saw. Like outside, he saw no electrical fixtures on the inside of the house. Candles were everywhere. Some had clearly been used. Upon closer examination, he saw aluminum foil covering something that was located in a place one would normally find an electrical wall socket. The drawing made sense now. He had read about people who were considered disturbed being treated by electroshock therapy. Most accounts were brutal; downright sadistic, in Abe's opinion. Abe tried the doorbell a last time. When no one answered, he left.

"Can't get me here, doctor, doctor," Felton whispered to himself hiding in the crawlspace, watching Abe leave. "Buzz, buzz, no fireworks today, cool here, no shock, no burn, no hurt, buzz buzz, safe here, no fireworks today. Felton hide good. Bye, doctor. Can't get me here, can you? No fireworks today."

CHAPTER TWENTY-NINE

Dwight and Winona shared a pleasant breakfast of hot waffles, whole strawberries, and fresh squeezed orange juice on the first day of Dwight's return to school. Time alone with Dwight had become precious to her, of late. Niobe's presence made Winona more attentive, less judgmental, and receptive to Dwight in a way she had not been since he was a young child. She competed with Niobe at every opportunity. Everyone noticed, just as they noticed Dwight's resemblance to Niobe. Winona did not care. It didn't matter what was thought, gossiped, or believed. Dwight was her son. If Niobe wanted him, she would have to pry him from her soul. A stint in purgatory would prove easier. In itself, that knowledge made Winona feel secure, invincible.

It was a clear, sunny morning. September breezes drifted into the kitchen. Yesterday morning, Winona awoke nauseous. She rushed to the bathroom, where she sporadically vomited for the better part of an hour. The nausea returned repeatedly that morning. Each time, she would vomit and remain in the bathroom until the nausea passed. Today she felt fine.

Winona sat at the kitchen table wearing her robe and slippers, with a fresh-brewed cup of black coffee and the morning newspaper. Her skin glowed from her morning bath; her body still sensitive in the erogenous areas Abe had explored. There were no chores requiring her attention. Abe had plans to take everyone to a dinner downtown. He felt Winona deserved as much, after all she'd been through lately.

Winona was reading the newspaper comics when Niobe entered the kitchen. Beetle Bailey had brought a chuckle out of her. Niobe said a chipper "Good morning." Dressed in her green housecoat and slippers, she walked past Winona to the cupboard for a coffee cup. Niobe poured a steaming cup of coffee, dumped in four heaping teaspoons of sugar and a generous portion of canned milk, and then sat across the table from Winona.

Niobe had been a houseguest for a week of the twelve days she had been in Pittsburgh. Dwight had remained obstinately confused as to why his favorite aunt could not stay with them. The guest room was ready and available. His cousins had returned home when Curtiss said they would. Abe was stunned when Winona bowed to Dwight's wish of allowing his supposed aunt to stay with them. Niobe had an open return ticket to St. Louis. She revealed that fact during dinner on Wednesday. When Niobe planned to use it, no one had a clue.

"Dwight get off to school okay?"

Winona pulled the newspaper down far enough to see Niobe's face. "Of course," she said, her tone sharp. Niobe had become accustomed to Winona speaking to her in such a fashion.

"It's a shame what happened to the Brown's house. Burning down like that. Some people seem to think that Felton man had something to do with it."

"Wiring was old. That's all there was to it." Winona had returned to reading her newspaper.

"Calvert says you always got to be careful with wiring. One hot spot and *whoosh*: up in smoke." Niobe waited for a response. Winona kept reading.

"Seems to me like Mrs. Powell is the one taking it the hardest. Last time I saw her, the poor thing looked like she was about ready for the grave."

"Used to be her house, went up in flames. Her and her husband lived there all of their lives together; *raised* their children in it. No different than if she watched her own house burn down." Niobe noted Winona's emphasis on the word 'raised'. It sent another dart into her heart. Winona had punctured it so many times, she had become numb to the pain.

"I see your point. Is she goin' be all right?"

"We'll take care of her, and the Browns."

"That's nice of you and Abe."

"Not only will we help; but this entire community will lend a hand."

"Of course. I didn't mean anything bad by that. I was just saying."

After an uneasy pause, Niobe said: "What's that minister's name?"

"You mean Reverend Wilshire?"

"Yes. Hear tell he's marrying a woman he got pregnant?"

"Don't know. He's getting married, all right. I suppose the baby's his," Winona lied. She knew everything about Rebecca and Reverend Wilshire. Word of Rebecca's pregnancy had blazed through Sisterhood. She felt no need to share that information with Niobe.

"Mrs. Powell seemed to think that's the case. Mabel Brown and Lisa Palmer, too."

"They know more than I do." Winona turned from the comics to obituaries. She scanned down the list of deceased. Nobody she knew. There was a twisted hope she would see Niobe's name.

"What about Jesse's fiancée?"

"What about her?"

"She really a stripper?"

"Was, she quit as soon as Jesse proposed."

"That's good; the way it should be. A wife shouldn't be taking off her clothes for no other man but her husband." Niobe looked to Winona for a response. Winona was reading Dear Abby by now. Niobe puckered her lips, tapped her fingernails on the side of her cup, and then let out a sigh.

"Poor Curtiss," she said after a healthy sip of coffee. "Don't make no sense what Roberta did."

"No, it doesn't."

"Leaving him like that. Who'd she run off with?"

"Jackson Foster."

"Seems I heard him called something else?"

"Melon."

"Yeah, why y'all call him that?"

"Because of the shape of his head."

Niobe laughed. Winona ignored her.

"Right out the hospital? Where was security?"

"Don't know."

"I hear tell Virginia and Curtiss were a hot number before Roberta came along."

"True."

"Appears they picked up where they left off." Niobe waited for a response that never came.

"Sure is a shame, leave behind two kids and a good looking, hardworking man like Curtiss for some no-good, poor-ass drunk."

"How you know he's a poor-ass drunk? You've never met him. For all you know, he might be a rich-ass drunk."

"Heard y'all talk enough about him."

"You've never heard me call Melon poor-ass or a drunk."

"Abe did." Winona said nothing. "Melon sounds like a loser, the way Abe and them was talking about him at the store the other day. Curtiss probably better off without her. According to Flea, the woman was quicksand. Virginia will take good care of him. Now, there's a good woman." Niobe brushed Winona across her forearm. Winona glared at her. Niobe said nothing. Niobe rose and ambled over to the screen door. She was surprised Winona did not leap at her slip of the tongue about Roberta leaving her kids. Perhaps that was a sign that Winona was beginning to forgive her.

The back door was open, allowing Niobe to view the back yard and some of the homes across the street. Niobe sipped her coffee. It was cool. She preferred it that way. Over the past week, Niobe had met almost the entire neighborhood. People were friendly and polite, putting her at ease—except for Winona. When they were together, she felt stalked. Every move she made, each word she spoke, was ammunition, stockpiled to be used against her. Not once in all that time did the question surface as to who would tell Dwight that Niobe was his natural mother. Niobe had wanted to until she saw Dwight and the words stuck in her throat. Her biggest question was answered. Niobe now knew, without a doubt, who Dwight's father was.

"Do you miss Alabama?" Winona detected a hint of melancholy in Niobe's voice.

"Sometimes."

"Me too—sometimes."

"You can always move back."

"I'm very happy in St. Louis." Niobe turned from the screen door. Her eyes pointed toward her chair. Winona folded the newspaper, laid it on the table, and then sipped her coffee. Her expression told Niobe there was something about it she did not like. There was a momentary pause. Niobe walked over to sit as Winona walked toward the stove. They nearly collided. Niobe stepped around Winona, who refused to change course. Winona refreshed her coffee.

"Your home is beautiful, Winona. Nice neighborhood." Winona sat. She sipped her coffee. Again, there was a pause. Winona sensed uncertainty in Niobe.

"You and Abe have done a great job taking care of Dwight." Winona's eyes fixed on Niobe.

"One of these days, Dwight will need to know the truth."

Winona's eyes narrowed. Niobe looked down at her cup.

"When that time comes, Abe and I will handle it. You can bet it'll be the whole version of the truth. Not some syrupy Aunt Niobe tale."

Niobe's finger circled the gold rim of her cup. Winona fought a strong impulse to choke Niobe.

"We found your child wrapped in a ratty burlap blanket on our porch. We gave him a name, love, shelter and support. For years, I knew you would come back. I couldn't believe my baby sister could do this kind of thing. Not the Niobe I knew. When we didn't see you and didn't hear from you, I gave you up for dead. That was the only thing I could think of that would keep a mother away from her child. Now you expect to walk in here and pick up as if nothing's happened. No chance, honey. Dwight is our son," Winona said, pointing her forefinger at her own chest. "Nothing you do will ever change that."

Niobe stared into her coffee.

"I bet you don't even know when his birthday is?"

Niobe thought for a moment. Her finger stopped circling the cup. Winona had been right. When Niobe arrived, she did not recall Dwight's birthday.

"September 18."

"That's only because Dwight told you."

Dwight had told Niobe, but she would not give Winona that satisfaction.

"And where's his daddy? Moses Sumpter, wasn't it?"

"Yeah, Moses was his daddy. He's dead." Niobe looked up. Winona was staring toward the screen door.

"I know about you and my father."

Winona slowly turned her head. She probed Niobe's eyes for her exact meaning. "What are you talkin' about?"

"You know."

"You're as crazy as you are stupid."

Niobe leaned forward. "Fishing, summer, Jackson Pond?" Niobe briefly grinned. Winona searched her face for the truth. How could she know? She was a child then. Had her father told her? Did her mother discover it and tell her daughter? No way could that have happened. Cleavon Waters was known for his ability to keep secrets, especially those most damaging to himself.

"He held you in his arms, Winona. I saw him take off your dress. I saw him get on top of you and do his business. Be glad you didn't get pregnant." Niobe leaned back. "I was in the bushes."

Winona remembered. She had dismissed the rustling bush as a breeze. Suddenly Winona felt small and dirty; less than Niobe, worse than a mother who had abandoned her child.

"I watched you two. He was teaching you how to fish when you kissed him. You and my daddy got all hot and bothered kissing and rubbing all up against each other."

"What were you doing there?"

"I followed him. I did that a lot when I was a little girl. I worshiped my father. He was God to me. When he left you, he saw me trying to sneak away. Before I could say anything, he started talking to me about how a man is at times given to indiscretions. It was like a fever only one thing could cure. Once it was done, it was done. He told me it didn't make him a bad person. What happened weren't your fault, but his. It was the fever. He couldn't control it. Think you the only one noticed him shamed-face when he looked at you. Mama figured it out. I overheard them whispering about it. He prayed after what you two did. Prayer didn't cure him of his fever."

Winona was speechless. Niobe seemed distant.

"My father is why I had to see Dwight. When he had the fever, even his daughter wasn't taboo. He started in with me when I was twelve. Fourteen is when I realized it was wrong. What my father really was. Everybody thought I got so wrapped up with Moses because he was good looking and kinda wild. Not so; not so at all. My father hated him. By the time Moses showed some interest in me, I hated my father. Moses was my revenge for what he'd done to me." Niobe continued to stare. Winona reached for her arm, then retracted before she touched it.

"I couldn't be sure if Dwight was Moses's baby. When I saw him, I knew. People think Dwight resemble me. If they'd seen Moses, they'd know different. Soon as I saw him smile, I knew he's Moses's, for certain."

"That's what you're here for?"

"Yes, and to see my boy, spend a little time with him—that's all. Left a hole in my heart…" Niobe did not finish. She placed her hand on Winona's folded hands.

"You doing a fine job with him. Winona, he goin' need to know the truth someday. I promise he won't hear it from me."

Her smile was faint, but sincere. Winona attempted a smile, but could not find the strength. Niobe patted Winona's hands. Niobe rose, eyed Winona for a moment, and then left the kitchen.

Winona stared into a moment of their shared past. She had assisted in the birth of Dwight. Niobe was fifteen; old enough to have a child. Winona had been envious of her. Try as she had, she had never been pregnant. When Dwight arrived, Winona was the one who bathed him. Hers was the first face he saw in his new world.

The baby passed from Winona to midwife to Niobe. Winona was so proud for her. Niobe's brothers and sisters came into the room first, followed by her parents. Sarah Waters had been angry with her daughter for becoming pregnant out of wedlock like so many common girls in the area. Cleavon Waters was furious for what he claimed were the same reasons. Sarah Waters held her grandchild. With the baby in her arms, many of her disappointments melted away. Cleavon Waters never held Dwight. When he looked at Niobe holding her child, his face became as it had when he looked at Winona for the longest time…ashamed.

CHAPTER THIRTY

"Good morning, Abe."

Abe raised a hand in greeting to Mabel Brown, nodding in agreement to a point Neville Carter made about Cassius Clay.

"He's a baaaaad man. I've never seen a heavy weight with that kind of speed; that kind of power."

"Talks too much for me," Abe said as he added up the last of Neville's groceries.

"But he can back it up with jabs, hooks, uppercuts, crosses, and footwork. Nobody's ever had an arsenal like that."

"That'll be $17.78, Neville."

Neville pulled out his wallet. "I used to do a little boxing myself when I was in the Navy."

"Really?" Abe could not imagine Neville boxing. He could see Neville wearing dark suits, doling out consoling expressions to ease death for the living for a fee. In his eyes, Neville was a born and bred funeral home director.

"I wasn't bad, either, but Clay's phenomenal. Did you see what he did to Henry Cooper?"

"Somebody will bring him down a peg or two."

"Doubtful, Abe. See you later."

Winona had become vigilant of Dwight since Niobe had arrived in their home. Her wariness gave them little time alone. Abe found it a relief to come to work. It gave him the opportunity to remove himself from the tense environment he deemed unnecessary. In his mind, Niobe had no plans of taking Dwight from them. With three children, a husband, and a full life awaiting her in St. Louis, he could not comprehend her absconding with a child who was the center of their universe. Isn't that what all parents want for their children: to be given love and the best opportunities in life?

Mabel bought a few household items. Abe and she made small talk about the church. Abe asked her if they liked their new home over on Paulson Avenue. She said they were getting used to it and felt blessed that no one was hurt in the fire and that they had found such a nice place to live in so short a time. Abe refused to take her money for the groceries and reemphasized his offer to assist in any way possible. Before she left, Mabel thanked him and asked that God bless him and his family. Abe wished the same for her.

"Hey, Dad."

Dwight, Kevin, and David walked up to the counter.

"What you boys up to?"

"We're going to play touch football over by David's house."

"Make sure you're home for lunch." Abe waved a finger at Kevin and David. "That goes for the two of you, as well."

"Yes, sir," Kevin said. David nodded.

"Can I have a box of Lemonheads and a box of Red Hots?" David asked.

"Sure thing." David gave Abe a dime in exchange for the goods.

"Bub's Daddy for me, Cousin Abe."

"What kind?" Kevin looked over the four flavors of bubble gum behind the glass case.

"Grape." He pointed and laid his nickel in Abe's hand.

"And what would you like, young Mr. Stone?"

"Boston Baked Beans."

"Aisle Three, middle section, second shelf."

"The candy right there." Dwight pointed.

Abe winked at Kevin and David. They laughed. "Why didn't you say so in the first place?"

"That's what I meant."

"Five cents, please."

Dwight paid.

"Thank you," Abe said.

"Later, Dad." The boys rushed out of the store.

"Watch out for traffic over there," Abe yelled after them, "and don't break anything."

They waved, disappearing around the corner. Rebecca added the last of her goods to those she had already set on the front counter.

"Looks like you're eating for two," Abe said.

"Afraid so; feels like a boy the way he keeps fidgeting, already getting on my last nerve."

Abe smiled. "When are you and the good Reverend going to tie the knot?"

"January 24th, my birthday."

"When's the baby due?"

"Not until April."

"Don't forget our wedding invitation."

"You'd better quit," Rebecca said with sweet sincerity. "You and Winona at the top of our list."

Maybe your list, but certainly not Embry Wilshire's, Abe thought.

"Are you going need help with this bag?"

"I'm fine."

"If Niobe's still here, she can come, too. I like her. She's good people."

"I'll tell her you said so."

"That Niobe sure looks an awful lot like Dwight. If I didn't know better, I'd swear she was his mother."

"It's a good thing you know better."

Rebecca laughed. She rubbed her swollen belly.

"This one will probably turn out looking like God knows who."

"Long as it's healthy, nothing else matters."

"You're right. Can I get one of those Milky Way bars and a box of Good and Plenty?"

Abe playfully frowned at Rebecca. He liked her spirit. Now that she was marrying Embry Wilshire, he liked her even more.

"Tell you what. Why don't we hold off on candy until after the baby's born?"

"It's for the baby."

"The baby doesn't have any teeth. How's it going to eat Good 'n Plenty?"

"I'll chew it for him."

Abe stood firm, with a playful frown. Rebecca gave in.

"All right, Dr. Stone."

Abe placed the bag of groceries in her arms.

"Sooner or later I'm going get me something for my sweet tooth. And I always get what I want."

Ron walked in. He stepped to the side and held the door open for Rebecca.

"Thank you," Rebecca graciously said.

"You're welcome."

"What can I get you?" Abe asked Ron.

Ron closed the door then walked up to the counter.

"Quart of milk and half a pound of cotta salami."

"Coming right up."

Abe got the milk and left it on the front counter. Ron joined him in the butcher's section while Abe cut the salami.

"How's that Larimer Laundromat doing?"

"So far, so good. I had no idea how many people use those machines. Even people with washers and dryers at home sometimes go to coin-operated laundromats."

"Why would they do that?" Abe wrapped the sliced salami, priced it, and then returned to the front. Ron followed.

"To wash and dry all of their clothes at the same time, instead of one load after another. Plus, we've got four heavy-duty washers to handle things like quilts and throw rugs and sleeping bags. Articles your regular washer doesn't clean very well. I hardly ever do my laundry at home anymore."

"Maybe I'll give it a try."

"We're open seven days a week, six to eleven."

"Cash or on account, Ron?"

"That's the first time you've ever asked me that."

"Really?"

"Yes."

"How about 'would you like a receipt'?" Abe asked.

"That's a constant," Ron said.

"Would you?"

"No; and it'll be cash, Abe."

Abe handed Ron change from a ten. Arthel and Earl Farmer walked in, followed by Frank Turner, Tina Russel and Elise Kale. They said hello to Abe and Ron, who greeted them in kind. Frank waited his turn, standing off to Ron's side.

"You said 'we' a moment ago. Would that be your business partner?"

"Yes." Ron declined the paper bag Abe had started loading in his groceries.

"The mystery woman?"

"Not to me."

"When are some of your friends—we *are* your friends?"

"Of course."

"When are we going to meet her?"

"Soon enough."

"Why don't you bring her to our Christmas party?"

Ron thought for an instant. "Sounds like a good idea. I'll do that."

"What's her name?"

"You'll find out at the party."

"Just wanted to know so I could put it on the invitation."

"Right," Ron said before he turned to leave.

"You two will still be together by then?"

"Goodbye, Abe."

Abe and Frank chuckled.

"What can I do for you, Frank?"

"Where's your Kotex?"

"For you?" Abe smiled.

"Don't be stupid, Abe."

"All the way in the back, second shelf from the bottom."

Frank had ventured halfway to the back shelves when the door flung open. Tony rushed inside. Jessie hurried in behind him before the door shut halfway. He grabbed Tony's shoulders. Tony turned and pushed him away. Jesse hardly moved. They stood facing each other. Tony was breathing hard, his eyes shifting from Jessie's face to his chest to his hands.

"You're coming home with me to apologize to your mother."

"I ain't going nowhere."

Jesse grabbed Tony's shoulders. Mrs. Powell came forward. Abe raised his hand in a gesture that suggested it would be best for her to remain where she was. Tony shoved Jesse. Again, Jesse grabbed him. Again, Tony shoved him away. Jesse grabbed Tony hard by his shoulders. Tony repeatedly tried to shove him away. Frustrated, Tony punched Jesse in the jaw. Earl stepped forward. Abe raised his hand. As Jesse turned his head to face Tony, hands still on Tony's shoulders, Abe could see the fury in Jesse's eyes. The slap sounded like a canon blast. Tony flew five feet before he landed on his backside. He sat upright. His eyes were dull. Jesse grabbed him by his arm and yanked him onto his feet with one hand.

"That was a baby slap. Care to try for a punch?"

Tony, groggy, shook his head no.

"You are going to apologize to your mother. But before you do, you are going to apologize to everyone in here."

Tony's wits were returning. The store was quiet. He looked around. Not one face of sympathy. He said a faint "I'm sorry." Jesse jerked Tony close to him.

"I tell you this now. Your mother and I are getting married. That means I'll be your stepfather."

Tony started to speak.

"Don't say a word." Tony looked away. "As long as I am your stepfather—which I consider myself to be, presently—you will never, ever, in your natural, black-ass life, speak to your mother in the gutter-like manner I heard you use a few moments ago. Am I making myself clear?"

Tony nodded his head. Jesse hissed directly into Tony's ear, "Do I make myself clear?"

"Yeah."

"Apologize to these good people."

"I said I was sorry."

Jesse stood up straight and folded his arms across his chest. "Say it like you mean it."

"I'm sorry," Tony blurted out.

"For all the trouble I've caused this morning."

"For the trouble I caused."

"And I promise."

"I promise." Tony rolled his eyes. Jesse moved closer to him.

"That I will never…"

"I'll never."

"Do such a thing…"

"Do such a thing."

"Again."

"Again—you happy now?"

"It's going to take a lot more than that to make me happy with you, Tony. But it's a start. Now we're going home. When we get there, you're going to apologize to your mother."

"Whatever."

"You're also going to mean every blessed word." Jesse leaned in close and his hand encircled Tony's upper arm. "Because if you don't, I'm going to break my foot off in your ass," Jesse straightened, "for starters."

Tony did not move. He was angry and embarrassed. Jesse led him toward the door by his arm. Jesse stopped by the counter, turned, and spoke in an eloquent voice.

"I sincerely apologize for this unfortunate disturbance. Let us all hope it will be the last of its kind witnessed in our neighborhood. At the very least, regarding Anthony Peoples."

"Amen," Mrs. Powell said.

"No problem," Abe added.

When Virginia walked in wearing a burgundy miniskirt and a white jabot blouse trimmed in gold, and brown clogs, the incident involving Jesse and Tony was an amusing discussion. Everyone in the store stopped what they were doing to look at Virginia. Frank and Earl were the only two whose faces did not disguise their shock. Others maintained differing degrees of composure. Virginia held firm Marvin Bankhead's little hand, who was delighted about it.

"Hello, Abe, darling."

"Good morning, Virginia." Scattered greetings came from all parts of the store. Mrs. Powell moseyed over and asked Virginia what she was wearing.

"You mean this?" Virginia pirouetted like a runway model, using Marvin as her guide. Out of their peripheral vision, women were watching their men.

"Like it?"

"It's a bit...revealing."

"It's called a miniskirt."

"Looks good on you."

"You can say that again," Frank said. Earl chuckled. Every woman except Ruth Powell furrowed her brows.

"Abe, how much for the canned peas?" Mrs. Powell asked.

"Twenty-one cents."

Mrs. Powell looked Virginia up and down. "Girl, you are something," Mrs. Powell said before she returned to browse Aisle Three.

Virginia turned to Abe with an alluring smile. "Abe, dear, may I have a Baby Ruth for Marvin and a pack of spearmint gum for myself?"

Abe reached inside the glass counter for what she asked.

"Are you behaving yourself, Marvin?"

"Yes, sir," Marvin answered, still grinning.

"We're going to see that Disney film—"

"The Sword in The Stone," Marvin interjected. Virginia looked down at Marvin. She seemed pleased. Abe noticed. Virginia grazed Marvin's nose with her finger, then looked back at Abe.

"They're having a morning matinee for kids at the Roosevelt Theater. That reminds me..." Virginia paid for her items out of her purse. "If Curtiss comes in before we get back, would you mention to him where we'll be? He was sleeping when we left. I didn't want to wake him. I left a note, but he might not see it."

"Will do."

"Did you see Kevin?"

"He and Dwight and David left a little while ago."

"On their way to play football over by David's house?"

"That's what they told me."

"Me, too."

"Why didn't you ask them to the movies?"

"I did."

"They said it was for babies," Marvin said.

"Don't believe them, Marvin," Abe said. "They just don't know a good movie when one comes along."

Marvin nodded in energetic agreement.

"Bye, Abraham. See everyone later."

Varied goodbyes followed Virginia and Marvin out of the door. Earl gave a low whistle when the door closed. Arthel elbowed him in his arm. Abe smiled and shook his head.

Frank bought Kotex, potato chips, pretzels, sodas, turnip greens, salt pork, tomatoes, green peppers, potatoes and cabbage. He and Abe bantered about politics and sports while he checked Frank out. Tina had come before Frank, followed by Elise—single purchases; single sentences each. Earl and Arthel were next in line. They bought chipped ham for themselves and candy for their grandchildren, who they were on their way to visit. Saturday morning rush was at an intermission. Another wave of customers would come through soon. Mrs. Powell moved her browsing to the freezer section. Abe began reading the latest copy of *Ebony* magazine.

"Hi, Mr. Stone."

"Hey, Abe."

"Clyde, Wallace. I see your wearing your fishing vests. You two going fishing?"

"Yes, sir." Clyde was excited.

"Came in to get some canned corn. Allegheny catfish love that stuff." Wallace stepped toward Aisle Three.

"Clyde, you know where we keep the canned corn?" Clyde appeared uncertain how to answer.

"Aisle Three, last row, top shelf."

Clyde was on his way before Abe finished. Abe leaned in close to Wallace.

"You shouldn't be eating fish from those rivers," Abe whispered. "Water's packed full of pollution. If anyone should be aware of that, it's you. It's a wonder anything can live in those waters."

Wallace turned his back toward Clyde, who was fingering each can on the top shelf, carefully reading their labels.

"I know. If we catch anything, we'll throw it back."

"Does he know that?"

"No."

"Why are you going fishing down at the Allegheny? Take him out to Crooked Creek, or up to Lake Arthur."

"Don't have enough time. I have to be at work by six. Figure this is better than nothing. Don't get enough time to spend with my boys as it is, working these twelve-hour shifts at the mill. Last time I remember going fishing, Clyde could hardly walk." Abe patted Wallace on the shoulder.

"I hear you, man. Dwight and I need to spend more time together."

"You do, all right."

"Could do a lot better."

"Is this the corn we want?" Clyde showed his father two cans of Del Monte Whole Kernel Corn.

"That's it: one for you, one for me. How much I owe you, Abe?"

"On me—under one condition." Abe leaned on the counter. His face was inches from Clyde's. "If you catch anything, you'll name it and throw it back."

"Why?"

"Allegheny fish are like pets. We don't eat them. It's our way of having fun. Like playing fetch with Moe. You wouldn't eat your dog, would you?"

"No."

"Same thing."

"What do you name a fish?"

"Anything you'd like. Deal?" Clyde extended his hand. Abe shook it. He noticed how much Clyde put him in mind of a miniature Wallace, with hair and eyebrows.

"Where's the rest of your gear?"

"In the car," Wallace answered.

"I got my own pole and everything," Clyde said.

"Listen to your daddy. He'll teach you how to use it the right way."

Wallace thanked Abe for the corn before they left.

CHAPTER THIRTY-ONE

Niobe set her vanity case next to two large suitcases near the front door. The house was vacant. It was peaceful inside and sedate outside; a warm, overcast late afternoon. Niobe wore a lavender suit much the same as the pink one she had worn when she arrived. A soft curl of hair dangled midway down the center of her forehead. Her face glowed. Sadness swirled in her eyes.

She picked up the living room telephone receiver and dialed long distance. The faint ring made her realize how far she was from home.

"Hello?"

"Calvert?"

"Baby, is that you?" She blushed. The sound of his voice made her wish he were there.

"How you doing?"

"Missing you like crazy."

"I miss you, too. How are the kids?"

"Missing their mother—other than that, they fine." It felt good to hear the word 'mother'. She held the receiver closer to her ear and her bottom lip glanced the mouthpiece as she spoke.

"I'll be home soon."

"How's it going?"

Niobe thought before she answered. "Not like I expected. But it turned out better than I hoped."

"How they treating your boy?"

"He's theirs now; not mine."

"That's good—ain't it?"

"Yeah, honey, that's good. I'm leaving on this afternoon's train. Are you going to be able to pick me up at the railroad station?"

"You know it. Get you home so you can get some rest. You sound exhausted."

"I'm a little tired."

"You okay?"

"Yeah." Niobe paused. "I'll tell you 'bout it when I get home."

"I love you, Niobe." Niobe cradled the telephone with both hands.

"I don't know what I would do if you didn't, baby. I love you, too."

"See you soon."

Niobe hung up. She looked around the living room. Photographs of family and close friends were everywhere. They made the room cozy. Her particular favorites were those of Dwight, Winona and Abe. Family is what she experienced when she walked into that room; into their house. Her family was considered affluent, where they lived. Their home had little of the coziness she now felt. They had things—family photographs and physical comfort—but the sense of belonging; that unconditional surrender of self; she had not learned how to nurture, until now. She wanted to pocket its aura and carry it back to her home. Show her family this is how home should feel, smell, and taste. She did not hear the front door when it opened behind her. Winona startled Niobe when she touched her shoulder.

"Leaving?"

Niobe nervously smiled. She turned and cupped Winona's face in her hands.

"It's time," Niobe answered.

"Dwight is going to be upset with you for not saying goodbye." Niobe's hands dropped to her side.

"I couldn't." Winona nodded her head.

"At least allow me to take you to the train station?"

"Jitney's on its way."

Winona looked toward Niobe's luggage. Niobe walked over and stood beside them, her back to Winona.

"You never opened your present."

"I will."

"It's a wood carving of an Appaloosa pony. Just a little something to remind you of when we were sisters and used to play horsy." Winona did not know what to say.

"I left my address and telephone number on the dining room table. Use it." Niobe looked over her shoulder at Winona. Her eyes were teary. "Please." Winona nodded. Winona stepped toward Niobe. "Don't," Niobe said. Winona stopped. They both heard the car horn. Niobe dabbed at her eyes with her handkerchief. She opened the front door, stepped onto the porch, and waved. Earl Farmer acknowledged her wave from where he stood by the passenger door of his 1960 tomato-red Ford Falcon.

Niobe walked back inside, head down, put her vanity case under one arm, and lifted her two suitcases. Winona watched. Niobe struggled with her luggage. Earl relieved her of both suitcases at the foot of the steps. He said something to Niobe that Winona could not discern as he put the suitcases in the trunk of his car. Niobe set her vanity case beside her luggage. Earl slammed the trunk shut. He walked around and opened the passenger door. Niobe stepped forward, and then asked him to wait a minute as she ran up the steps.

Winona saw Niobe rush through the doorway. She imagined a playful girl that flashed to a strong woman before her eyes. They stood arm's length apart, facing each other.

"Will you say goodbye to everybody for me?"

Winona nodded.

"We'd like it if y'all visited us sometime in St. Louie."

"We will."

"Promise?"

Winona crossed her heart with her forefinger. "Promise."

Niobe smiled. "It would do a world of good for Dwight to meet his brother and sisters, even if he doesn't know what they are to him. Tell Dwight to enjoy all moments of his life. Don't let anger or sorry or bitterness make him do things he might regret."

"I don't think he'll understand what you're getting at."

"Do you?"

"Yes."

"However you got to say it, make sure he understands."

"I will."

Winona hugged Niobe. Winona could feel Niobe shivering. Niobe's arms encircled Winona. "You're always welcomed here, baby sister," Winona whispered into her ear.

"Fremont."

"What?" Winona leaned backward.

"Fremont. That's the name I gave Dwight a couple of days after he was born. I always meant to tell you; thought you'd like to know."

Earl honked his horn. His car was running. He had left the passenger door open and settled in behind the driver's seat.

"You'd better go."

They hugged again like sisters once more. Winona walked Niobe to the car. Winona said hi to Mr. Farmer. Winona cautioned Earl to be extra careful driving her baby sister. He said he was always careful. Through the rolled-down window Niobe and Winona held hands. They looked into each other's eyes. There was an airy sense of unity; mirrored images of the same soul. They were forced to let go when Earl pulled away.

Winona went inside when the car was out of sight. She found a white piece of notebook paper Niobe had left on the dining room table. Carefully written in blue ink were Niobe's full name, her husband's full name, those of their children, and their address and telephone number. Winona copied the information into their address book. When done, she wrote on the bottom of the piece of paper, "FREMONT."

Winona took the paper upstairs with her to her bedroom. From her night table, she took a battered, gilded-edge, black leather-bound Gideon Bible her mother had given her when she left Alabama. She leafed through the Bible for the Book of Psalms. After folding the paper in half, Winona placed it between the fragile pages of Psalms eighteen through twenty-one and laid the Bible inside her secret shoebox, returning it to its hiding place.

CHAPTER THIRTY-TWO

The festive crowd filled the Stone's living room, cleared of furniture on the final Saturday before Christmas. Guests overflowed into the dining room, dressed in their finest attire. When the doorbell rang, whoever stood closest to the front door that was plastered with a foil poster of Santa Claus, welcomed their neighbor. Invitations were not verified. If the person at the front door was not a neighbor, then they were someone associated with an invited guest. That person experienced the same affection given a trusted friend. Guests bearing meticulously wrapped gifts attempted to hand them to Winona or Abe. They were graciously thanked and then kindly instructed to place them around a heavily-decorated Douglas Spruce in the far corner of the living room. Finding room under the green-skirted tree, mountainous with gifts, had become a problem. Gift bearers did their best.

Amongst a spread of food and punch bowls brimming with fruit punch or eggnog in the kitchen, Louis Russell, Tina's husband, commented to Eva Hearn on how popular the Stone's Christmas party had become.

"I remember their very first party," Eva said, examining one of the two white tablecloths with large printed images of mistletoe and garlands. "Wasn't but a handful of people. You wouldn't know it to look at it now." She rubbed a corner of the tablecloth between her forefinger and thumb to verify that it was cloth. "Now there's hardly room to breathe."

"Lotta' love in this house tonight." Louis said. "You can feel it soon as you walk through the front door."

"God blesses those with good hearts." Louis handed Eva a plate and held onto one for him.

"And good food," Eva laughed.

"Amen to that, sister," Louis said. They piled their plates high with slices of glazed ham, macaroni and cheese, cranberry sauce, potato salad, and buttered sweet potatoes. What would not fit on their plates could wait for seconds or thirds. Then there was dessert (if there was room in their stomachs by that time). To get their eggnog, they set down their plates.

"Sisterhood certainly did a fine job getting all this stuff together for the party," Louis said. Eva held a paper cup in each hand.

"We helped with the cooking. Sister Winona and Brother Abraham did the rest."

Louis filled one cup to the top. The other he stopped midway. Eva handed him the half-full cup.

"I noticed something about Winona today I hadn't noticed before," Eva said.

"Her breasts have gotten a little bigger."

"What you doing looking at Winona's breasts?"

"A man can't notice things?"

"You better hope Abe don't notice you noticing, or he's going to introduce your eye to his fist."

"Now, you know it ain't like that."

"Um-hum."

Louis topped off his drink with brandy from a silver flask stashed in the interior breast pocket of his tweed sports jacket.

"Well, her cheeks look fuller, but I bet you didn't notice that?" Louis remained quiet. "Seems to me her hips have gotten a little wider, too. If I was to take a guess at why, I'd swear she was pregnant."

"Could be." Louis stirred his drink with his middle finger, extracted it, and sucked it clean. He took a healthy drink and then licked the tight lips of his egg nog smile.

"Does Tina know you have alcohol?"

"Who do you think filled the flask?"

"Let me have a little taste?" Eva gulped down a third of her eggnog. Louis poured until she said stop.

"That's scarcely a shot."

"I'm not a drinking woman. Don't take much for me to fly." Louis shook his head. Eva found a plastic spoon and stirred her drink. She sipped it as if expecting it to bite. Louis suggested they return to the party.

Eva and Louis took up residence in the dining room just outside the kitchen. Their spouses joined them, nibbled from their plates, and shared their drinks. In every direction, people were milling around or standing still. Food, drink, smiles, and lively conversation abounded. Abe and Winona were listening to Phillip Davenport describe a recent discrimination case he was handling for the local Porter's Union against the Pennsylvania Railroad. Winona nudged Abe. She saw Ron wading through the crowd, holding the hand of a baby-faced, petite woman wearing a long red dress that complimented her smooth dark skin.

"My God, it's the mystery woman," Winona whispered to Abe out of the side of her mouth. Phillip's eyes followed their stare. He stopped talking. Ron stood the young lady in front of him, proudly smiling, one hand on her shoulder, the other indicating who was being introduced.

"Miss Colleen Tyler, I'd like you to meet some of my friends. This is one of our gracious hosts, Winona Stone."

"Hello," Colleen said with a warm smile. Winona took Colleen's hand in hers. "So nice to finally meet you, dear. Ron has told us so little about you."

Ron continued, "And this is her husband Abraham."

"Everyone calls me Abe." Colleen made a curt nod.

"The gentleman to his left is Phillip Davenport." Phillip cordially bowed.

"It's a pleasure to meet you, Miss Tyler. I understand now why Ron has kept you to himself for so long. 'She walks in beauty, like the night; Of cloudless climes and starry skies; And all that's best of dark and bright; Meet in her aspect and her eyes; Thus mellowed to that tender light; Which heaven to gaudy day denies.'"

Abe raised an eyebrow in Phillip's direction. Ron spoke into Colleen's ear. "Phillip's an attorney. He's also a bachelor, which makes him off limits."

"Yes, dear," Colleen said in a sprightly, ingratiating voice. "Allow me to introduce you around." Winona took Colleen by the hand and led her toward the dining room. Colleen finger waved goodbye to Abe and Phillip. Ron, she kissed.

Next to be introduced to Colleen were Mrs. Powell and her daughter and son-in-law, Rachel and Martel, followed by the Hickmans, the Browns, Curtiss and Virginia, Embry and Rebecca, Theresa and Jesse, Neville, Avery, the Jenkins, Drake, the Hearns and Russells, Darius

Muhammad (formerly Darius X) and his parents the Divers, Ralph Lingle (who had to leave early to catch his Miami flight), Flea and the Turners, and the Kales; concluding with an introduction to the Farmers. Arthel proclaimed Colleen Her Majesty greeting her court, for so many had flocked to meet her.

Phillip had recognized her last name. It took time for him to recall from where. When he was a graduate student at Florida A & M Law School, he had followed a story in the newspaper about a Negro family who were first to occupy a home in segregated Penn Hills. Racist residents who wanted them out continually victimized them. There were cross burnings, windows shattered, manure dumped into their car, threats on their lives, and their children were viciously accosted and sometimes assaulted. On several occasions, reluctant police had to be called to protect the family from possible lynching. Phillip wondered what sort of hell it must have been for them, living in constant fear. He waited until Colleen settled before he discreetly asked her if she were a member of that family.

When it was learned that Colleen was the eldest daughter of the first family of Negroes in Penn Hills, people gathered around. They looked upon her with pride and awe and compassion. Phillip coaxed her into sharing some of her experiences. He was unprepared for her candid truths.

"We were recruited by the NAACP," Colleen began in a firm voice. "The organization had been scouting for families to move into neighborhoods that have a racially exclusive history. They provided funds for half of all costs involving the move, house, and property. When they approached my father, he told them no. My mother saw it as an opportunity to spearhead civil justice while getting a great house in a good neighborhood to boot. We voted on it. That's what we do on any issue that affects the entire family. My Dad and Ryan and my baby brother voted against. Mom, Jordan, my little brother, and I voted for. Dad insisted he live alone in the house for a while, until things cooled down. That, too, was put to a vote. Six-to-one, it was decided against."

The guests had become quiet. They nodded, sighed, and made low, audible sounds confirming their solidarity in her family's impending anguish. Colleen's brown eyes appeared focused on whichever distant tragedy she conveyed. Courage, dignity, and faith were terms she used to describe her family during those times. Every person in that room applied those valiant characteristics to her. There were times when she appeared to be overwhelmed as she told her family's story. Ron comforted her.

Others patted her back or arm or shoulder; whatever part of her person they could touch.

"We know, honey," Ruth Powell said. "We've all been there."

Gentle comments of support were given. Expressions of anger, anguish, bitterness and torment spread like lapping flames throughout the room.

"Three other Negro families live around us, now. We look out for one another. Racism hasn't vanished. What surprised us most was that the racists were in a minority. The majority of whites were more concerned about their property values rather than the color of our skin."

Colleen had somehow been positioned in the center of the living room. Ron stood to her right, holding her hand tightly and giving her a shoulder to lean on when she needed it. Others stepped forward to share their personal experiences of persecution. The party descended into a melancholy confessional. As if summoned to his pulpit, Reverend Wilshire took center stage, handsome in his green cardigan sweater and creased wool pants.

"That which does not kill us makes us stronger," Reverend Wilshire began. "We must trust in The Almighty. Believe in His plan. Truth will be our beacon along the dismal path of gloom. Mercy will prevent the erosion of our souls with acidic thoughts of revenge. Justice will be our legacy of life forever on. It is trying times such as these that travail our humanity. We must dig deep to tap that infinite pool of strength we possess. Sisters and brothers, every day we witness His miracles; be they from the magnificent valor of Sister Tyler or the daily good deeds of the people in this very community. Reflect not on that which scars us, but on the multitude of joys. God has blessed each of His children. Health, clothing, shelter, food—many are denied such luxuries. We gather tonight due to our generous hosts, the Stone family. In a few days, we celebrate the birth of Jesus Christ, Our Savior, Our Lord. Christmas is a time of giving, a time of renewed faith, and a time for thanks. Let us rejoice in the celebration of God's greatest gift to humankind, his son, Jesus Christ. Let us give thanks."

Everyone, including Darius, bowed their heads in silent prayer. The Reverend's sermon lifted an invisible weight from the somber party. God was with them. They felt Him in their hearts. Abe experienced it, as well. He had been impressed at how Embry Wilshire moved his guests from despair to hope.

At the end of prayer, Jesse suggested it was time for music. Abe was quick to respond. Christmas music by The Temptations permeated throughout the house. The party returned to its festive mood.

Near the party's end, Abe asked his friends and neighbors to fill their cups and join him in a toast. Abe thanked everyone for blessing them with their company, their gifts, their friendship and their love. Blade commented that Abe had slipped too much brandy into his eggnog. When the laughter died, Abe responded. "Truth from a drunken man—or a sober one—is nonetheless the truth. Merry Christmas, everyone!"

"Merry Christmas," everyone replied in a unified chorus.

Abe and Winona stood at the front door and thanked each person for coming to their party. For many, it was well past their bedtimes. A light snow flurry had begun. People walked to their homes; some accompanied by acquaintances that did not live in their neighborhood. No woman went without an escort. Sisterhood aided Winona with cleanup. The men were not allowed to help.

Snow flurries had thickened when the last of their guests were bid goodnight. Dwight was spending the night at the Bankheads, a house jokingly referred to throughout East Liberty as the Lovejoy-Bankhead residence. Abe checked the door locks and extinguished all downstairs house lights. The drapes were open. Their colorful tree glowed in the corner of the deserted living room. Across the street the Farmer, Hickman, and Hightower homes shone with Christmas lights. Abe gazed at the bright display.

Felton Dobbs stood on the sidewalk in front of Ron's home, staring directly at Abe. He marched to the edge of their front lawn, his expression oddly sympathetic as he stood at attention. Abe watched him stand erect, snowflakes basking his person. Felton winked. Abe winked back. Felton saluted Abe, turned on a dime, and marched away.

Upstairs, he could hear Winona. There were languid splashes of water as she bathed. *Embry Wilshire was right, for a change*, he thought. *God was with them.*

Abe climbed the stairs, peeling away his clothes. Winona answered a light knock on the bathroom door with "Come in." Abe entered. All that remained of his clothing were his boxer shorts. Winona encouraged him with a seductive smile and a beckoning forefinger. Abe removed his shorts before he closed the door behind him.

www.ingramcontent.com/pod-product-compliance
Lightning Source LLC
Chambersburg PA
CBHW020506120726
47904CB00003B/725